BLACK HEART

KETLEY ALLISON

Copyright © Mitchell Tobias Publishing LLC, 2024

This book is a work of fiction. Names, characters, places and incidents either are products of the author's imagination or are used fictitiously. Any resemblance to actual events or locales or persons, living or dead, is entirely coincidental.

All rights reserved. Except as permitted under the U.S. Copyright Act of 1976, no part of this publication may be reproduced, distributed or transmitted in any form or by any means, via artificial intelligence or stored in a database or retrieval system, unless to be used as snippets or excerpts for a review, without the prior permission of the publisher.

Visit Ketley Allison's official website at www.ketleyallison.com for the latest news, book details, and other information.

LAYLA'S PLAYLIST

Revenge (DBSC) - tan feelz

Some Say - Adam Ulanicki

Marble - Neptunica, Shockz, Rebecca Helena

Zombie - The Cranberries

Survivor - 2WEI, Edda Hayes

Let Her Go - lost, Honeyfox, Pop Mage

The Blackmoor Mansion (3 AM) - Martin Egger

you should see me in a crown - Billie Eilish

Saints - Echoes

Doin' Time - Lana Del Ray

Listen to the rest of the playlist on Spotify:

PROLOGUE

Former Second Lieutenant Kaden Black loved his morning runs along the coast.

There wasn't much to look at, considering the ocean was always covered in fog and the sand beneath his feet was dense and clumped, but he enjoyed the cold puffs of exhales leading his path and the chill of the salted air keeping his sweat at bay.

And he *absolutely* adored being away from his computer, if only for a little while.

He'd recently transitioned to civilian life, securing a job as a cybersecurity consultant for a high-profile tech firm. Because the sedentary work was so demanding on his mind and body, his quiet hour of running beside the rising sun grounded him. He'd finish by doing deep stretches on his driveway, then creak open the door to the screened-in porch and make a Sunday brunch for him and Cassandra on a Friday.

His daughter just graduated from middle school and made the swim team for next year. He was so proud of her, he wouldn't even comment on the red licorice he was positive she was sneaking while he was out. She was obsessed with that candy.

Being a single dad, a former officer, and now a cybersecurity consultant made for a busy, adrenaline-induced life that even had his weekends fully booked, but he fucking lived for it and wouldn't trade it for anything else.

Engrossed in whimsical daydreams of smoky bacon and velvety pancake stacks drizzled in honey, he was oblivious to the rhythmic thumping echoing nearby.

Far too absorbed in planning the start of his weekend with Cassie, Kaden turned a blind ear to what should have arrested him on the spot.

He'd never register the blood-curdling female screams for help.

His daughter, it seemed, was buried far too deep underground for her desperate cries to reach him.

1
KADEN

10 Years Later

The hazy glow of the neon sign outside bleeds through the grimy windows, painting the world inside the bar with a blood-red sheen. I sit in the corner, shrouded, nursing my whiskey. The sharp burn as it slides down my throat doesn't faze me anymore. It's just another sensation, like the buzz of the worn-out fan overhead or the sticky residue on the glass from a hundred other careless hands.

A man—a weasel in an ill-fitting suit—slides into the booth across from me, his beady eyes flicking around the room before they latch onto my face. I resist a sardonic pull on my lips as his attention slides to my left temple, and with the awe of passing a gruesome car accident on the interstate, he follows the jagged scar up the side of my face, curving under my eyebrow, and ending halfway down the side of my nose.

Just like the Reaper's scythe.

Many of my new associates and rivals believe I received

such a maiming from an assassination attempt gone awry, that one of my victims was able to get in one last mark of vengeance before I ended their life. Ironically, the wound isn't from my life now. It's from what I call my Old Life, the Time Before, the Good Life, when the other HUMINT operatives and I had to infiltrate a rebel group in a foreign, volatile region where we were subsequently ambushed. One of the rebels had a nice piece of shattered glass he slashed across my face before I escaped.

The only person who didn't gasp or gag at the time of my healing was my baby daughter, who seemed unperturbed by the whole thing. She recognized me despite my disfigurement; she knew my love for her was unchanged.

This weasel before me, however, receives no such devotion. His presence irks me, a reminder of the petty pawns I'm often forced to interact with.

"It's done," I announce, my voice as rough as the edge of the whiskey glass in my hand.

He flinches as though the words were a physical blow but recovers quickly under my unrelenting, and I'm told very off-putting, stare, offering a jerky nod. His hand trembles slightly as he pushes a plain envelope across the beer-stained wood. It's thick with the promise of freshly printed bills.

I don't bother to check the amount; the numbers are always right. They have to be. People who short me don't get the privilege of making the same mistake twice. I slip the envelope into my jacket, feeling the slight shift in weight.

Without another word, I finish my drink in one final, burning gulp and rise. The chair legs scrape against the floor, the grating sound echoing in the subdued space. The few scattered patrons turn their gazes toward me—silent revulsion playing across their shoulders when I move behind them.

I step outside, and the night greets me with its cold

embrace. The chill doesn't bother me. It's an old friend, one that's been with me since the nights I spent without my daughter—3,648 of them. I pause for a moment, letting the darkness settle on my skin, the only cloak I've ever needed.

Behind me, the door to the bar closes, cutting off the murmur of voices and the tinny music that had been trickling out. It's quiet out here, muted. My eyes scan the street—a desolate stretch of forgotten city, my footsteps silent against the cracked pavement as I make my way through the winding backstreets.

Up ahead, a lone streetlamp flickers, its pale-yellow glow revealing two figures lingering in its halo. Their hushed voices stop as I approach, spines straightening in recognition. These are my contacts, the crooked cops on the take who keep me informed.

I pull my mask out of an inner pocket and slip it on, a seamless, matte black piece that covers my entire face, molding perfectly to my features. The most striking feature is the eyes. In normal lighting, they appear as two narrow, horizontal slits, barely discernible from the rest of the mask. However, when activated, a faint, eerie green glow emanates from these slits, indicating the night vision is in use. This glow is subtle enough not to give away my position in darkness but noticeable enough to unnerve anyone who sees it.

"Scythe," the bulkier of the two rasps in greeting as I approach, his breath fogging in the icy air.

I offer a curt nod in return. "Do you have something for me?"

The other man reaches into his coat and retrieves a sealed manila envelope. "Fresh from the top. High-priority target."

His gloved hand trembles as he passes me the envelope, from the cold, or fear, or both.

They've been waiting a long time. They have no choice but to wait until I'm ready to appear.

I tuck it away without inspection. "Payment will be in the usual manner."

They dip their heads in acknowledgment. Our business is concluded.

As I turn to go, the first one calls out, "This one's personal, Scythe. Watch yourself."

I pause, then continue. In this world, it's always personal.

And I trust no one.

Once out of their eyesight, I lean against a grimy brick wall and open the envelope. Unfolding the papers reveals an address, a time, and a photograph.

I pause on the photo.

A woman, striking even in the low resolution as she crosses a busy street, one slim arm up in a thank you to the cars as she's frozen mid-run, her long, bright blond hair flying behind her in waves. Her dark denim jeans are tight, rounded in just the right ways along her backside, with a sleeveless white button-down doing the same amount of justice to her front.

I glide over her body in a short time snap of assessment. It's her face that stops my professional perusal and for much too long.

Haunting multicolored eyes stare out from the image, one pale blue, one dark brown, a genetic rarity that makes her appear otherworldly. They're framed by a pale, heart-shaped face and full pink lips.

I force my gaze away from her high cheekbones, the line of her jaw and confident notch to her chin.

Her eyes.

I frown, turning the photo in my fingers and reading the back.

Layla Verona, age 25.

My next target.

Something about this feels off. My contracts typically target those ensnared in the web of the underworld. But this woman's features are untainted, devoid of the lingering evil I see in so many.

I need to return to my safe house, but I hesitate against the rough brick wall.

This goes against my code, the lines I swore never to cross. My contacts *know* this.

Why would they give me this girl despite it?

With a quiet curse, I tuck the photo into my inner pocket and burn the rest of the dossier with my lighter.

Some contracts aren't worth the cost.

But the information I gain?

Always priceless.

2

LAYLA

The clock ticks past midnight as I hunch over my desk, bleary eyes straining against the harsh glare of the computer screen.

Another impossible task from Emmitt Dawson to add to the never-ending pile of "emergency" deadlines. This internship was supposed to be my golden ticket into the tech world, but instead I've become a slave to the whims of a lecherous supervisor.

My fingers fly across the keyboard, racing against exhaustion to de-bug this code before going home. The office is eerily quiet, most employees having gone home hours ago. Only the low hum of sleeping computers and the click-clack of my typing break the silence.

Until heavy footsteps echo down the corridor, sending a spike of dread through my weary body. I know those languid footfalls all too well.

Dawson slinks into my cubicle, reeking of stale cigarette smoke and cheap cologne.

"Burning the midnight oil again, Layla?"

Dawson's voice drips like poisoned honey behind me.

Before I can respond, his hands grasp my shoulders, thumbs pressing into the knots of tension.

I flinch, skin crawling at his unwanted touch. Bile rises in my throat, but I force it down. *Endure*, I remind myself. *You need this internship*.

His hands linger a moment too long before finally falling away.

"I admire your dedication, Lay. You'll go far in this company."

His implications slither down my throat like the midnight oil he's so fond of. I want nothing more than to flee his presence, but I'm stuck in place. All my life, I've fought against men like him, yet here I am, allowing him to paw at me like an object.

No. I refuse to be cowed. I shrug out of his grip and meet his beady eyes. "I should get back to work, sir. I have an early morning."

Dawson's smile turns icy. He knows I've rebuffed him. "Don't stay too late. They're shutting off the heat soon for some work on the system and testing the air conditioning. Place'll be freezing."

He skulks away, but his stench lingers like a disease.

I let out a shaky breath, skin still crawling from his unwanted touch. This would be the tenth time he's invaded my space after hours, and I've worked here for five months. But I can't dwell on it. My future's too important.

Raised by a single mother after my father abandoned us, I've had to learn to be self-sufficient and independent—especially when the boyfriends came along. The power of invisibility is something I gave up a long time ago. With my eyes the color that they are, I'm an immediate curiosity to anyone I inadvertently make eye contact with.

Doll Eyes. Ghost Girl. Vampire. Witch. Temptress. Whore.

The cruelest moniker of all, spat at me by one of Mom's more articulate Lotharios. As if the color of my irises alone could bewitch a grown man, absolving him of any accountability for his own wretched behavior.

The screen blurs as hot tears sting the corners of my eyes. I blink them back, refusing to let Dawson or the memories of my fractured childhood distract me any longer. I owe it to myself and to the memory of the broken woman who raised me to rise above the role of victim.

Mum's Men, as I've termed the assholes who came in various forms but with the same type of brain, came up with these nicknames throughout my life until I found my escape hatch out of that house at eighteen.

My mother may have chosen the fleeting affection of despicable men over the well-being of her own daughter. She may have looked the other way while her boyfriends lewdly objectified a child. But her mistakes, her weakness, do not have to define me.

I draw in a deep breath, imagining I can expel the rancid odor of Dawson's cologne on the exhale. Conjuring an image of wide-open skies and sprawling hills, I let the dream of freedom that saved me as a child flow through my veins, steadying my hands.

The office air conditioner kicks on with a wheeze, blasting frigid air into my cubicle. Goose bumps rise on my arms. I've been so involved in my work, I didn't realize the heat must've shut off some time ago. I pull my jacket tighter around me and continue typing.

As the progress bar inches toward completion, my mind wanders to the box of Mom's belongings sitting in my closet. I haven't opened it yet. Part of me wants to throw it away, to sever that last connection to a past I've tried so hard to escape. But something holds me back.

The clock on my desk reads 1:37 a.m. when I finally finish debugging the code. I save the file and email it to Dawson, cc'ing the project lead. I envision going home and curling up in front of a warm fire in the new, slightly ramshackle home I inherited after my mother was in the wrong place at the wrong time and was killed for it.

How did Mom get caught in a shoot-out at a bar? My questions only multiplied when her ex, an attorney, read me her will and her long-kept secret that she—*we*—owned a decrepit lighthouse in a remote coastal town, left by a father I never knew.

My mother dated men with all kinds of occupations, from deadbeats to lawyers, but a lighthouse keeper wasn't one I ever would have predicted.

Or that he'd be my father.

He's dead, too. He was killed in a drunk driving accident on one of the many narrow, cliffside roads in Greycliff twelve years ago.

Maybe you think I'm cold for talking about my parents this way. But for so long, I was the only parent I knew. I supervised myself more than these two ever could, and while I'm sad that I'm *actually* an orphan now, I've kind of always felt that way.

Which is why the foggy coastal town of Greycliff was perfect for me and the resulting internship at one of the latest start-up tech firms in the industry. My skills and the atmosphere were a perfect match.

Until Emmitt Dawson.

I swallow down my gag reflex, remnants of adrenaline and repulsion, as I slip out of my cubicle. The floor-to-ceiling window completes my small office square, dark and bone-chillingly cold at this late hour.

With a warm fire and maybe a hot bath still on my mind, I grab my trench coat off my chair and—stop.

The glow of the other computer monitors on this floor covers my arms in a creepy blue light as I reach down and tap on my keyboard, and before I know it, my ass is following my reach and returning to my seat.

I've *had* it with meaty, asshole men. Thinking about my dead mom, my dead dad, and my dead past causes a spiral of rage inside me when I equate them with Dawson.

I'm not going to be used again. I refuse.

But I'm also non-confrontational and extremely passive-aggressive.

Using skills I learned not in college but in college basements with the other tech nerds in darkened, monitor glow rooms, I hack into my company's surveillance in just under ten minutes and pull up all the times I remember Dawson approaching me, touching me, and giving those gross one-liners of his. And calling me *Lay*. Ew.

Dragging them to a folder I've falsely titled **HR Compliant Files,** I unclip my *Hello Kitty* USB port from my keychain and insert it into the computer's tower.

Then I hit *copy files*.

I lean back with folded arms and a smirk. I don't know what I'm going to do with the evidence quite yet, but I'm happy I'll have it in case Dawson gets smart and decides to cover his ass.

While I'm smirking, I hear the low rumble of voices in an enclosed office behind me—Dawson's. I guess he never left despite his warning that the office would turn into a fridge after two.

Curious, I pull up real-time surveillance in his private office from a camera he's long forgotten about. He believes himself invincible, what with his Nepo-baby managerial title.

I watch and listen with half-interest, and then my smile falls.

"Project Oracle's complete. Don't lie to me, Dawson."

"I never denied it!" Dawson's voice rises to a panicked pitch. "I was merely running it through last-minute tests. It's not easy, you know, having a floor's worth of analysts write hidden code without them knowing about it."

The stranger with Dawson, a man I can't see, has placed himself just outside the camera's peripheral view. But I hear him just fine. His low tone is easy and calm.

"We don't have time," the man says. "Give the AGI to me."

I tense so hard, the tendons of my neck strain. AGI? Did I hear that right? Artificial General Intelligence. That's a highly illegal form of AI. AGI can learn and understand any intellectual task that a human can.

Minimizing the surveillance feed, I open the company's project files and search for any mention of Project Oracle. Nothing.

As if he can hear my racing thoughts, Dawson says, "Look, the progress on Oracle is exceeding our expectations. Its predictive models are already influencing the trial markets we've tested. But I can't hand it over to you this second."

"It should have been operational yesterday."

"We're moving as fast as we can without arousing suspicion," Dawson responds, using his hands as if to calm the situation—though the mysterious man is *more* than calm. "This isn't a simple algorithm. It's closer to Pandora's box. If you want it to influence the economy, elections, Wall Street, then we have to—"

"You promised a deliverable, Dawson. The organization doesn't take kindly to lies."

Mystery Man advances, his silhouette slithering over Dawson's desk. Between two blinks, he grips Dawson's throat, bringing him halfway over the desk like a rag doll bent the wrong way.

"Do you understand the kind of people you're dealing with?" Mystery Man hisses. "We're not some corporate investors you can pacify with jargon. You are at the edge of our knife."

"I understand. Please..."

"Shit. *Shit*," I hiss under my breath.

Heart hammering, I bolt out of my chair and grip my coat like a lifeline before rounding my cubicle and getting the fuck out of here.

Wait. The flash drive.

Hunching over so I'm hidden by the rows of cubicles, I stealth-crawl back to my computer and detach my USB, pocketing it before Dawson's door rams open.

My clenched jaw catches my gasp. I melt to the floor, huddling under my desk.

A tall man in a dark suit emerges. But from this angle, I can't see his face.

"You have very little time left," he growls over his shoulder at Dawson. "If you so much as—"

The man stops, his head turning toward my desk lamp.

"Is someone else here?" he barks.

My muscles tense. I could run, but they'd see me. I could stay hidden, but they'd find me. Either way, I'm fucked.

The man's hand disappears into his jacket. I bite down on a whimper.

"Dumb interns," Dawson's scratched, raw voice responds in his office. "They're always leaving shit on before they leave, like a high electric bill will really stick it to the man."

Heavy footsteps approach my cubicle. I press against the wall under my desk, my mind going blank with terror, the USB drive burning a hole in my pocket.

The steps pause. A shadow falls across the cubicle entrance.

My fingers curl, ready to claw or flee. The man's hand reappears from his pocket, holding a pistol.

Dawson pokes his head out.

"Hey," he says to the *gun-wielding* man. "The office cleaning crew will be in here any minute. If you don't want to be seen, you'd better make yourself scarce."

I see enough of the man to watch him pocket his gun and straighten his suit before receding out of view. "This warning is the last courtesy you'll receive, Dawson. Next time, it'll be far less friendly."

Huddling my knees to my chest, I wait for the elevator to *ding* its presence, taking Mystery Man with it to the ground floor. Yet I'm still not alone.

I listen to the sounds of Dawson collecting himself, clearing his throat multiple times, and muttering hoarsely under his breath as drawers bang and keys jangle when he steps out of his office and locks the door behind him.

His silhouette comes next, the edges illuminated by the city's lights through the windows as he passes by at a fast clip, his briefcase clutched close to his chest.

Thank God for Dawson's inflated ego—he's so convinced everyone jumps at his commands, he'd never imagine I'd still be here after he told me to leave before two o'clock.

After the second elevator ding comes and the doors slide shut behind Dawson, I allow my shoulders to relax and lift my head. But I still don't move.

Fifteen minutes pass before I'm comfortable enough to slide out from the cover of my desk and take the same route Dawson and Mystery Man did to exit to the ground floor.

The rain pelts my back as I slip out a side door, the wet rivulets seeping through my thin jacket. I quicken my pace, head down, hurrying through the empty streets. The cobblestones shine slick under the streetlamps, the fog swirling around my feet.

My mini-Coop is parked a half a block away. I pay for street parking because the garage is for full-time employees only, and right now, I've never been more thankful for that.

The engine rumbles to life, its vibrations slinging through the driver's seat like the fizzing of my blood as I navigate my way home, checking the rearview mirror religiously, praying that I won't notice headlights through the wash of rain. It becomes more of a terrifying possibility the farther I drive from the main expanse of Greycliff and into the narrow, winding road that snakes along the peninsula's spine, a precarious path lined with gnarled trees bent from the relentless sea winds. The road is an undulating ribbon of asphalt, offering glimpses of the rocky shoreline on one side and dense, tangled woodland on the other.

The lighthouse itself, an imposing structure of weathered stone and iron, rises stoically from a grassy outcrop up ahead. Its base is encircled by old, salt-stained boulders that have borne the brunt of countless storms like this one. The narrow piece of land it stands on extends into the restless sea like a slender finger. I speed toward it like one that beckons me closer.

With the help of the blanket I keep in the back seat because of the constant temperature drops, I scuttle into my home with it draped over my head—a plaid, wet-blanket-ghost seeking safe harbor.

I discard the blanket and peel off my damp clothes in the small entryway, my skin prickling with a residual chill. Clad in my bra and underwear, I wrap a quilt that's draped on the couch around my shoulders and light the stone fireplace that dominates one wall. I'm happy to report that the small house retains its historical charm by having no central heating.

The tempest rages outside, but in here, all is still but for the crackling of the growing fire.

Curling up on the couch facing the flames, I drag my laptop onto my lap.

It hums to life, casting an electronic glow that battles with the dancing light of the natural fire. With trembling fingers, I stick my USB in and click open the files, dreading what I'm pretty sure made it onto the stick in addition to Dawson's subtle groping.

I click on the newest file and the footage starts, the top of my supervisor's balding head darting across the screen as he seeks shelter behind his desk from a figure just out of view on the right.

Mystery Man knows where the camera is.

He edges near the frame but never comes into it. His dark suit, topped with a black fedora that I didn't notice before, obscures any profile I might screenshot.

I slam the laptop shut and shimmy away from it, biting my nails, wishing I could unsee the footage and un-hear my boss's damning words. But it's too late. I know his secret.

Who is the mystery man? What kind of organization would risk creating an AGI capable of influencing global events?

I've always been a loner, keeping to myself and avoiding conflict. A people-pleaser who never makes waves. But now fate has dropped a live grenade in my lap, forcing me to make an impossible choice.

Outside, the wind shrieks as if mimicking the churning in my gut. Do I keep quiet and pretend I never saw the video? Turning a blind eye goes against my conscience, but whistle-blowing could place me directly in sight of a gun. Powerful people seem to be at play here, and I have no allies.

If they realize what I know, there's no telling how far they'll go to silence me.

Illegal AI ... a black market sale ... *Jesus*, Emmitt, what the fuck were you thinking?

I sink further onto the threadbare sofa, head in hands.

It finally occurs to me how my mother might've found herself in the middle of a shoot-out that cost her life.

Sheer and utter bad luck.

3
KADEN

The blade slices through his carotid artery in one fluid motion. Blood spurts, warm and wet across my hands. His eyes bulge in shock and pain, hands grasping futilely at his throat to stem the crimson tide.

Another mark off the list, another ghost I've created to haunt the earth for eternity.

When I'm satisfied his eyes are soulless, I check the time, the hands of my blacked-out Rolex informing me it's 1:04 in the morning. Pulling a cheap, plastic wristwatch from my pocket, I ensure the time matches up, then remove the battery, freezing this man's final moments, and wrap it around his wrist.

A token, if you will, or a calling card, a kill signature, or most importantly, confirmation to my client that the Scythe met his end of the contract.

Sometimes playing a role in public keeps the real operation hidden to throw off suspicion or create false leads. But true clients? They never see my face.

It's only through a long, twisted binary road that their

message can reach me, and I never write back. Once the money is deposited up front, the only answer they receive is the person they wanted dead.

My hands are stained with the blood of the wicked, the corrupt, the guilty. And with each life I take, a part of me dies as well. But it is a sacrifice I'm willing to make for justice.

I leave the body cooling in the basement of its multimillion-dollar brownstone, stepping over congealing pools of blood. The night air is damp and heavy with the promise of rain, diffusing the streetlights into halos. I take a winding, circuitous path to my car, using two buses, a subway, and three outfit changes before I slip into a nondescript black sedan in a pristine business suit and join the interstate exit out of the city.

Back in my spartan apartment, I rinse the blood from my skin, watching the pink-tinged water swirl down the drain, one of my hands black with intricate ink from my fingernails up to my shoulders, and the other as bare as it was when I was born. My inked arm is compromised of an intricate patchwork of symbols and designs, but three always catch my attention. A clock with no hands is tatted on the top of my hand. A phoenix rising from the ashes flows up to my elbow. My eyes stray to the coordinates tattooed on my inner forearm—a place I can never forget, where I lost everything.

Greycliff.

It's as if all the ghosts I've dispatched have clawed their way back to me, howling as they drag me back to where I lost my little girl. It's not to give me a second chance to save what I couldn't a decade ago. I have too many sins to be given such salvation.

But ... Layla Verona.

An innocent caught up in a tangled, lethal web I doubt she fully grasps.

I groan, my steel-blue eyes disappearing as I shut my lids on my reflection.

There was another caught under the legs of a similar spider. Cassandra Black. Cassie. My daughter.

Despite my refusal to make Layla a target, I'm compelled to research *why*. Why her? What has she done, or not done, to deserve to have her time frozen by the Scythe?

With a hot cup of coffee by my side, I sit at my makeshift desk, my four computer monitors humming to life. It doesn't take long to pull all her public information. Her address, social security number and passport are all child's play. Using that, I spend an hour attempting to access her private data.

I expected to have her personal passwords fifty-five minutes ago.

I grunt, leaning forward on my elbows, my fingers flying like an expert pianist at a concert hall, using all the backdoors I can think of.

Each time I have to restart or try something new, my temper flares. Yet so does my intrigue.

"Come on, sweetheart, drop those firewalls for me," I growl and croon at the same time.

Like stroking a sensitive inner thigh while the woman under my touch whimpers with want. I'm gentle and patient with the promise of tongue.

At last, she opens in submission, and I'm scrolling through Layla's life, from the beginning of her birth certificate (born in Santa Fe, California) to her new internship at Pulse Dynamics, a mediocre tech firm with below-average accolades and a bare-minimum clientele list.

I snort. It's as if whoever named the company thought slapping the promise of a heartbeat and "Dynamic" together would magically spawn innovation. The kind of person who deserves the Scythe at his doorstep.

Within two hours of scouring behind the scenes on her personal laptop, I have all the information I need on Layla Verona. It becomes clear very quickly that Miss Verona is massively overqualified but desperate for a job matching her degree in this flailing economy.

I sit back, folding my arms as I mull over her files, projects, and what catches my eye last—a drive she left open named HR Compliant Files containing recent security footage.

The most recent recording catches my attention first, and within seconds, I get my answers on why she's being offered on a platter to assassins for hire like me.

The footage continues to play after the preening supervisor, Emmitt Dawson, gets his throat worked over by a cleverly concealed attacker. I switch cameras when the attacker stalks out of the office and into the main area.

All my training should have me focused on the back of the attacker, taking note of his gait, his approximate height, and any habitual tics or marks identifying the man. Fuck, I should be able to tell if they're male or female at *least*.

I can't tell you a thing.

Because all my attention goes to the light-haired beauty darting around the cubicles like a lost, wingless dove as she attempts to hide from the attacker.

And I think, *Hide. Come on, conceal yourself before he finds you.*

My chest tightens when she slides under her desk and cowers just in time for the attacker to pause at her cubicle. With my lashes providing the only flicker of tension on my expressionless face, I note the pale sliver of her hand pulling a USB stick from her computer tower before huddling deeper into her small crevice of safety.

And I release a long exhale as the attacker leaves the frame, a stumbling Mr. Dawson following suit a few minutes after.

Layla pokes her head up after fifteen minutes of no movement. I watch every millisecond of her pulling herself together, collecting her things, and tentatively making her way to the exit, her head twisting and turning under the threat of getting jumped.

She has no idea that as easily as she overheard and made personal copies of this conversation, she signed her death warrant. The sheer danger of knowing about this piece of tech could bring every crime lord down upon her pretty head. I should take her copy from her, give it to whomever wants it, and bargain to keep her out of harm's way. Yet ... that is not my first thought.

She intrigues me, this gentle wraithling with her moon-pale skin and wide, supernatural eyes.

Not a single muscle in my body moves as I watch her on the screen as if I'm hiding in the shadows behind her, sharing her same air.

I replay her movements ten times before I decide to rewind and give the attacker a better look. Inexplicable rage uncoils from my gut toward the man who put the fear of God in her, a woman too smart for her job, too innocent to acquire such information, and too beautiful to wear such terror on her face.

And when I dig deeper into company security footage history, that rage becomes an inferno.

Mr. Dawson has some explaining to do, touching her the way he does.

Feeling her the way he wants to.

Trailing fingers across her shoulders, holding her arm too tight when he stops to converse with her in the hallways, ensuring his palm brushes across the side of her breast...

The small tent inside his pants when he turns to leave.

He deserves death.

It's a simple thought. Unbidden. And similar to the one running parallel to it: *no one touches her.*

I rise from my chair five hours later, only now registering my full bladder and growling stomach. I relieve both before resuming my online prowl, beginning with Emmitt Dawson and finishing with the attacker.

My blood runs cold once I use my personal facial recognition software on the millisecond when the attacker turns his head and scans Layla's cubicle before pocketing his gun and taking the elevator. It's enough to make a 60 percent link to a face in my diligently collected crime files.

When that face stares back at me through the screen, I can't blink. I stand completely still, holding my breath until the silence becomes unbearable, and I break my rule of never drinking while hunting. I search through my kitchen until I find a dusty bottle of whiskey and take a long sip that burns all the way down my throat.

It lands on my counter with a shatter, my fist clenched around broken shards of glass and blood-soaked cuts burning with whiskey fire.

Frank Morelli.

I've caught your trail, motherfucker.

The attacker on the footage is an associate of his. Morelli is shrouded in near-mythical status and has mastered the art of remaining unseen despite leading a vast criminal empire. Unlike other capos, he rarely appears in person at his clubs or establishments. Instead, he uses a complex network of proxies, doubles, and encrypted communication. I've been tracking and losing him for years.

He is the man who killed my daughter.

With a shaking, blood-soaked fist and my head bowed over the counter, strands of dark hair falling into my vision, I make a vow not to lose him. Not again.

Cassie deserves her justice.

I start by packing a multitude of weapons in a plain canvas duffel, using a second bag for my electronics, wrapping the expensive equipment and vicious weapons with clothes I'll need on the go.

I changed my mind. I'm traveling to Greycliff for selfish reasons because my return to that godforsaken city isn't about saving or protecting Layla.

I confess this to myself as dawn eats the shadows on my floor with cheerful orange and pink teeth.

She's marked by Morelli. Therefore, the Scythe's next move is clear.

Haunt her every step.

4
LAYLA

The heavy fog clenches around me like ghostly fingers as I make my way down the winding cliffside road from where I was forced to park.

Rush hour on a Friday morning is never enjoyable, but it's even worse on a gloomy day like today when visibility is at an all-time low, and everyone comes into the city anyway, taking all the street parking available.

Wispy gray tendrils snake through the trees and swallow the iron lampposts. My breath fogs before me, and the rocky shoreline looms below, obscured by mist and stone.

I quicken my pace, shoes clicking on the damp cobblestones and my makeup fast becoming morning dew. The familiar walk to work has always brought me fresh air and comfort before sitting for hours in a cubicle, but today, nervousness prickles my skin through the fog.

I glance over my shoulder, unable to shake the feeling of unseen eyes tracking my every movement. And when a murder of crows bursts from the cluster of trees to my left, my harsh cry joins theirs, shattering the eerie hush blanketing the atmosphere.

That's it. I'm taking the road more traveled instead of enjoying my normal solitude through the side streets.

With a quick look both ways, I dart into the empty street, intending to cross to the other side and slip through a short alley before I reach Main Street.

A set of headlights pierces the gloom ahead. I freeze, blinded by the glare. The car's tires let out a piercing screech as it slides across the wet asphalt. I'm rooted in place like a deer caught in the headlights—though I always assumed that deer could *fucking* move out of the road if it really wanted to. Panic rises in my throat as the car barrels forward, no longer in control.

A strong arm wraps around my waist, yanking me back onto the sidewalk. My shoulder collides painfully with cold pavement, and we tumble to the ground in a tangle of limbs. The car rights itself and zooms past in a blur, horn blaring.

Gasping for breath, I clench my fingers tightly around the sturdy arm enveloping me like a shield. My rescuer meets my startled gaze, his eyes like metal left out during an unforgiving winter storm and surrounded by a torrent of jet-black lashes. But—his *face*.

A symmetrical masterpiece of creation. Angular, sharp, *beautiful*. His nose, straight and adorned with a faint scattering of freckles bearing testament to hours spent under an unforgiving sun, leads down to stern lips that are slightly parted as he catches his own heavy breaths. His scent is mind-blowing—leather, gunpowder, and underlying it all, a crisp note resembling the sea breeze mingling with forest pine.

Relief floods through me so fast, I fail to immediately register the jagged scar marring the perfection, running like a crooked river from the corner of his jaw and curving under his left brow.

Which, if I were in a better mental state, could signify he's not my savior but a potential kidnapper.

He slowly withdraws his arm from around my waist and pushes off me, his lean, muscular frame rising in a fluid motion that hints at a disciplined rigor. I remain sprawled on the sidewalk, struggling to process what just happened.

I stare up at him with wide eyes, still a deer.

"Are you alright?"

The voice is low, rough like gravel under the tires that nearly killed me but oddly soothing, lending an unexpected warmth to this horrible morning.

I nod mutely as he extends a hand to help me up. His grip is firm and steady, easily pulling me to stand. My legs wobble, but he keeps me upright with another hand on my shoulder.

His touch seeps through my windbreaker, unravels my sweater, and all but hands my breasts over to him.

"Thank you," I manage to stutter, my voice trembling as much as my limbs.

I'm acutely aware of his palm still pressed against me and radiating heat while his eyes stare into mine, dark and fathomless yet a startling blue.

How can someone's eyes be both? Yet his are.

Being the center of his focus makes my cheeks flush. I take in the jagged scar cutting across his cheek, the tension in his broad shoulders clad in a long black trench coat. He seems coiled like a spring and ready to react to any threat.

His hand on my shoulder relaxes, and for a split second, there's a flicker in his frostbitten gaze, like he regards me as more than just another wayfarer in this gray city who nearly got flattened by a car. I'm no stranger to people giving me a second look once they notice my different-colored eyes, but this is new. He's taking in everything—the curl of my hair against my cheekbone, the trembling of my lips as I try to regain my composure, and the way the chill has painted color across the apples of my cheeks.

His grip moves from my shoulder to my arm, fingers sliding down my windbreaker, but not before brushing over the dip in my collarbone—a touch light enough that it might have been accidental if it hadn't been for the way his eyes followed it.

I watch him curiously, my heart pounding a fierce rhythm against my ribs.

An irrational fear that he could be yet another danger pricks at my senses, but I discard it. He's just saved my life.

"Layla," I finally introduce myself, a little breathlessly.

He withdraws his touch as if burned. "Be more careful next time."

"I usually am," I sputter, still trying to regain some semblance of control over the situation. My legs feel like they could give out at any second.

He just gives a curt nod. I feel utterly exposed, as if he can see right through me. Nervous energy thrums through my veins.

"Well ... thank you, again." I repeat because gratitude seems inadequate against the weight of what he just saved me from.

The corner of his mouth quirks up slightly as if he can read my thoughts. But it falls as quickly as it came. He glances back toward the road, where the car has vanished into the foggy ether. "Don't make me do that again."

He studies me for a moment longer before he turns away. One moment, a savior; the next, a stranger detaching himself from my life as easily as he entered.

I shake my head, clearing the haze in my mind. "Hey! What's your name?"

He doesn't answer, his long strides carrying him down the fog-shrouded street until the mist swallows him whole.

I'm left standing breathless on the sidewalk, tracing the space where he stood only moments ago. Shoving my hands into my pockets for warmth, I force myself to walk in the opposite direction.

The fog has slightly lifted by the time I reach Pulse Dynamics. Its imposing glass building reflects a distorted image of Greycliff's oldest district, a reminder of how easily the new encroached on the old. I swipe my ID through the scanner and try to shake off thoughts of my early morning encounter.

Who *is* that guy?

And why does a part of me wish he hadn't left so soon?

————

My grumpy savior was terrifying to look at.

And gorgeous.

It takes four hours and a long wait at Whispering Waves Café, as well as downing two salt spray espressos before his face becomes a little more blurred in memory, and I can focus on the day ahead.

Emmitt was mysteriously absent this morning, and I can't say I'm not grateful for his lack of presence. In fact, I get way more work done than usual and clock out at five, getting in a light jog to my car and carefully, *reluctantly,* looking both ways before I cross the road.

I say "reluctantly" because a part of me kind of wants to do it again and see if he reappears.

I laugh as I slide into the driver's seat. So dumb. Why would I want to put myself in danger just to get a good look at him again? I have enough scary-crazy on my plate. I don't need to test if I have an angel in the form of a phantom protecting the road to my lighthouse. Or maybe it's just his job to collect my soul when I inevitably crash into the rocks below.

He probably would've saved anyone. It just happened to be me today.

Not with his kind of scars, my subconscious whispers. *And certainly not with the pissed-off expression he used while he peeled you off the asphalt.*

I reach the lighthouse just as darkness envelops the sky, turning the sea into a vast black void. The familiar sight of the old structure should comfort me, but tonight, it feels different.

Something's off as I approach the door to the keeper's cottage. I can't shake the idea of being watched. I look around for eyes in the shadows, but there's nothing. Still, that creepy sense sticks with me.

The porch stairs groan under my weight, a familiar sound playing along with the unfamiliar shiver of the wind at the back of my neck. I fish through my purse, feeling for the key ring and dreaming about the fireplace I'm about to light when I find it and fit my key into—

CLANK.

Frowning, I jab the key against the lock again. It makes the same sound, refusing to fit.

My head falls back with a sigh. Once again, I've forgotten to turn on the porch light for myself when I come home, making it too dark to see the problem.

Finding my phone amid the debris lining the bottom of my purse, I angle the flashlight, then recoil with a frown, my hip banging into the salt-damaged railing and nearly cracking it all the way through.

"What the hell?" I whisper to myself.

The lock on my door isn't the old, worn one I'm used to grappling with. Instead, a new, high-tech lock with a pristine nickel finish is centered within my flashlight's beam. Where dread once resided, I'm feeling a swirl of confusion now.

Who would change my locks without telling me? I don't have a landlord, and the previous resident is dead.

Being located on the tip of a peninsula presents its own set of issues, one of which is not having neighbors nearby to ask if there was any suspicious activity while I was at work.

My arm drops to my side, taking my useless key ring with it.

It's a smart lock, featuring a small, illuminated pad for keyless entry. Above the keypad, a small, inconspicuous camera lens is embedded, almost invisible unless one knows where to look.

I let my purse fall to the floorboards so I can bend and study the lock further. Then I look around for instructions or a code left in my mailbox but find nothing.

A less stubborn woman might spin around and drive straight to the police station after seeing this, but I am no such thing. I will *break* this lock if I need to. This house is the only thing I have that's mine.

Cursing under my breath, since that's a lot better than panicking, I call the sole locksmith in Greycliff, who was out on a call, but whose wife adamantly denies ever booking a job for the cute young thing with the crazy eyes staying at the light-house. I believe her.

Drawing a deep breath, I lean closer, examining the keypad. My mind shifts gears from the perplexed new home-owner to the tech-savvy computer scientist I am. If this is a game, I'm not backing down and just breaking a window to get inside. No way am I inflicting such damage when I'm basically broke and drowning in student debt.

First, I check for the simplest solution—a factory reset

code. But a quick inspection dispels that hope. This lock is far from standard.

Next, I observe the wear. It's brand new. No worn keys give away frequently used numbers.

"Think, Layla," I mutter to myself.

Then it hits me—what if the code is something related to the house itself? A historical date, maybe?

I try the year the lighthouse was built, running my fingers over the numbers. Nothing. I follow with the year it went from a manual lighthouse operator to an automated system. Again, the door remains locked.

Frustration ranks high on my list of emotions right now, but so does my determination.

This fucker is keeping me from the warmth of my home.

Then an unsettling thought crosses my mind. What if the code is something intimately personal to me? My stomach goes cold at the thought of a stalker's close observation.

Is this something Dawson did? Or the Mystery Man? With my near-death experience this morning, I hadn't given much thought to stumbling into Dawson's illegal side-job, but now...

Almost on autopilot, my mind drifts to the day I inherited this lighthouse—a strange legacy from a father I never knew, a man who was a mere afterthought in my life. Could it be?

With a tentative hand, I enter the date I officially became the owner of the lighthouse, five months ago on May 13, the day my life took an unexpected turn. The keypad responds with a soft beep, the lock clicking open in affirmation.

A creeping apprehension quickly overshadows my shout of triumph. The code is a date that only a few know and marks a significant shift in my solitary world. Whoever set this lock knows me and knows my life far better than I'm comfortable with.

If I think logically, the only strange occurrences I've experienced lately are my accidental recording on a USB and being saved by a dark, mysterious stranger on the street this morning. It'd be insanely coincidental if the two were related, and to top that off with the gift of a top-of-the-line lock I could never afford, I don't know what the hell to do with this puzzle.

Whoever installed this knows their tech, and now, they've seen my skills, too. But why challenge me like this? What's their game?

Fitting the phone into my hand to bludgeon an intruder if I need to, I slink through the front door. As my eyes adjust, I notice more small differences that were made to my home since I left.

The living room, usually bathed in the warm glow of my thrifted lamps, is now under the watchful gaze of small, unobtrusive security cameras perched in the upper corners of the wall.

With shortened breaths, I walk slowly, my footfalls heavier than usual. Next to the front door, where an old coatrack used to stand, there's a sleek, new control panel with a touchscreen interface.

In the kitchen, I find more upgrades. A small device on the counter blinks with a green light, a state-of-the-art air quality monitor.

The feeling of intrusion grows as I ascend the stairs to the upper level. I half expect to find more gadgets, and I'm not disappointed—or perhaps I am. My bedroom door now has a lock similar to the front door, promising a level of security I'm not sure I need. Or want.

Thankfully, it's not pre-coded like the front door, and the wood swings open at my touch.

Inside my bedroom, my eyes are drawn to the window, as they always are. The primary bedroom is set in what used to be the watch room, offering a panoramic, if not melancholic, view of the surrounding waters. The glass is often misted over from the sea spray, and the waves crashing against the cliffs are a constant lullaby.

But even this isn't free from the silent invasion. A slim, almost invisible sensor is attached to the frame, likely an alarm trigger.

My breath catches when a realization hits me—*my thumb drive.*

I run to my window and latch onto the curtain when I slip, nearly taking it down with me. Crashing to my knees, I fumble with the curtain's hem, searching for the tiny hole I made and running my finger through it until my shoulders fall with the weight of relief.

It's still where I hid it. Thank God.

Rising, I wander into the middle of my room with the drive biting into my palm as I clench it, staring wide-eyed at a place starting to feel like a sanctuary. I'd added soft textiles to my biological father's barren space, like throws, pillows, and rugs, now transformed into a stranger's idea of a fortress. These types of gadgets are meant to protect and make you feel safe inside your home.

But I never gave them permission to come inside.

So I wonder, are these meant to keep me safe?

Or keep me locked in?

5
LAYLA

I wake up to the soft but incessant beep of a security panel.

Groaning, I roll out of bed and rub my swollen, sleep-deprived eyes.

I spent hours last night deactivating every damn electronic device I could find and covering camera lenses with sticky notes, nearly breaking an ankle and stubbing two toes as I balanced on chairs and tables to do it.

The moment I was satisfied I got them all and changed the code to the front door and all other codes I located, I crawled into bed, resolved to report this to the police in the morning.

But the beep.

I slide my hands down my face.

There's a fucking survivor.

Grumbling, I throw an oversized cardigan over my white tank and sleep shorts, tying up my hair while I pad down the stairs and into the entryway, glaring at the blinking green lights next to the door.

"I thought I killed you," I mutter, tapping the screen to shut it down. "Die, Satan."

The light goes out, and the screen goes black without argument.

"Good. Now stay that way."

I'm in desperate need of coffee on a good day, which makes this morning an absolute emergency. But as I'm filling my carafe in the kitchen, the system springs back to life, its lights winking at me like tiny, mocking, *beeping* eyes.

"Seriously?"

Setting the carafe on the counter, I move to stab at the panel again. After a few more curses, threats, and disengage codes, it shuts down again.

Satisfied, I dress in gray sweats and leave for my morning jog. Staying in routine is the key to not panicking. Praying I'll be able to leave my home, so electronically invaded, is instinct.

In the event I *can* leave, I planned on collecting as much of the gadgets as I could, in pieces or whole, and dumping them at the police station as evidence.

Evidence of ... what? My mind continues to needle at me as I run down the shores of the peninsula and back. *Does this qualify as stalking? Harassment? What even* is *this? Definitely an invasion of privacy.*

When I get back, out of breath and my hands on my knees, I find the security system active yet again.

But I'm outside, not locked in. I can escape. If I contact the authorities, maybe I can make sense of the madness.

But this is my *home*. Everything I have, sequestered into a lonely lighthouse cottage my unknown father barely furnished.

And what's stopping my electronic intruder from taking down everything in the time it takes me to drive into town and file a report as quickly as they put it up?

I don't have friends. No one can protect the property or *me*.

"Shit," I mumble, then climb up my porch steps and crack open the front door, ensuring I'm alone.

Throughout the day, the pattern continues. I disable the system, and it reactivates itself. I do it three more times before I resort to a baseball bat, which after my first swing sets off such a raging set of alarm bells that I scream along with it until I disable it by *reactivating* the damned security system until it happily blinks green again.

I'm so busy fighting the type of technology I used to love that the day flies, and by evening, I'm half convinced my house is haunted.

I think about the mysterious benefactor behind all this. It's like having a secret admirer, but instead of flowers and chocolates, I get gadgets and surveillance.

"Romantic," I say to the empty room, my voice thick with sarcasm.

Well, joke's on them—I've named the control panel Bob. And Bob's about to have a very tough time with me because he's about to die.

———

Bob wins.

Tamper-proof hardware, encrypted locks on devices, reinforced mountings, backup power sources, and self-healing technology all prevented me from sending Bob to hell where he belongs.

I'm gasping for breath, my hair plastered to my face and body covered in sweat. A ratty gray sports bra and my jogging pants are still on, but I must have taken off my shirt at some point during the intense stand-off.

I've yanked off the neon pink sticky note from one of the

cameras mounted to the left of the fireplace, clambering down the ladder and positioning myself in the middle of its lens.

And I'm currently giving it the finger while mightily waving around the bat with my other hand.

"I know you're in there!" I yell. "What's your game, huh? What the hell do you want?"

I get a steady green light in response.

"I used to like the color green," I seethe. "It's calming, means nature is bountiful, leprechauns love to wear it, and most people see it as a new beginning. But because of you, I *hate it!* Turn it off!"

I volley the bat at the camera, missing it by inches.

"*Aagh!*" I fist my hands in frustration, storming around in a useless circle.

Then my chin snaps up. I squint at the cold, black lens through long tendrils of tangled hair. "Dawson, is that you? Is this your idea of intimidation? Are you getting your kicks from watching me now?"

"Comparing me to that handsy bastard? Layla, I've killed men for less."

I suck in a breath so suddenly, I almost choke on it.

A voice. An actual response.

It's distorted, altered to be unrecognizable and coming across as cryptic, unnerving, and definitely *not* Dawson.

Mystery Man. The name comes unbidden into my mind, the sound of Dawson choking, the easy gait as he left our offices without a care in the world despite leveling a gun at my cubicle's lamp and death threats at my supervisor.

"How do you know my name?" I ask, backing up a step. "What do you want from me?"

"What do I want? To keep you breathing. As for your name, I know everything about you, Layla Verona. Everything."

I scoff, annoyed when my voice shakes, and my heart reaches for my throat. "So you're a stalker with a tech fetish."

With a surge of annoyance, I snatch up the baseball bat and hurl it again, this time with a lot more accuracy. It clangs off the circular camera, cracking its lens, but not much else.

I huff in disappointment.

The voice chuckles, a sound that sends tremors through my chest.

"Calm down, Wraithling. Wouldn't want you hurting yourself."

"Wraithling?" I echo, my voice laced with a mixture of apprehension and curiosity. "That's a new one. Who are you?"

The voice seems to sigh, a static-filled sound that fills the room. *"You're in danger, Layla. There are worse things than cameras watching over you. Trust me."*

A shudder ripples through me at the repeated mention of my name, stated so easily, it's almost personal.

"Isn't it obvious?" The voice feels closer now, almost inti-mate, even though it comes from an electronic eye in the corner of the room. *"You're not just precious. You're vital. And what's vital to me, I protect ... or destroy. I haven't decided which yet."*

The words send a forbidden thrill through me, mixed with a healthy dose of fear. "You sound like a predator, not a protector."

The voice chuckles, a sound that's terrifying and strangely compelling. *"Maybe I'm a bit of both."*

I wrap my arms around myself, suddenly feeling exposed now that I'm not storming around my home with a vendetta. "If you're really here to defend me, then show yourself. Stop hiding behind your gadgets."

There's a pause, and I can almost picture him pondering the idea.

"Patience, Wraithling. When I finally reveal myself to you, it won't be through a camera. It'll be with my hands around your throat, deciding whether to end you or claim you. Until then, sweet dreams."

The speaker falls silent, and I'm left standing in the wreckage of my once peaceful home.

6

KADEN

I'm slowly, delightfully driving Layla mad.

She's been working tirelessly to outsmart her mysterious watcher.

First, Layla covers all the cameras—that she can find. I'm nothing if not meticulous and choosy on where to install my backup surveillance. Using the hidden lenses she'll never find around her modest home, I watch her carefully assemble a homemade signal jammer, hoping to disrupt my wireless communications.

She fails, of course, but she uses up a good amount of my time in stopping her.

Next, she returns to the basics. Homemade decoys made out of her clothing shoved over pillows and mirrors clutter her living space, creating confusing reflections and movements that aim to mislead my cameras. That alone signals to me she's aware her watcher would have installed backup, unseen surveillance. Clever girl.

She also experiments with high-frequency sound emitters, attempting to scramble any audio surveillance.

Layla's resourcefulness is undeniable, but she underestimates her opponent at every turn.

"Persistent, isn't she?" I murmur to Reaper as he's winding between my legs.

Layla makes a final attempt to hack into my security system's network again, seeking access to the controls or, at the very least, the identity of her mysterious watcher.

"Good luck with that." I smirk, confident in the military-grade encryption protecting my system.

My fingers dance across the keyboard, ensuring the encryption is in place on the surveillance system. It's nearly impossible for her to hack in, but I find myself silently cheering her on.

As Layla disrupts one signal, my system automatically switches to another frequency. The high-frequency emitters she uses cause a brief disturbance, but I've installed sound filters that quickly adapt and clear the audio interference. Despite the decoys, I use sophisticated image recognition software that can differentiate between Layla's real movements and the false signals.

"Such tenacity, Wraithling." I admire her skills while ensuring I remain one step ahead. "But you won't find me that easily."

As Layla's attempts to outsmart me continue to prove futile, my interest in her deepens. I'm more captivated by her personality and ingenuity than I ever anticipated.

She's quick thinking, I'll give her that. But what impresses me the most out of all this is her outright refusal to *leave.*

Throughout the weekend, Layla plants herself in the light-keeper's house like a poisonous mushroom, ceding no ground to my new but deeply implanted roots. I had a whole plan in place if she did—access to her credit cards and bank accounts, shutting them down if she so much as attempted a hotel room or escape from town.

Yet it turns out, my efforts to block her freedom were unwarranted.

This slip of a girl wants to play.

Hours skipped by as I counter-attacked her methods, my time transgressing as quick as the fog hugging the city of Grey-cliff like a shroud. As time ticks by, it wraps itself around the ancient buildings with a ghostly embrace outside the iron-railed windows near my perch in an abandoned fisherman's warehouse on the docks. The fisherman's warehouse appears timeworn, with rickety wooden beams and the salty ocean air that seeps through the cracks, leaving its mark on the once vibrant floorboards, now a sun-faded gray. Yet it's strategically advantageous. It offers an unimpeded view of Layla's home and the city in general while remaining hidden from prying eyes.

When I initially broke in, I thought I'd be alone with the dust and solitude. The only signs of life were some long-forgotten fishing nets cast haphazardly aside and the soft lapping of waves against the docks outside.

I was wrong.

Plunged in the farthest corner, hidden by stacked crates, I found I wasn't the only squatter. There in the dim light, I noticed green eyes glittering with a fierce protectiveness over a litter of kittens bundled together against the cold drafts that filtered in through the warehouse cracks.

My initial reaction was to drive them out. To eliminate any possible disruptions to my work here. But the sight of the kittens, barely a week old and so vulnerable, had stirred something in me. A flicker of compassion, a protective instinct that seemed so alien now that I've paved it over with ruthlessness.

I'm driven by need—an insatiable hunger for justice, or

perhaps revenge—but also tethered by a code that forbids harm to the innocent. And what is more innocent than these small lives, blindly mewling for their mother's comfort?

Their mother, with her ominous demeanor and emerald eyes promising death, immediately deserved my name.

"Good evening, Reaper," I murmur as she returns to me and prowls around my legs, her coat an obsidian shadow against the faint glow of my machines.

I sigh through gritted teeth. "All right, I guess you're staying."

A soft purr reverberates from her slender throat, a begrudging acceptance of me as her kittens' uninvited guardian.

Rising on stiff legs, I bundle her litter to my chest using the fishing nets she'd collected. I glance down to find the runt of the litter nuzzling into my chest, its tiny heart beating like a trapped bird. Its trust is immediate and without question, something so pure it stings.

I create a little corner for them in the warehouse, cordoning off a part that traps the least breeze and is warmest. At the edge of this space, I place bowls of water and tuna cans for Reaper.

Reaper carefully stalks my movements until I've settled the kittens in their new space and she curls around them. Her low growl reverberates through the quiet evening, but she doesn't attack. There is an understanding between us. Two predators, different by nature but bound by a silent pact to protect the weak. Almost akin to respect.

By Sunday at midnight, I'm chastising myself for becoming so distracted. I've ignored one contract kill already, and from the buzzing of my encrypted phone, I'm avoiding another. But I can't stop.

Layla is so very intriguing, and while I don't yet need to kill her, I also don't want to give her up.

I lean back in my chair, a mixture of admiration and frustration simmering inside me. She's good, damn good. But I can't afford to stay inside and battle her, not now, not when Morelli is still out there.

I watch Layla through the feed—her determined expression as she stalks into her bedroom and the way her brow furrows in concentration. She's become more than just a mission; she's under my skin, in my head. And that's dangerous.

I type a quick command, pausing the feed.

But as I continue to stare at the monitor, I can't shake the feeling of regret. What am I doing? This isn't just surveillance anymore. It's bordering on obsession.

I stand, pacing the length of my hideout. I need to refocus and remember why I'm here. Morelli is the target; Layla is just the bait. But the thought leaves a bitter taste in my mouth.

I glance back at the screens, Layla's image frozen.

My brows tighten the longer I stare.

She has one hand up to her shoulder as if she's about to lower the strap to her tank top, a move I have yet to log in my growing spreadsheet of her activities.

Usually, she goes into her attached bathroom to change, and while I installed cameras behind her mirrors and it takes all my manpower to turn away when she undresses, I'm not into the fetish of watching someone relieve themselves, so I give her the privacy and dignity of walking away from my monitors when the need arises.

This time, it's different.

She's not walking into the bathroom and slamming the door shut, not-so-subtly informing me to stop looking.

I prowl back to the computer. My hand hovers over the mouse. I'd like to fucking look.

Click.

The video plays, revealing her bedroom in high-definition clarity. This camera is behind her jewelry box on her vanity and is directly centered on her bed.

I watched her sleep last night. It was soothing. I've always been in the dark, and the silence is welcome. I return to my seat and type rapidly on the keys, bringing up security footage from multiple angles, all trained on Layla's bedroom. Her movements are mesmerizing, like a dance only for me. Every breath, every glance, every flick of her hair or sip of wine is captured.

This night, however, she's dressed in pink satin.

My eye twitches at the sight. I didn't notice that before, and I notice everything.

I'm glued to the screen as she lets her hair down slowly, savoring the moment. Her lips part in a slight smile that sends a shiver into my groin. A rustle of cloth fills my ears, her body moving fluidly under the thin fabric. She runs her fingers along the hemline suggestively, daring me.

My heart pounds, my breaths shallow. Layla's taunting me, that much is obvious, but if someone were to sneak up behind me and shoot me in the head, I still wouldn't look away.

Suddenly, she looks directly into the camera, our gazes locking. A smirk curves her lush lips upward.

"I know you're there," she whispers, her voice a low purr that sends an ecstatic shudder down my spine.

"Wraithling."

My palm sweats as I grip the mouse tighter. Her nickname rolls over the tongue like a whiskey burn, a name she can't truly understand, but I croon it like she's mine.

Yet her bicolored eyes flash. Layla's still so defiant, so unafraid.

She could be my undoing.

"You would taste so sweet," I say, my voice a husk of itself.

I clench my jaw, trying to focus on priorities but finding it impossible.

Layla purses her lips and begins to dance—a sultry waltz to silent music that makes the air heavy around me. Each undulation accentuates her hips, breasts, the curve of her neck. She's too tempting, both spectral and tangible, like I could reach out and stroke my screen, able to touch her skin.

I struggle to breathe as she leans closer, palming her vanity and putting the tops of her breasts on display. My fingers twitch in reflex, longing to trace the outlines of those curves. Her eyes lock on mine once more, rolling her lips in an invitation.

"You like what you see?" she purrs, her voice a low rumble that makes me swallow hard. "I thought you might."

She trails a fingertip over her collarbone, down to where her breast peeks through the lace fabric. Her other hand slides beneath the thin material, cupping herself intimately. She moans softly, and it's like a knife to the gut. The sound of her arousal rings in my barren warehouse, mixing with the grinding of my teeth.

But I lose myself in the image, hypnotized by her every move.

Her fingers move faster, her nails dragging lightly across sensitive skin. My own palm presses against the cool glass surface of the monitor, my dormant heart reawakened. I bite back a groan as she arches her back, her breast rising to meet her seeking hand. When she closes her eyes and throws her head back in modest ecstasy, I can't bear it anymore.

Pushing away from the desk so violently it nearly topples, I flick off the monitors, the room plunging into darkness again. I can still feel her, though—her presence permeating every pore of my being.

This isn't right. She shouldn't be doing this.

But I can't deny that I want her.

I spin, pressing myself against the cold wall behind me, trying to find some semblance of calm amid the havoc she's created. My hand fists, knuckles white from the strain. I know I should stop, but I can't.

My mind races, imagining what she's doing, what I could be doing to her. The softness of her skin against my rough grip, the slick, wet sounds of her pleasure echoing through the empty room. I close my eyes tightly as I try to picture it, try to feel it.

It's not enough.

An ache grows deep inside, a hunger only she can satiate. And so I succumb, dropping to my knees before the blacked-out monitors.

I stroke myself, imagining her hand instead, guiding me with those delicate fingers. Her gasps of pleasure become my gasps for breath, and soon, they mingle together in a symphony of need and longing. My hips jerk forward, faster and faster, my entire being consumed by this forbidden fantasy.

I roar, my orgasm overwhelming in one powerful release, my back curving as if hit by lightning. Cum splatters against the cool glass screen, warmth spreading between my fingers.

I fall forward, trembling, panting like a beast unleashed.

This shouldn't be happening—no one should feel this way about their captor or stalker or whatever she thinks I am or what she is to me.

I wipe my hand on my pants, still unsteady from the intensity of my release. When I finally gather enough strength to stand, I glance at the blank screen, wondering if she's done with her performance.

The screen flickers to life, and there she is—Layla near the side of her bed, sipping her wine, setting it down, then guiding one strap down her shoulder.

My blood runs cold.

"Wraithling," I say, low and feral as I lean closer to the screen. "What have you done?"

Layla must have set up some sort of loop, taunting me with an endless replay of her undressing to incapacitate me and give her time to escape my watch.

I growl under my breath, snatching my phone from the desk and storming out of the warehouse. My fingers hover over the screen for a moment, but I decide against sending Layla any threatening messages.

Words are unnecessary. Punishment is what matters now.

7
LAYLA

The night air hits me like a wet slap—cold, damp, and angry.

I can actually *taste* my heartbeat as I scramble out of my house and into my car, like my heart just might slip over my tongue and out of my mouth in a similar panicked escape attempt.

All I've taken with me is my red cross-body purse, the thumb drive safely tucked into my bra, and a kitchen knife I impulsively tucked in the front pocket of my hooded sweatshirt.

My hand shakes as I turn the key into the ignition, then I skid over gravel and over-correct when I press on the gas too hard.

Earlier, I amazed myself at how calm I was while figuring out how to outsmart my watcher, first by ensuring his focus when I used tactics trying to break into his system, then subtly recording pleasuring myself to upload.

His system went through routine maintenance reboots—brief windows I observed over the weekend. During this short period, I uploaded the loop directly into the system's local storage via a hidden access point I discovered in the house's network infrastructure, bypassing the main security firewall that my watcher monitors. I figured my striptease would be surprising enough to give me precious time to escape.

Grinning, I imagine the shock he must've felt at the sudden appearance of his victim in barely-there silk pajamas, fondling her breasts. I didn't have to imagine the heat pooling between my legs as I did it or how hard my nipples became when I pinched them, thinking of my invisible watcher on the other side, watching me with hooded eyes.

It turned me on when it should have repulsed me. I actually felt the beginnings of an orgasm when my hand wandered down my stomach, reaching for the ache between my legs.

He could be anyone. A pervert. A greasy, elderly, moth-bitten man. Yet I, the large, scarred man who saved me, all angles, muscle and jagged lines, came into my mind the minute I cupped my breast, and then it never left.

It's him I pleasured myself for.

And holy shit, that is so unlike me.

Maybe that's why I'm out here now, driving as if for the first time, adrenaline shooting out of my hands and throat and into the road ahead.

I'm so consumed by what I've done and who I put myself on display for, that it takes me a full three minutes to figure out if this watcher outfitted my home, he sure as fuck would've put a GPS device on my car.

"Shit!" I pull over to the side of the road, slamming on the brakes.

My phone pings the instant I turn the engine off.

"Double-fuck," I hiss.

Clambering out of the driver's side, I pull the SIM card out of my phone then throw both on the ground, stomping on them multiple times.

See, this is why one should never record naked or sexual videos of themselves. The possible repercussions become so mentally all-consuming, you then make stupid goddamned mistakes like me.

With all possible electronic monitoring behind me, I race into the surrounding forest, scrambling over rocks, downed branches, and bushes full of thorns.

I don't hike. My hobbies include napping and reading, so with only my wits about me and a visual map of Greycliff in my mind, I take a circuitous route through the outskirts of town, staying off the path and the full moon to give me guidance.

Within fifteen minutes, I can't breathe. I'm used to computers as my muse, my mouse as my movement, my mind as the ultimate weapon.

But here in the forest, my body is in charge.

And it sucks.

"Keep moving," I heave out to myself, forcing my legs to push forward despite the agony coursing through them as I trek up a sharp incline.

The ground beneath me is treacherous, uneven, threatening to trip me up at every turn. But I have no choice. The fear of what might happen if I stop is far worse than any pain I'm currently experiencing.

The farther in I go, the darker it gets, and I curse my decision to seek refuge in this godforsaken forest. In my haste to escape, I'd failed to consider just how disorientating it would be to navigate through the oppressive gloom. I can barely see a foot in front of me, let alone find my way back to civilization.

"Stupid, stupid, *stupid*," I mutter under my breath, my voice shaking as much as my body. Yet, even as I chastise myself, I know I couldn't have stayed where I was. Not with him watching me.

Branches claw at me, tearing at my clothes and scratching

my skin. The once comforting chirps of forest creatures have given way to an eerie quiet that leaves me exposed and vulnerable. It's as though the very trees are conspiring, closing in from all sides and trapping me within their suffocating embrace.

My pulse hammers in my ears, ragged breaths escaping my lips. But still, I listen, praying for some indication that I've managed to put enough distance between myself and the man who's haunted my every waking moment for the past forty-eight hours.

"Please," I sob, my voice barely more than a breath as the weight of my terror threatens to crush me.

I was so brave with my hacking skills, so cunning with my erotic idea to escape. Now? Not so much.

But even as the words leave my lips, cold tendrils of fear wrap around my chest. Because deep down, I know that it's only a matter of time before he catches up with me. And when he does...

I force myself not to think about what might happen next, focusing instead on putting one foot in front of the other. It's all I can do to keep moving, to keep fighting for the chance to escape this sudden nightmare.

"Keep moving," I urge myself again, trying to ignore the fear that rises within me like bile in my throat. "You have to keep moving."

And so I break into an uneven run, my body fumbling with exhaustion and terror, my mind filled with awful thoughts of the man who shadows my every step. The invisible man who will soon overtake me.

I hear it.

The sound of a twig snapping not too far behind me. The knowledge that he's out there, relentlessly pursuing me with his uncanny tracking skills, sends relentless shudders into my bones. The fear grips me tighter, making it hard to even wheeze.

My legs grow weaker by the second. Panic threatens to consume me entirely. My mind is a jumbled mess of thoughts, a jumble of emotions crashing against each other like waves upon the shore. But above all else, I feel betrayal—the bitter sting of my smarmy supervisor who put me in a position where I'm being hunted down like prey.

It has to be that, doesn't it? The thumb drive, now coated in sweat, shoved in my bra is the culprit of all this.

I can't shake the feeling that I'm being observed even now, hunted for entertainment, and that every step I take only brings him closer to capturing me.

"Stop!" I cry out, my voice breaking with exhaustion. "Just leave me alone!"

The shadows seem to come alive around me, reaching out with sinister intent as if urging their phantom to claim his prize.

I whimper, feeling my strength waning and my resolve crumbling.

"Please," I whisper one last time, tears streaming down my face as the moon becomes trapped behind clouds the minute I find a clearing. "Someone help me."

There's no answer, only the oppressive weight of the forest trapping me in my own terror. The isolation is maddening, making me question if perhaps I'm imagining it all—if the threat of pursuit is nothing more than the product of my own fractured mind.

"Am I going mad?" I murmur, my breath hitching as fresh tears pool in my eyes. "Is this what you want? To drive me insane with fear?"

A sudden, deliberate snap of another twig shatters the stillness, and my heart leaps into my throat. Every muscle in my body tenses, preparing for the inevitable confrontation. The surrounding shadows seem to shift, and I squint, trying to discern any movement in the murky darkness.

"You poor thing," said a voice cold and smooth as ice, so close I can practically feel his breath on my neck. "I'm already here."

My skin erupts in goose bumps, and I whirl around to find him standing just inches away, his light-dark eyes boring into mine under strands of thick, ebony hair.

Then the clouds part, and the puckered scar on the side of his face glows, his cheekbones curved like a skull when the moonlight touches them.

A broken whisper comes out of my throat. "It's you."

He chuckles, a low and dangerous sound that echoes through the night air. "You're brave, Wraithling. I'll give you that. But courage won't save you."

"Is that a threat?" I ask, my voice wavering despite my desire to keep it steady. "You saved me once only to kill me on your terms?"

"Consider it a warning," he replies softly, his eyes never leaving mine. "You're not safe. And running away from me won't change that."

"Then I guess I'll have to find safety elsewhere," I declare, rebellion burning bright within me now that I've caught my breath.

He hesitates for a moment as if considering his options. Then, with a sigh, he steps aside, granting me passage onto the logging road appearing behind him.

It could be a trick. After all the effort he put in, he shouldn't let me go so easily.

I take a look behind me, then turn back to the front. I've proven I'm no wilderness expert. If I run back the way I came,

I'll end up in the same position. The logging road looks much better traveled.

Swallowing, I tuck my hand inside my hoodie's pocket. "I have a knife."

He cocks a brow.

"And I'm not afraid to use it if you try to touch me when I walk past you."

A ghost of a smile plays across his lips. "Noted."

As I sidestep around him, his eyes follow me. Even in the misty air, his gaze shines like he's seen too much and experienced so little when it comes to human emotion. My breath catches. A muscle in his jaw ticks. The clearing shrinks, air thinning. My skin prickles, hyperaware of the bare inches between us. I force my feet to move one step, then another. Even with my back turned, I feel the heat of his gaze searing my spine.

I stripped for you, I almost say, until my brain tells me to choke on those words before ever allowing them out.

Once at a safe distance, I hurry down the road, enjoying the taste of freedom, as fleeting as it is.

"You're good."

His words stop me. I turn, showing him my profile so he can't see my puzzled expression.

"At what you do," he continues. "A rare few have ever managed to keep me so occupied."

My throat works as I force myself not to shudder. "You're just trying to scare me. You're nothing but a psycho, breaking into my home, watching me, studying me, and probably jerking off as you watch me undress. It's *you* who wants me in a cage."

He doesn't flinch. "If I wanted you in a cage, you'd already be there. Tied up and at my mercy."

I recoil, disgust and—*arousal*—warring within me. This

man, he scares me, but I can't deny the thrill of the unknown that comes with being in his presence.

"Then why aren't I?" I ask. The question is bold, but my voice is barely above a whisper.

"Because," he says, prowling closer. "You're not my prisoner. You're my lure. And I need you exactly where you are."

"Lure?" I repeat, confused.

"Yes," he says, his voice low. "I want to keep you until Morelli can't resist coming for you himself. Until then, I will own you."

"You're sick," I spit out, trying to keep my voice steady. "And I don't know why I'm still talking to you."

His chest rumbles before he moves so fast, he seems to teleport into my space and catches me mid-spin, preventing me from going anywhere. It's an amused sound that sets my nerves on edge.

"Admit it. You're curious. You want to know more about me."

"I don't want to know anything about you," I grit out, trying to wrench out of his hold.

He matches my backward dance, keeping our unnerving proximity to each other. "That's not true. You're drawn to me, just like I'm drawn to you."

"I'm *sickened* by you," I say, but my voice is weaker this time. "I'm afraid of you."

He reaches out with his free hand and brushes his fingers against my cheek. And instead of flinching, my lips go slack under his touch. "But fear can be so exhilarating, can't it? The rush of adrenaline, the pounding of your heart. It's been a while since I've felt that. But watching you experience it. Fuck, it's like an entirely new high."

I push his hand away in a surge of anger.

"You need help," I repeat. "And it won't be from me."

"Is that so?" he says, his eyes gleaming with his own personal vendetta. "By now you realize the mistake you made. That strip-tease you did for me, you thought it was enough of a ruse to allow you to escape. Instead, all it did was mark you as mine. I've seen you, Wraithling, and I want all of you now."

A panicked noise comes out of my throat, one I've never heard before, but I wriggle enough to get out of his hold and stumble into a run.

His laughter follows me, carried by the wind, caressing my cheeks with the damp air.

No. My cheeks aren't wet from the atmosphere.

My hand comes to my face to confirm, puffs of air bursting out of my mouth as I sprint down the dirt road.

The tears burn trails down my face, each drop a shining scream of rage—at him, at myself, at this new life I never knew I had to fear.

8

KADEN

"Idiot," I mutter under my breath as I crouch behind a large, overturned rowboat, partially buried in the sand near the lighthouse.

Its paint is peeling, revealing weathered stone and rusted metal. The abandoned structure casts a long shadow in the fading light of the day over Layla's small house.

I watch the silhouette of my next victim skulk around a craggy outcrop of rock, edging closer to what's mine. The person's cautious movements and frequent glances over their shoulder suggest they're not just a curious trespasser. But he fails to pause or check his surroundings in detail, his overconfidence in hunting down a twenty-four-year-old girl clouding his judgment.

He has no idea that a scythe has attached itself to her shadow.

In the past twenty-four hours, Layla's property and Layla herself have been silent. She ran from me in the forest, which was expected. Her return to the lightkeeper's cottage was a possibility but not a certainty. Yet when I resumed my watch, there she was, curled up on her bed and sobbing.

I don't feel guilt. The wraithling needs to understand the seriousness of her situation.

A situation that's just become more complicated when I noticed movement on the shore twenty minutes ago.

I knew another assassin would come after my refusal to accept Layla's kill contract, and I'm not disappointed.

The air is thick with the scent of salt and decay. Gulls cry overhead, circling the lonely tower that has long ceased to guide ships. The surrounding area is strewn with debris from the sea—driftwood, tangled seaweed, and the remnants of old fishing gear.

Lowering my binoculars, I creep forward, moving with practiced stealth, keeping low, and using the natural cover of the terrain. I navigate through patches of tall beachgrass and behind clusters of rocks, closing in.

Every step is calculated and silent despite the crunch of gravel and dry seaweed underfoot. My focus is absolute, my senses tuned to any sound or movement from the lighthouse.

I freeze when the silhouette moves not to where Layla is undressing and getting ready for bed but to inside the lighthouse.

Curious.

As the assassin enters it, I sprint for the door, slipping inside a few minutes after him. Inside, the lighthouse is hollow and echoes with the sound of the sea. The interior is dank and smells of mold and rust, with puddles of sea water dotting the floor. A fragile metal staircase winds up around the crumbling walls.

Taking cover under the stairs, I wait until my new friend is a few steps above my head, then lunge.

I grab his ankle, yanking it sharply. The assassin's surprise is audible—a sharp gasp cut short as he tumbles down the stairs. I move quickly, my actions honed by years of training and real-world combat.

I don't let confidence overshadow the situation. The assassin, a trained killer, recovers quickly and swings a fist. I deflect the blow with my forearm, using the momentum to deliver a precise elbow strike to his ribs. The impact is sharp.

As the assassin doubles over, I grab his shoulder and spin him around. Driving a knee into the assassin's abdomen, I further knock the wind out of him. Every one of my moves is designed to incapacitate without causing unnecessary harm.

Yet.

The assassin, now struggling to catch his breath, tries to retaliate with a wild, desperate punch that I sidestep, grabbing the assassin's extended arm and twisting it behind his back in a classic arm lock.

"Looking for someone?" I whisper in his ear while baring my teeth.

With my other hand, I reach into my tactical vest.

In a swift, practiced motion, I secure the assassin's wrists behind his back with black zip ties. I force him to his knees, and with another zip tie, I bind his ankles.

As I stand over the subdued killer, my breathing is steady. There's no anger in my study, only a cold, professional necessity.

With the assassin now securely bound, I take a moment to survey my surroundings, always vigilant for any further threats. My vision stays cold and calculating, my features betraying no emotion as this attempted threat to Layla looks up at me with shocked, flared eyes, but my mind races ahead to the information I'm about to methodically extract.

All to protect my wraithling.

———

"Fuck," the hitman groans as he opens his eyes and sees me standing over him.

I've dragged him onto a wooden chair, securing him tightly and waiting for him to come around.

The lighthouse is silent, the darkness broken only by the soft glow of the moon through the broken windows overhead, laced with the neon green that glows through my mask.

He squints as his vision comes together and notices my snack. "Is that...?"

"Red licorice?" I ask, snapping the rope of candy between my teeth, chewing, then swallowing. I hold the other half between us. "Would you like some?"

"Who the fuck are you?" The would-be assassin spits on the floor, the chair creaking under his weight.

I move faster than he can react, wrenching his chin back to face me.

"Wrong question," I growl, punching him under his jaw and almost sending his entire tongue down his throat. "What you should be asking is how much pain you're about to endure."

The hitman's bravado falters. Fear flickers in his eyes, a delicious sight that sends a thrill down my spine.

I decide to add to it.

Lifting my arm in a high arc, I plunge a knife behind his kneecap.

He screams but doesn't scream loud enough. I twist the knife. "Who hired you?"

"Fuck you!"

I pause my torture. "I've asked you a question."

"Fuck yourself." The hitman spits blood in my face.

I shove the knife farther, my knuckle nearly touching his thigh.

"All right, all right!" he gasps out, the desperation in his voice palpable. "It was the Morellis! They hired me!"

"Who specifically?" I demand, keeping a firm grip on the knife for emphasis.

"Franco Morelli ... Frank ... The Ghost," he stammers, dread dancing over his face as he stares unblinking at the hot steel embedded in his leg.

My expression hardens. I knew he was behind this, but to hear it from this amateur's lips is something else entirely. I take another bite of my licorice, my gaze never leaving the hitman before standing and taking my blade with me.

He screams through clenched teeth.

"What's your name?" I ask idly, wiping my blade clean with a cloth.

"M-Madman."

I arch a brow over the fast-cooling silver, though he can't see it. "Madman? Really?"

His throat bobs so deeply, beads of sweat fall off and into his collarbone. "A contract went out on the dark web. I'm not the only one coming for L—"

I glance up sharply. "I'll kill every last one of you."

Then I pause, pretending to be in thought and picturing a graphic, graphic death. "If any of you tries to so much as utter her name, I'll make sure you live without a tongue or eyes for a few days first."

The idiot turns smart. He shuts his mouth.

"I know who you are." His swampy brown eyes rake over me, watching me chew my candy with considerable unease, muscles pulsing in his jaw.

"Oh?"

"I recognize that mask. You're the Scythe. Never seen but … always felt."

That gets a laugh out of me. "Is that what they say? How amusing."

Madman regards me like—well, like *I'm* the madman.

"You torture your kills." His voice reverts into puberty. "Prolong their deaths."

"I find it fun."

Madman's shoulders slump. "Why are you here, man? This isn't—she isn't your type. Of kill, I mean," he corrects quickly when my cold neon-green stare claims him. "You usually go for guys like me. Men. Not women."

"I'm here for her." That's all I'll admit.

I watch the tiny clock of his fate start ticking in his head. "Okay, well, good for you. The Morellis have a whole file on her. But I … I don't know all the details. They just tell me what I need to know. Grab the girl, find what she's hiding. That's it."

"What's she hiding, then? Be specific."

Snap goes another rope of licorice through the mouth-hole of my mask.

Madman looks increasingly nauseated. "Why are you eating through that thing? So fucking creepy, man."

Snap. Chew. Swallow.

He breathes deeply, bracing himself. "Okay, fine. She has some sort of evidence against the Morellis, I guess. I don't know, man, they don't tell me everything!"

"How many have you killed, Madman?"

He blinks, sweat now coating his lashes. "Maybe … ten?"

"And you take any contract given out, don't you? Women, girls, boys, kids, the elderly. Am I right?"

His blinks turn rapid.

"The truth, Madman," I prod him kindly.

He answers, his voice thick with unease. "Whatever pays the most."

I incline my head.

Then I drive a fist into his abdomen. His gasp fills the circular room, bouncing off the walls.

"Go to hell," he wheezes, defiance sparking in his gaze. It's a fleeting spark, however, and one I fully intend to extinguish.

I snatch the man by his hair. This man—young, likely in his early twenties, with a lean build and short, unkempt hair. Too arrogant for any sort of disguise.

His eyes dart around nervously. I push him backward until his chair balances on two legs. "Do you truly believe I haven't already been there?"

I lean in close until our noses almost touch, his flesh, mine cold metal. My fingers dig into his scalp, drawing blood as I angle him farther. "You won't be leaving this lighthouse alive, but whether you die quickly or suffer for hours is entirely up to you."

"WAIT!" he screams, surrender finally overtaking the bravado now that his throat is exposed. "Look, Scythe, I'm just a hired gun, like you. I'm not given a ton of info on my hits. But I can tell you something ... Morelli is not directly calling the shots here. It's someone else, someone close to him."

I still. Not even the breeze coming through the upper windows dares to flick my hair. "Someone close to Morelli? Who?"

"I don't know, I swear. I just heard whispers. Morelli's got a right-hand man, someone who's been with him for years. They say he's the real brains, the one who's been keeping Morelli untouchable."

I release my hold, sending Madman crashing onto four legs. His head sags, and he groans with relief.

Processing this new information, I ask, "And you think this man is behind Layla's targeting?"

"Yeah. It's all about whatever she's got that they want. It's big, whatever it is."

I face him. "You've done me a favor, Madman. It's only fair I return it."

"Thank—wait, what the fuck?"

He watches me pull out not a knife or a gun, but the remaining bag of licorice, dangling it between my fingers. "Hungry?"

I smile a slow, sadistic smile behind the darkness of my mask as I cut a single strand from the rope of licorice, stretch it taut, and slice it cleanly.

Madman's eyes widen as I make a second cut, then a third, until I have a handful of bright red licorice.

His breath catches as I raise the bundle, bringing the candy closer to his face.

"What is this? W-what are you doing?"

"Whatever you do," I croon in a low voice, "don't swallow until I say you can."

I feed him the licorice, piece by piece, as his eyes slowly close in relief. Madman's fear made him hungry.

"I won't lie to you," I begin. "I can't simply kill you. I have to send a message."

When I'm finished stuffing as much licorice into his mouth as I can, I take the plastic bag the candy was in and twist it.

"Ready?" I ask.

Madman shakes his head in denial, his cheeks bulging like a poor, cornered chipmunk.

"Swallow," I command.

His head bobs as he works to ingest the licorice, his hair matted with sweat, his face more scarlet than the candy. When I notice the bulge in his throat, I take the bag and tie it tightly around the man's neck, creating a tourniquet that works nicely with his sweetened suffocation.

"You do get a quick death," I explain to Madman as the chair bucks beneath him and his garbled cries transform into chokes. "But I never said it wouldn't be traumatizing."

9
LAYLA

My cubicle mate, Ethan, is hunched over his computer and typing like a madman when I walk into our office.

"Morning, Layla," he says without looking up from his screen. "If you hear me talking to myself today, just ignore it. I'm debugging code, not slowly losing my mind. Well, at least that's what I keep telling myself."

I smile when I take my seat next to him. "Got it. If I hear any arguments, should I side with you or the other you?"

He grins, his glasses reflecting the scrolling code. "Always side with the me that's winning. It's good for morale."

As I stare at my black screen, my stomach churns. Somewhere in this sea of data hides the secret AI responsible for my current predicament. What else does it know? What else is it capable of?

Sensing my wary study, Ethan finally looks up, his forehead puckering.

"Rough night? You look like you've been battling some serious code. Or a dragon. Though I guess in our world, bad code is the dragon."

I huff in amusement. "Let's just say I had a night of intense ... Netflix bingeing. You know, the kind where you have to keep reminding yourself that sleep is actually a necessary human function."

"Ah, the Netflix vortex. Dangerous territory. I once watched an entire series about hacking into government databases. For research purposes, of course."

"Of course. Purely academic."

I force myself to wake up my computer and act like this is another normal Wednesday and not another day I've managed not to get killed. My furtive glances above my computer to check for any sign of danger might give me away, though.

Despite my nerves, returning to work was intentional. As tempting as it is to disappear and assume a new identity, I don't have the money for it. I barely have enough to cover my current cost of living. I can't suddenly quit and run underground, mostly because I wouldn't know the first way to do that. Instead, I scampered back to my home like a spooked possum since I didn't know what else to do after my watcher bluntly explained that Mafia people wanted me dead.

Which he then assured me would never happen because he's deigned himself my stalker. No, sorry, *protector*.

This very large man has invaded my home, chased me down in a forest, terrified me, yet I keep returning to the time he saved me, and I finally got a good look at him.

Because yes, I've done the math.

He was a good two heads taller than me but lean in the most lethal way. Same with my watcher. In the forest, he was dressed entirely in black tactical gear. The thin material covered his arms and enhanced the ridges of muscle under his skin. His hands hung loosely by his sides, but his fingers curved in a way that could strike at any moment. His face was partially obscured by a plain black ball cap, pulled low over his brow, with a hood from his shirt covering the rest, but it wasn't enough to hide the jagged scar that ran from his left temple to his jawline.

I wasn't afraid of his scar during the day, like I should've been, and what it could represent. The scar somehow adds to his allure, a flawed perfection. In fact, I can't picture him *without* it, though there must have been a time when he was flawless.

He's a predator, and I'm his prey, yet part of me yearns to close the distance, to understand the man behind the scar, the gear, and the tormented stare.

Maybe he's lying, and no one is after me. It's been three days—five since I recorded a conversation that's changed my life—and nothing's happened. Maybe he's cornering me for his own sadistic pleasure and said the name "Morelli" as a red herring. As soon as I looked it up, there was only one Morelli family to be concerned about—the most vicious Mafia on the West Coast.

However I want to label it, my new stalker is both the most terrifying and compelling person I've ever encountered.

"Want some?"

Ethan shoves a bag of gummy worms in my face so unexpectedly that I yelp.

"Whoa. You okay?" Ethan's warm brown eyes, magnified by his thick lenses, blink at me with concern.

"Yes, just..." I rub between my brows. "Sleep deprived."

"Then you absolutely need some. I find it helps with the post-Netflix brain fog. Or any brain fog, really."

I force a smile and reach for a few gummy worms. They're sour and sweet, and the taste is a welcome distraction from the constant fear boiling inside me. My gaze drifts to the window. But as I chew, I can't help but think about the dark predator who has taken an interest in me. I can feel his eyes on me even when he's not there—and not just electronically.

But I can't let myself get distracted. I need to stay focused on my survival, on finding a way to protect myself.

I take another handful of gummies and turn back to my computer, determined to keep working. I'll have to be cunning, strategic, and careful. I'll have to use all my skills to stay one step ahead and gain any information on this AI that I can.

Information is power, after all. I'd like to know more about what's so important that it brought a stalker to my doorstep and the Mafia clipping at my heels.

"Hey, Layla," Ethan says. "Did you know I almost cracked that new encryption algorithm yesterday? I swear, it's like a digital fortress."

I smile despite the heaviness in my chest. "That's impressive. Maybe the CIA will finally realize what they're missing out on."

Ethan laughs, a sound full of genuine warmth. "One day, Layla. One day."

He's so unaware of the poison lurking within our own workplace. I watch him, wondering if his unrealized dreams of CIA cybersecurity would make him a confidant or place him in danger too.

Throughout the day, I play my part to perfection. Smiles, nods, casual chats by the coffee machine. But beneath the surface, I'm on high alert, scanning every email, every document for anything that might shed light on the Oracle project.

My eye keeps going to Dawson's office, his door closed and lights off. It's almost time to leave, and he hasn't made it in. In fact, he hasn't been in for the past two days.

I'd worry about it if he weren't such a smarmy, shady asshole.

I exit the office when the sun almost dips below the

horizon and head to my car. There's a thickness to the air as the burden of another day of uncertainty clings to me.

I reach for the door handle on the driver's side, sensing something out of place even before the door swings open. It's the faint scent of cologne, a musk that doesn't belong here, but my nose tingles with recognition.

It's not cologne. My brain only thinks it is because it's so inviting: earth, salt water, fresh male exertion.

I've smelled him before.

My heart races as I slide into the driver's seat, and there it is—a small, velvet pouch resting on the passenger seat as if waiting for me. The fabric is a rich, deep crimson, its hue reminiscent of fresh blood. My curiosity piqued, I reach for the pouch with trembling fingers, feeling a shudder run through me as the soft material glides over my skin. It's unexpectedly heavy in my palm.

My curiosity, mingled with a sense of foreboding, nudges me to loosen the ribbon.

Inside, I find a jar, small enough to fit in the palm of my hand but large enough to hold something ... liquid.

Lifting it, I peer through the glass, using the lowering sunset's rays to illuminate the—

"Jesus *fuck*!"

The curse flies out of my mouth at the same time I release the jar. Just as fast, another curse flies out, and I scramble to catch it.

The last thing I need is pickled human remains staining my interior.

Yes, pickled remains.

Floating in the clear liquid is a square of skin, a tattoo my brain processed enough to understand it *was* a tattoo before I wanted it out of my hands.

I catch my breath, my heart deciding to slow down, too, then lift the jar back to my eyeline.

The ink illustrates something Celtic maybe, or Viking—*why do I even care?*

Disgusted, I shove the jar back in the velvet pouch. In doing so, a slice of pain hits my finger. I've brushed against the sharp edge of a piece of paper.

I want to cry.

Instead, I pull out the small, folded rectangle and read.

Layla,

This skin is your trophy. His screams, my gift to you.

Your name is on too many lips.

Next time, I might not be there to paint the walls red for you.

Your Scythe

"Oh, good," I say in a high-pitched voice bordering on a mental breakdown. "He's given himself a pet name I can call him."

10

LAYLA

"Scythe!"

I storm around my home, yelling into every camera lens I can see. I didn't even give myself time to drop my purse or go to the bathroom. I'm so mad.

"Show yourself! Now!"

The purse smacks against my side in time with my pacing. The grotesque jar sways and bangs inside, a brutal reminder of its presence.

Halting in the middle of the main room, I glare up at the camera installed in the corner and point at my bag. "What is this? What have you *done*?"

Silence.

I laugh under my breath, half insane with the images my imagination created on the rest of the drive home. "It must've been you who left me this in my car. My *car*, you asshole! The only other thing that's mine other than this house you've also invaded!"

No response.

"You don't get it, do you?"

The purse's strap slips off my shoulder. I let it fall on the banged-up sofa chair next to me. "I don't require much. Hell, I don't come with much. But what I do have, I'm proud of. So scare me all you want, but I'm not running away. This half-rotten piece of land is my only legacy, okay? It's more than just a home to me. I'm not abandoning that part of myself. I'm not."

My arms fall to my sides. I blow a piece of loose hair out of my face, waiting ten more seconds before I lose my mind.

I'm about to give up and just toss this haunted pickle jar into the ocean when the camera's speaker light blinks to life.

"*Wraithling,*" my Scythe drawls, his tone dripping with casual indolence. "*You keep forgetting you're prey. I'm just making sure you live long enough to learn how to be a predator.*"

"By presenting me with pieces of human skin?" I snap, my outrage reigniting. "I should just take this to the police. Show them what you're doing."

"*Don't.*"

The single word chills the air.

"*Consider it a warning,*" he continues coolly. "*Each assassin I eliminate will be laid out as evidence for you. You should start listening to me.*"

"Assassin?" I echo, my attention drifting from the camera and to the floor as I think.

"*I warned you they would come because of what you know.*"

"What is it you want me to do? Unsee what I saw? Unhear what I heard?"

"*Stop going to work. I won't make you leave your home, but I will lock you in it if you keep testing me.*"

I pull my lips in. My mother would have called my current expression a lemon face, but I still feel like going toe-to-toe with this jerk. "I can't do that."

"*Then you will die.*"

The finality of his words rings in my ears.

I take a deep breath and look back up at the camera. "I'm not afraid of dying. But I'd rather not."

My Scythe laughs softly.

The speaker hums with static, the green light flicks off, then the voice is gone.

I take a deep breath and exhale slowly. Before I can second-guess myself, I grab my purse and trudge outside, my heart heavy and my mind spinning.

The lingering echo of his words snakes through my thoughts, an ominous reminder of the duality that defines this man: self-proclaimed protector and deliberate executioner.

I can protect myself. I've always been able to.

And he's not going to execute me.

He's had plenty of chances, and he's avoided each one. Starting with my almost being run over by a car. It would have been so easy to let me go *splat* under the tires. All of this could've been avoided, like the rewiring of my house, the skin sample from an alleged professional killer, this *fucking* thumb drive wedged permanently in my bra that's become my death warrant. Maybe I should just give it to him. I'm not sure why he hasn't grabbed it from me already.

What keeps him here?

As if responding to my thoughts, a gust of wind whispers through the trees as I walk down the gravel path to the light-house, their branches scraping against each other like the skeletal hands of lost souls.

I shiver, pulling my jacket tighter around me. The light-house looms ahead, its once-white paint now faded and peel-ing. I use my entire body weight to shove open the door, entering the empty circular chamber with an odd sense of doom.

Nothing is out of place since the last time I drummed up

enough nerve to explore the barren lighthouse floor. Dirt and debris cover the ground in the same windswept pattern, clicking and chittering every time I open the door and let the breeze in. It's still lonely and musty in here. The previous light-keepers' lives are a permanent mystery since they've left nothing behind of themselves.

It's the smell.

My nose twitches once I realize the subtle shift. A metallic, feral scent, almost like sweat, lingers where it never was before.

Swallowing, I climb the stairs to the top, trying to ignore it.

The top of the abandoned lighthouse, known as the lantern room, is a circular chamber encased in weathered glass panes, many of which are cracked or broken. The room, once housing the beacon, is now empty. I tentatively step through it and outside to the gallery, the exterior circular balcony encircled by a corroded metal widow's walk offering a panoramic view of the rugged coastline and churning sea below. The wind here is relentless, howling through the cracks and carrying the scent of salt and seaweed. I pull the jar from my purse, clutching it to my chest and looking down at the dark, angry water.

I take a deep breath and unscrew the lid. I hold it out over the edge of the railing and dump the contents into the water below, then toss the empty jar behind it.

As I watch the waves swallow it, I feel a sense of relief and dread. Relief that it's gone, but because I'm being so reckless and defiant, fear that the Scythe might actually kill me if he corners me up here.

But I was tired of arguing with a surveillance system. Now that his advantage of surprise is gone, I could finally confront him and ask the questions I couldn't a few days ago.

I turn around to face the lantern room, waiting. Minutes

pass, and I start to doubt myself. Maybe he won't come. Perhaps I was wrong about him.

But then I hear a sound.

I whirl, my hair whipping into my face, and see the eerie, glowing mask at the top of the stairs, neon eyes fixed on me.

He's dressed in all black, his hair tousled by the wind. He takes slow, measured steps toward me, his gaze never leaving mine. I try to fight against the urge to run but fail miserably when my knees go weak. The tension between us is so palpable, a thick current of lightning crackles in the air.

He stops a few feet away, angling his head.

For a moment, we hang in silence, staring at each other, the sound of the wind and crashing waves the only background noise.

"You're playing with fire, Layla," he says, his voice muffled but no less dangerous.

"I figured it was the only way to get your attention," I reply, trying to sound confident even though my heart is beating through my chest. "You said you wanted to protect me, so I put myself in enough danger for you to decide to show up again."

His mask glints in the moonlight. "You called. I came."

"I didn't call you. I just made myself an easy target."

He laughs softly, the sound sending a jolt straight to my core. "You're always an easy target, Layla."

I bristle at his words but can't deny their truth. "Why are you doing this? Why are you protecting me?"

"Who said I'm protecting you?" He takes a step closer, his breath hot against my face. "Maybe I'm just using you to get to them."

"Them?"

"The people who are after you."

"And who are they?"

He shakes his head. "You don't need to know. Just know that they're dangerous."

"And you're not?"

I hear the smirk in his next words. "I never said that."

"Then why should I trust you?"

"Who said you have to?"

"I think you owe me some answers. You've been following me, breaking into my house, and sending me threatening messages. I deserve to know why."

He takes a step closer, and I can feel the heat radiating off his body.

"You want to know why I'm here?"

His words send a thrill through me, and before I know it, I'm leaning in closer to him, my heart pounding.

He cups my face. My eyes flutter closed of their own volition.

And then he murmurs near my lips, "A man wants you, Layla Verona. For what you're not supposed to have. You've taken something very important to him."

The cold grip of the wind snatches away his heat.

"I knew it was about the AI," I whisper to myself, backing out of his hold.

He hears me despite the crashing waves below. "More than that, Wraithling. If what I've discovered about you in a mere two days is anywhere near an indication of your talents, he'll want you for more than what you've recorded."

It's enough to make me lift my chin and meet his eyes again. "What are you talking about? And who is *he*?"

"Frank Morelli. A crime boss known as a Ghost Leader."

"Ghost Leader?"

At my confused expression, he elaborates.

"Someone nobody sees, but everybody knows in the underground. Ruthless, a true cold-blooded killer, and greed-driven in ways even nightmares avoid."

Something fluctuates in this man's voice as he explains. The first emotion that comes to mind is *agony*, but that can't be right. His face is so cold, so closed off. He's so smooth, I bet wrinkles don't line his skin.

Just that scar.

"He sounds successful and set for life," I say, my voice taking on an edge. "So why would he want someone like me?"

"Morelli always wants more. And you would be an asset in the black market. Sold to a terrorist organization, maybe, to help with their technology. Or forced to marry one of his made men to keep you in the family. Hmm." He cuts himself off, pretending to think. "Those are the best-case scenarios, of course. He could always keep you in a cage and take you out when he needs you."

I refuse to let his words terrify me—yet. I can burrow under my covers later. "And what do you want with him?"

"He took something from me." His tone is a venomous whisper that carries such hate, even the waves seem to hush. "Something I can never replace."

It's like my question flipped an off switch inside him. If I thought he was cold before ... he's barren now.

But I don't look away. I can't. Something about the raw intensity of his confession compels me to stay put despite the fear gnawing at my insides.

"And how does that involve me?" I ask, holding his gaze despite the very real urge to run away screaming.

He leans in, his lips brushing against my ear. "You are the key to my vengeance."

"I can't help you with that." Desperation creeps into my voice.

A sudden gust of wind pushes against us, and I stumble. He

catches me before I fall over the railing and pulls me into his arms. While my heart scrambles senselessly, I can feel his steady, unhurried pulse against my ear.

"You can. Start by not dying, for one."

My hands latch onto his shirt, the soft fabric crimping between my fingers in an effort to both clutch him and push him away.

"Please," I whisper against his chest, my body starting to shiver. "I don't want this. I didn't ask for it. Just—take the thumb drive. Take it and give it to them. I need both you and him to *leave*."

He stills. I can't tell if he's staring over my head at the ocean in thought or looking down, watching me. "Then give it to me."

Trembling, I slink out of his hold. He steps back, and I'd like to think it's giving me space, but my survival sense has kicked in, and I'm fairly sure it's so he can take all of me in one bite.

Even though I'm clenching and releasing my hands in an effort to stop them from shaking, they flutter like panicked bait for the predator in front of me as I reach into the V of my shirt.

You brought him here, you idiot. What did you think would happen? A happy exchange of peace before he exits my life forever?

"I'm waiting."

His voice is a terrifying caress while his eyes, so empty and light at the same time, target my chest.

My fingers brush against the skin-warmed metal of the thumb drive, and I pull it out of my shirt, holding it out to him. The wind whips around us, my hair tangling into my face, but I don't dare make the sudden move to tuck it behind my ear. His mask never shifts as he takes the thumb drive from my hand, his fingers brushing mine in the process.

I harden my muscles against the shiver that wants to ignite my blood at our skin-to-skin contact. And I pay particular attention to the fact that a man like this, honed in black and carved with muscle, metal and skill, now holds a pink and white *Hello Kitty* USB drive in his considerably scarred hand.

He tucks the thumb drive into his pocket but doesn't leave. Instead, he becomes so motionless that my stomach does somersaults.

"Okay, so is that it?" I ask. "Are we done?"

He says nothing.

I step back, my ancestral lizard brain taking over and only wanting to get the hell out of here.

He reaches out and grasps my wrist, yanking me toward him.

"We're not done yet," he says.

I try to pull away, but his grip on me is too strong.

"Release me," I say, my voice shaking.

He doesn't listen. Instead, he pulls me closer to him, his other hand wrapping around my waist. Despite the fear coursing through me, I can't deny the way my body responds to him. Every inch of my skin is on fire even though every synapse in my brain screams *MONSTER*.

"You think this is over just because I have the thumb drive?" he murmurs with almost casual amusement. "You're wrong. I could end you with a flick of my wrist."

I try to yank free, but he only tightens his hold when he holds a blade to my throat.

Despite the shriek building in my chest and demanding to be let out, I hold his cold, bottomless gaze. "Then why don't you?"

"Because you're the first thing in years I've wanted to keep alive." His mask tickles the shell of my ear. "I won't let you go."

I open my mouth to scream, but he cuts me off, his hand sliding up my arm, a snake coiling around its mouse. "Don't try to deny it, Wraithling. I can smell the sweet scent of your arousal and feel the way your body trembles for me."

"Out of *fear*."

I try to pull away again, but he makes it impossible for me to escape. He tilts the point of the knife until it presses under my jaw, forcing my head up.

"I could take you right here, right now," he says offhand. "If I ever let you scream, it will be with my name on your tongue, begging me to touch you again."

I gasp, but I'm not sure if it's with apprehension or surprised delight that a man like this, so feral and beautiful, could be drawn to someone like me.

Pathetic, I know, but I've never discounted my flaws. I can feel the heat between my legs building, the ache becoming almost unbearable.

"But I won't," he continues, angling his head. "Not yet. First, you need to understand what you're getting yourself into."

I catch the hunger in his tone too late.

He clasps me by the throat and pushes me back against the railing until I'm dangling, the toes of my shoes scraping against the floor as I grip his arm and beg him not to let me fall.

My heart pummels against my rib cage as I stare down into the white foam of the sea below. The salty mist bites at my cheeks.

"What are you *doing*?" I cry out, my words choked by his rough, calloused hand.

His hand slides under my shirt, the hem buffeting in the wind. His cold fingers tease the soft skin of my stomach before moving up to cup my breast over my bra. He squeezes gently, and I both cry out and gasp, arching my back involuntarily.

"Please—don't let me go. Don't let me fall!"

"But it's not the fall that scares you, is it?" Scythe's voice is as soft as a creeping shadow, the words like a gentle caress against my cheek. "It's me."

His free hand finds its way to the button of my jeans, flicks it open effortlessly, and reaches my soaked panties.

The railing could break underneath my weight at any moment. Scythe's hand under my jaw is the only thing to keep me from tumbling into the waves below.

Scythe's finger slips inside me, teasing the edges of my pleasure with a delicious torment that makes me whimper in spite of myself.

"No...it's..." I can't finish my sentence.

I grip the railing when his thumb finds the small bundle of nerves just above where his finger is buried inside me and rubs it gently. My hips jerk in response, and I release a gasp that drowns out the pounding sea.

"You like this, don't you? You like being at my mercy, your life in my hands as I make you come."

I want to say no and deny the truth in his words. But his fingers are relentless, and his control absolute.

My climax slams into me, my body responding to him in ways I find hard to comprehend. Despite the situation, I can't help but moan when he releases my throat. The sudden lack of friction sends icy terror through me and twist away from the railing and to the safety of the wall, gasping.

I have enough energy left to raise my head, enough defiance to glare at him.

With an emotionless, metal-rimmed stare, he raises his fingers to the shape of his mouth, painting the ingot lips with my arousal.

My own lips thin. If it weren't for the noticeable tent in his pants, I'd be convinced that his dangling me over the railing of the lighthouse and pushing his fingers inside me was just another evening to him. That *I* was just another inconvenience to be dealt with before he moved on to cut another piece of skin off someone else.

"I have your scent now," he says, at last finished with savoring me on his fingers. "And you've tasted what it's like to be associated with a man like me. Because I'm not going anywhere. I'll kill anyone who tries to get near you. And when it's time for Morelli to make an attempt..." He seems to mull over his last words. "I still don't believe I'll ever let you go."

"I'm not someone to be kept," I snarl while coming to a wobbly stand.

"That's where you're wrong, Wraithling."

He fishes into his pocket, tossing something small, metallic, and heavy near my feet.

"Your new phone," he explains. "Since you ran over your last one. Updated with advanced security features, including encrypted communication channels, a custom-built privacy firewall, and a discreet tracking app. All for my enjoyment and your protection."

I pick up the smartphone, staring at it like I've picked up a roach. "It's like I can't escape you. Everywhere I go, you'll track me down."

"Yes, but I've made it pink." His chin subtly dips toward the pocket he shoved my thumb drive in. "Which you seem to enjoy."

"I don't want—"

"Don't destroy this one. You won't enjoy my backup plan."

With a grim salute, he spins and disappears down the staircase, leaving me and my electronic handcuff behind.

11
KADEN

My daughter's laughter haunts me.

I sit in the shadows, her memory a relentless tormentor unleashing words of guilt and blame. The fateful morning she disappeared is etched on my soul, leaving an indelible mark of loss, black and all-consuming.

I imagine what Cassie saw when he intercepted her in the hallway of our home.

What she said as she struggled and cried:

I want my dad. Please, Daddy, help me...

The cold marble floor on her bare feet, the hallway lit by the early morning sun and adorned by our family photos—her elementary school graduation portrait, when she caught her first big fish with me smiling behind her, the one where she snapped a picture of me at the top of the cliff, overlooking the sunset after a long hike ... all those happy, proud father versions of me bore silent witness to Cassie's terror.

She would've stumbled backward, her small hands instinctively forming fists, preparing to fight with all the innocent courage a twelve-year-old could muster.

I imagine the sickening crunch of a blow, a monster's fist colliding with my baby's face. The cry she would have let out—a sharp, horrifying sound that bounces off the crumbling brick walls of my nightmares each night.

Maybe she bit him. Perhaps she kicked and scratched, using the self-defense maneuvers I taught her from when she could walk. My Cass was a fighter. She wouldn't have gone down without a struggle.

Then I hear the dull thud of her body hitting the floor for the last time before being dragged away, ripped from everything she knew and loved. Taken from me.

And I imagine how I'll kill him.

I'm on the hunt, Morelli. For ten years, I've followed your trail, and now I've found you.

One of his assassins attempted to grab his latest prize, Layla, which I easily prevented. Morelli will make the mistake of sending more, all of whom I'll dispatch, sending blood-soaked evidence to him, to anyone who steps between me and what's mine. Every person involved in this scheme will understand the Scythe's presence. I won't leave until I get my pound of flesh.

That will make Morelli curious, an emotion I've learned he does not enjoy.

While clearing my dinner this evening, I'm not worried. I've thought of strategies and counter-solutions for all of the above. My operational designs are all so second nature to me, I consider individual warfare to inhabit a reserved section of my mind.

It's the anomaly I never planned for that pisses me off. Layla is a variable that defies all my predictions, yet she's become the most crucial part of the equation.

With her uncommon beauty and impressive mind, she

makes me question everything I've become—a man consumed by vengeance and hardened by the cruel effects of violence. I know I can't let myself become distracted, but my fingers still thrum from burying themselves inside her. I've never worn lip balm, yet I would gladly paint my mouth with her pussy's scent every morning.

I study the abandoned fishing warehouse around me, its decaying walls, the salty scent of the ocean heavy in the air and mingling with the pungent aroma of rotting wood and rusted metal. The wind whistles through the cracks in the building's facade, the eerie sound accompanied by the distant cries of the seagulls circling above and soft mewls of kittens.

After leaving an open can of tuna for Reaper, I take the dilapidated staircase leading up to the loft. The old structure creaks and groans under my weight, as if protesting my intrusion into its forgotten realm. I reach the top of the stairs and enter the dimly lit room, the flickering glow of the monitors casting a spectral light.

My gaze is drawn to the screens, and there I see her, like an ethereal vision framed by the camera's unyielding eye. I only allowed myself to leave her watch for ten minutes while I slapped together a sandwich and guzzled water from the sink.

An inexplicable longing seizes me, making it impossible to look away. I'm captivated by Layla's every gesture, from the way she tucks a strand of wheat-blond hair behind her ear, to the soft curve of her lips as she hums a bittersweet melody while she turns in for the night. I doubt she knows she's doing it.

I cock my head at her nighttime routine. Either Layla's given up on destroying my electronic surveillance or the piece of the hitman I sent her has convinced her that she's better off with a guardian shadowing her every move.

My Wraithling is sensible. She understands the need for me.

Lifting my fingers for one last, delicious inhale, I take my seat in front of the largest monitor.

I'm also a sensible man. Coldly so. And I realize that I'm not just observing a woman who's unwittingly become entangled in my dark world; I'm witnessing the embodiment of everything I've lost and can never have again. Layla represents the innocence and light that have long since been extinguished within me, replaced by a void of despair and bitterness.

"Dammit," I mutter under my breath, the words a harsh reminder of the chasm that separates me from her.

Yet even as I berate myself for succumbing to the temptation of watching her, I can't tear my eyes away from the screen. The magnetic pull between us is undeniably powerful. She must feel it, too. Layla curved against that railing for me, the metal trembling under her orgasm, threatening to send her plunging into the ocean sixty feet below.

But she let me finger fuck her. She curved her pussy into my hand like she would gladly fall out of the sky in the throes of what I gave her.

I'd never let her fall. But I'm also never going to let her *free*.

As the night unfolds, I remain rooted to my post, the flickering images on the surveillance monitors holding me captive. I know I should leave and put distance between myself and the woman who threatens to shatter my carefully constructed barriers. But as the hours slip by, I find myself unable—or unwilling—to turn away from the haunting beauty of Layla Verona.

The weight of my original directive—to kill her—stirs around me, taunting and relentless.

On the screen, Layla moves gracefully about her room. She's wearing a short white nightgown that clings to her body, revealing every curve as she prepares for bed. My breath hitches, my heart pounding against my chest.

"Dammit all to hell," I curse under my breath, trying to distance myself from the visceral reaction her mere pixelated presence evokes.

As Layla settles into bed, I expect her to read a little, as she always does, making it three pages before she closes her eyes and drifts off to sleep.

Tonight, she does no such thing.

Her brows are tensed in thought. Layla keeps her eyes hooded, but I've watched her so often I'm familiar with every move, tic, or habit she falls into when she thinks no one's looking.

Her lashes flutter in a poor attempt to disguise where her focus is: on my camera. She starts chewing on her lower lip, her exquisite jawline tensing and releasing as she debates whether to unleash some sort of rebellion.

I smile.

After three days of uneventful patrols around her property, I'm looking forward to how she'll attempt to incense me next.

My Wraithling would never simply give up.

Leaning back, I rip open a package of red licorice and stare at the screen, chewing slowly.

Her hand slides beneath the sheets. The sight sends a jolt of electricity through me, straightening my spine and dropping the candy to the floor.

My mouth goes dry when the small tent of her hand moves toward her center.

I take a deep breath. She moves her fingers in a slow, steady rhythm. I can't look away, transfixed by the sight of her exploring her own body with a savage hunger that matches my own. I feel my restraint slipping with each passing moment.

But my resolve only lasts for so long. Eventually, I give in to temptation and engage the microphone.

"Missing my fingers, Wraithling?"

Layla's hand freezes. She looks up, directly into the camera, her mismatched eyes locking with mine. Something passes between us, primal and powerful.

"You better be thinking of me while fucking yourself," I warn.

"I was."

Her voice comes through my speakers, husky with both shame and desire.

My response is just as low and raspy. "Toss the sheets aside. I want my monitors to glisten with how wet you are."

Layla peels the sheets off her glorious body, her nightgown riding up as she squirms.

"Spread your legs," I command.

After a brief hesitation, she does, her knees bending slightly.

"Wider."

I zoom in while I make the demand, the details of her desire reflected back at me in high definition, from the blush to her cheeks, the swell of her bottom lip as she bites it, to the fluttering of those gorgeous eyes.

Layla shifts, her knees lifting on either side of her.

I smile when the pink folds of her pussy are centered perfectly in my vision.

"I'm very pleased to know that I'm keeping you up at night," I tell her, my voice a low growl. "Are you dreaming of me fucking you, Wraithling?"

I can hear her breath quicken, her center wet and ready for me.

"Yes," she whispers, her voice breaking.

Her fingers resume their frantic pace.

I can understand her need at this moment. Desire is so much better at consuming fear than hate. Layla wants to lose herself in what I did to her—what I will continue to do—rather than think about her life being cut short solely because she chose to stay late at work one time.

A respite which I am more than happy to give her.

"Stop playing with your pussy. Pull your nightgown up. Show me your breasts."

"What if I say no?" Layla continues to bury two fingers in her pussy, pumping and rubbing her clit with her thumb.

My upper lip spasms with both want and irritation. My Wraithling will bow to me if I have to storm over there and force her hands above her head.

"You wouldn't dare," I say.

"I can say anything I want."

"You can say no," I concede, my tone barely restrained with temper. It's not often I'm defied. "You can do anything you want, in theory. You can call the cops, come after me, do whatever the fuck you have to do." I pause. "But you won't."

"Won't I?" she asks, her brow arching along with her neck as she curves into her pleasure.

Amusement curves my lips at her attempt to provoke me.

"I've scared the absolute fuck out of you before—what's stopping me from raising the stakes the next time I see you? Using my cock instead of my hand, I could shove it inside that sassy mouth of yours, your plump lips rounded as you choke on my cum while I plunge in so deep, you can't bite down."

I throw my head back and groan at the tantalizing thought.

It's the most words I've ever said to her, and what does she do? She shoves her hips up, burying her fingers up to the knuckles at my words.

"Maybe next time I see you, I will," I vow, my voice tight. "You want the kind of pleasure only I can give."

"You're an arrogant bastard," she retorts.

"I know," I admit. "But I'm right."

Finally, she relents and pulls her shiny fingers out and uses both hands to lift the fabric of her nightgown. The soft silk pools around her neck, revealing the creamy swells of her breasts. They're small but perfectly formed, the nipples tightened into hard peaks.

"I want to see you play with your nipples, Wraithling."

She cups her breasts, gently tugging and teasing her tight pink buds.

"Keep going," I order.

"I hadn't realized you were so demanding," she says, breathless. "You know what they say about the quiet ones."

I smile, knowing she'll do as I instruct. Victory flows through me as I watch her fingers pinch and rub her nipples to the point of pain. Her movements become more urgent.

"Now fuck yourself, Wraithling. Come for me."

Both of Layla's hands dive for her starved pussy, stretching herself wide, showing me that tight hole. Layla's back arches off the bed when she plunges four fingers in. Her head presses into the mattress. Her pussy is so wet, the top of her hand is soaked. I imagine it's because she's been thinking of me since the moment I walked away from her at the top of the lighthouse.

The thought fills me with such satisfaction. I imagine how it'll feel to have her pussy clutching my cock.

Her chest heaves. The camera zooms in farther, and I can make out the glistening trail of her juices running down her thigh. I set the camera to record before I think twice. I don't want to take my eyes off her. I want this image of her forever ingrained. This is the best I can do.

"You have no fucking idea how good it feels to watch you. I'm as hard as a fucking rock, and I'm going to stroke my cock to you. Layla..." I whisper her name.

I undo my pants, and my cock springs free. My hand wraps around my shaft, and I groan, imagining her pussy stretched around my length.

Layla convulses, tensing as she races toward her orgasm. She brings her knees up to her chest, her toes curling as she comes apart, her pussy squeezing the fingers that are still inside her. I stroke my cock faster, wanting to come with her.

I pump my cock, the seductive sight of Layla writhing on the bed taking me into another, better world. She spasms, and her eyelids fall closed.

"You're close, aren't you?" I say.

"Yes," she moans.

"Eyes on me," I snap.

Layla blinks her eyes open, her head lolling toward the camera and her focus staying on the lens.

I stroke my cock fast and hard. I'm so fucking close. The rasp of my hand is loud in the room.

"Come all over yourself, Wraithling."

The sound of her orgasm starts a split second before she can't look into the camera anymore, and her lips part as she cries out. Layla's body shakes with wave after wave of pleasure. I'm driven over the edge. The sight of her has me spurting over my hand and my abdomen.

I lay there in a post-orgasmic stupor, my heart beating fast, my breathing labored. I don't know what the fuck just happened. I've never come so hard. I've never been so transfixed by a woman before.

The room is silent, save for my thundering heartbeat in my ears, and as her face lingers in my mind, a sense of foreboding descends.

Layla's not just under my skin; she's infiltrating the fortified bastions of my soul.

I've faced countless dangers and navigated treachery and near-death experiences, both in my patriotic past and this menacing present.

But Layla Verona is the greatest threat I've ever encountered.

12

LAYLA

My vagina is a traitor.

I'm squirming in my office chair in hopes of punishing myself by feeling the ache, over and over again, as a shameful reminder of what I did last night.

But instead of enduring any penitence, I'm creating desperate fuel for *more*.

If imagining what it would be like to have sex with him was that incredible, what the hell would it be like to actually—

NO, LAYLA.

That road doesn't lead to a happy ending. The Scythe insists he's protecting me, but his traits lean more toward a stalker than a defender. He sends me trinkets in the form of human skin as "proof" that other men are after me.

Not to mention his manners. He took my thumb drive without so much as a thank you.

I clench my fingers above my keyboard when the final, cutting thought hits me: I don't even know his name.

The fluorescent lights above my cubicle flicker like a warning, the mundane *click-clack* of keyboards around me now sounding like a countdown to something inevitable, something irreversible.

Like the Scythe will storm in here next, demanding I strip down so he can claim me in front of my startled coworkers.

Last night's encounter wasn't just crossing a line. It obliterated it. In one reckless evening, I flirted with danger and danced with the devil. And now, sitting here amid the drone of office normalcy, I'm electrified with a secret that's both exhilarating and terrifying.

I thought I could play him, thought I could weave through his defenses and pluck out his vulnerabilities like a needle through fabric. It was supposed to be a way to gain leverage. If he's so distracted by my body, maybe I could find a way to escape both the danger he presents and the people who don't want me talking.

Instead, what I exposed was a rawness within myself and a need for pleasure so deeply sown, I hadn't known it was there until the Scythe offered me relief.

I'm not sure what I want more. For these Mafia men to show themselves or to stay in this aggravating purgatory where I lay in wait for the next person who wants to hurt me.

If there even is one.

It could all be a ruse. I only think I'm in danger because *he* told me I was. He used it as an excuse to set up cameras in my home, monitor my every move, scare me, threaten me ... pleasure me.

But I'm not so innocent myself. I lured him to the top of the lighthouse, knowing what he is. I justified it as a right to an explanation for the jarred nightmare he left in my car, but we all know the real reason I drew him up there.

I wanted to see him again.

My mind replays last night—my fingers turning into his

touch and igniting my skin, his very real whispers weaving through the room like silk and steel.

How can I sit here, typing reports and sipping coffee, when I've lifted the curtains to this town and seen something darker, so much more intoxicating?

My screen comes to life, an email notification popping up. My heart skips a beat. Because now, every ping, every call could be him. The man who's not just ambushing my life but also creating a fire that's threatening to consume everything I am.

I'm still lost in my thoughts when I sense someone standing by my cubicle. Looking up, I see Ethan, his expression a mix of concern and curiosity.

"Hey, Layla, you okay?" he asks, adjusting his glasses. "You've seemed a bit off lately."

I pause, caught off guard.

"I'm fine, Ethan. Just tired," I reply, forcing a smile. "You know, long nights of Netflix."

I've been successfully avoiding everyone at Pulse Dynamics, especially Emmitt Dawson, who returned a few days ago after taking time off. He returned quieter and with shifty eyes, like he was constantly bracing for incoming threats.

I don't blame him. I've adopted the same attitude.

If he's aware that I'm an involuntary witness to his crimes, he doesn't give any indication. To my surprise, he hasn't come up to my desk, tried to massage my shoulders, or smell my hair when he thinks he's asked a distracting enough question to get away with it.

Dawson isn't avoiding me, exactly. He's still my supervisor. But he's not acting like himself. He's neither creepy nor interested. It's like I've stopped existing.

Like he's already marked me as a dead girl walking and I'm no longer worth his time, or he's been warned that he'll turn into pickled skin if he's seen talking to me?

Both are terrifying prospects.

Above me, Ethan's forehead creases with worry. "You know you can talk to me, right? We've known each other for, what, five months now?" He grins. "That puts me way above cubicle neighbor."

I appreciate his outreach more than words can say. It wasn't apparent to me until Ethan asked that I don't have anyone left to care about my well-being. "I consider you a friend, Ethan. And I appreciate it. It's just personal stuff, you know?"

Ethan nods slowly, his eyes still reflecting unease. "Personal stuff. Got it. But hey, everyone needs a break from their personal stuff sometimes."

God, if he only knew.

I raise an eyebrow, curious about where he's going with this. "What are you suggesting?"

"Well..." Ethan starts, looking uncharacteristically hesitant. "I was thinking, maybe a change of scenery would help. Something different from, you know, codes and screens."

"A change of scenery?" I echo, intrigued despite myself. Ethan's more of a hermit than I am.

"Yeah," Ethan says with growing enthusiasm as if warming up to his own idea. "Like going out. There's more to life than this office and our homes, right? I mean, I don't usually do the whole nightlife thing, but I think we could both use a night off. Just to unwind and forget about stuff. It's been tense in this place lately, have you noticed?"

I study him, surprised by his offer. "Ethan, you hate going out. You once described the club scene as 'a Venn diagram of loud music and poor life choices.'"

He laughs awkwardly. "I did say that, didn't I? But I also

said I wanted to try new things this year. So what do you say? A night out in Greycliff. Our choices are the one nightclub or the one dive bar. It might be ... fun?"

The idea of Ethan in a social setting is amusingly out of character, but his genuine concern is touching. "Okay, Ethan, let's risk some poor life choices together. But if we end up in a techno rave, I'm holding you responsible."

His grin is infectious. "Deal! It'll be an adventure. We deserve a little fun."

As he settles into his chair, I'm left with a feeling of warmth. Ethan, in his earnest and slightly awkward way, is trying to pull me out of my shell, to offer some normalcy amid the chaos of my life.

And maybe, just maybe, a night out is exactly what I need.

———————

At the end of the workday, Ethan and I hover at the crossroads of Greycliff's nightlife, the vibrant nightclub on one side and the low-key dive bar on the other.

"So your pick," I say, trying to sound enthusiastic.

He glances at the nightclub, then at the dive bar, and finally says, "Let's start with the dive bar. Ease into the whole 'wild night out' concept."

My lips curve at his tight voice. It's more than charming that he wants to cheer me up in the face of his own anxiety. I loop an arm through his, Ethan's well-worn plaid shirt soft and comforting against my hand.

And nothing like cold black tactical clothing.

I bat the unwelcome comparison away. *Not tonight.*

The Leaky Dinghy is cozy and dimly lit, with a jukebox playing soft rock classics in the background and crooked nautical decorations on the wood-paneled walls. We pick a booth at the back and order a couple of beers. I find myself relaxing, and the laughter and chatter around us are welcome distractions.

Ethan leans forward on the scratched, wobbling table, and asks, "Hey, so, are you enjoying working at Pulse?"

Light laughter escapes me before I can stop it. "Sure. Are you going to ask me about the weather next?"

His cheeks turn pink under his freckles.

"Oh—shoot, sorry." I reach out in apology. "I just meant that it feels like we're on a blind date, and I found it funny. I'm terrible at jokes. I should know better than to try to make them."

"Wait, so you're actually bad at something?" Ethan gives a lopsided smile.

That gets another laugh out of me. "I'm bad at so many things. Don't let my killer computer skills fool you."

"Oh really? Like what? I can't picture you struggling at ... anything, actually."

"I'm pretty sure my oven has a restraining order against me. The last time I tried to roast a chicken, it came out looking like a prehistoric fossil."

Ethan bursts into laughter, his glasses reflecting the lights above and obscuring his green eyes. "That's nothing. My culinary low point was attempting a 'romantic' dinner. The pasta was so undercooked, I think it still remembered the field it grew in."

I have to lower my beer before I accidentally laugh into it. "Pasta with a backstory, I like it."

"I took it as a sign. Some of us are destined for culinary greatness, while others are destined to support local takeouts."

"Cheers to that."

We clink our bottles together. I forgot how much I enjoyed that sound. Glancing down, I notice mine is empty—

a testament to how comfortable I've become in Ethan's company.

"It feels like ages since I've had a conversation this easy. No pretense, no subtext," I say, appreciating the moment. *No apprehension and fear.*

Ethan nods. "It's nice, isn't it?"

I glance at my empty bottle, then back at Ethan with a smile. "What's your poison? Another beer, or should we live dangerously and try the house special?"

Ethan peers at the chalkboard menu behind the bar, squinting slightly. "House special, huh? Is that the Fisherman's Regret or the Dockside Dregs?"

I snort. "Knowing this place, probably both in one glass. Come on, let's risk it." I call to the bartender, "Two Fishermen, please!"

It doesn't take long to get our new drinks, and it didn't take long to finish them. We're on our second round when the mood shifts, Ethan's open expression a little blurred, but serious.

He leans forward. "I can't believe we haven't done this sooner. You've always been so approachable despite how intimidating you could be, you know, given how you look."

I raise an eyebrow over my half-empty martini glass. "Intimidating? Me?"

If he only understood how easily I gave into the twenty-four-hour surveillance from a man with a fetish for bloodshed.

"Yeah," he admits, a little sheepishly. "When you first started at Pulse, I was kind of terrified of you. Thought you'd be like those girls in school who never gave me the time of day. But in the first team meeting you attended, everyone was throwing around tech jargon, trying to impress the boss. But you—you spoke about the project's potential impact on ordinary people. You had this way of seeing beyond the code, connecting it to real life. It wasn't just genuine, it was refreshingly human."

His honesty catches me off guard. "That's really sweet, Ethan. I had no idea."

Ethan nods, taking a sip of a mostly full drink that sloshes around the edges. My new bestie is a lightweight. "Yeah. I guess we all have our layers, right?"

I huff softly through my nose, glancing sideways. "Yeah. We do."

Ethan pauses in setting his glass down. "Something wrong?"

I return to his face, and the genuine concern I find there brings tears to mine. I want so badly to tell him everything: about my stalker, the terror that surrounds him, and the twisted hold he has on my heart. But to do so would put Ethan in danger too, and I can't bring myself to do it.

I'm not that selfish. Yet.

"Hey." Ethan reaches over and squeezes my hand. "You can talk to me about anything. Whatever it is."

His words are a comfort, a reminder that amid the madness, there are still pockets of kindness.

"Thanks, but it's nothing. I'm probably overthinking it."

No, you are fucking not, Layla.

He squeezes my hand reassuringly, not pushing me to reveal more.

We decide to check out the nightclub next, needing a change of pace.

As we leave the dive bar, the cool air hits us, sobering us up a bit, but not enough to remember the target on my back. Ethan and I are far from graceful when we spill out onto the sidewalk. He's telling me some absurd story about his one and only attempt at skydiving, where he apparently screamed so loud, the instructor thought a bird had gotten caught in the plane engine. I'm laughing so hard that tears are starting to form.

I'm wiping my eyes when I notice Ethan's jacket draped over my shoulders. When did he do that? It's a sweet gesture, and I'm touched by his thoughtfulness. I have to smile when his scent surrounds me—like fruity cereal and energy drinks.

As we reach the curb, Ethan reaches for my hand to steady me, our fingers intertwining naturally.

That's when the laughter dies in my throat.

My skin prickles, an alarm system firing too late. The streetlamps flicker, their light seeming to bend around a slice of night that refuses illumination.

And then he's there.

No fanfare, no warning. One moment empty space, the next filled with his presence. Tall. Immovable. A black hole given form, warping reality to his will.

The Scythe.

"Shiiiiit," I breathe out in a drunken, off-key melody. "I'm in so much trouble."

Ethan stares at our new friend. "Whoa, is Darth Vader in his mercenary era? Damn, I left my lightsaber in my other pants."

"Ethan. We need to leave. Now," I whisper.

The Scythe looms in the middle of the deserted street, a void punctuated only by the eerie glow of his mask's electronic eyes. They pulse with venomous green light, scanning us with cold precision.

His gaze locks onto our intertwined hands, then flicks to Ethan's jacket draped over my shoulders. I'm certain the temperature drops as his scrutiny intensifies.

"Hello, Wraithling," the Scythe purrs.

"Okay, yeah." Ethan blinks. "Definitely not a fellow

cosplayer. Unless he's really committed to the whole 'fear is part of the costume' thing."

I squeeze Ethan's hand hard, silently pleading with him to shut up.

The Scythe's focus shifts to Ethan, his voice a glacial command. "I'll be taking her now. Step aside."

Ethan glances between me and the Scythe, confusion and alcohol warring in his eyes. "Uh, Layla, you know this guy?"

I open my mouth but only taste the Fisherman's Regret churning in my belly. Words fail me.

Ethan, oblivious to the danger, throws an arm over my shoulders. "Sorry, Mr. Scary Mask. She's with me now."

The Scythe prowls closer, each step a silent threat. "Last warning, Ethan. Walk away."

Ethan, with drunken bravery I never knew he possessed, squares his shoulders. "Ooh, the cyber-ninja knows my name. I'm shaking in my ergonomic shoes."

I hiss at Ethan. "Now is not the time to discover your inner action hero!"

"Listen, my dude—" Ethan starts, and I nearly faint at his casual use of "my dude" to address the human embodiment of death.

"—we were having a great night until you crashed our party. I made Layla laugh. You made her frown. I think the scoreboard's pretty clear here—"

Ethan crumples to the ground mid-sentence.

"Ethan!" I cry, but the Scythe is already there, his gloved fingers digging into my arm.

"Are you insane?" I scream at the Scythe, lashing out at the arm that just executed some sort of cobra strike on Ethan's throat. "He's just a drunk nerd, not a threat!"

He deflects my strike effortlessly, trapping me against his side with inhuman speed.

"Ethan!" I cry, twisting frantically in the Scythe's iron grip. "Ethan!"

The Scythe yanks me closer, his hot breath a stark contrast to the cold metal of his mask against my skin. I shudder involuntarily.

"He's not worth it," he whispers, voice laced with venom. "No one is."

Fear ignites in my veins as his glowing stare pins me in place. "I warned you to stay in your home."

I struggle harder, but his hold only tightens. "Let me go," I hiss through gritted teeth. "You're hurting me."

"I could hurt you so much worse," he warns, voice dangerously soft. "You're so careless, Wraithling."

He spins us, half dragging me across the road. The cocktails in my system turn my limbs to lead, hampering my resistance.

I whimper, my heart squeezing my lungs. The scent of saltwater and decay fills my nostrils as the wind picks up, carrying with it the eerie whistle of distant ships. The moonlight casts grotesque shadows on the old, crumbling buildings around us.

"You belong to me, Layla," he murmurs, his voice deep and throaty. "Remember that."

"Ethan," I shout, craning my neck to keep his prone form in my view. "Ethan, wake up!"

There's a sharp intake of breath, and my heart leaps as his eyelids flutter open. Ethan sits up and shakes his head groggily.

Emboldened, I turn on the Scythe. "You are the only danger in my life. Everything else is normal except what you've sabotaged. Dawson hasn't breathed a word about what I overheard. And Ethan? He's just a nice guy, not part of your twisted kink."

The mention of all those names makes his grip tighten.

"You speak of other men in my presence," he warns, a

dangerous edge to his voice, "when even one is too many, Layla. Their existence in your life is at my discretion."

With an unyielding grip, the Scythe steers me toward a sleek black car hidden in an alleyway. The vehicle is modern and nondescript, almost swallowed by the narrow pool of black between the buildings. I try to pull away, my heart pounding a frantic rhythm, but his strength is overwhelming.

"Get in the car," he orders.

"I'll call a cab. I'm not going anywhere with you."

He leans in close. "Get in the car if you want Ethan to live."

His words hit me like a physical blow. My eyes dart back to Ethan, still on the ground, rubbing his neck and looking around in confusion, searching for me.

Ethan's hurt because I let my guard down. I wanted normalcy when it is so clear my life is far from ordinary.

With leaden steps and a heavier heart, I climb into the car. The Scythe closes the door with an ominous thud.

As we vanish into the night, leaving a dazed Ethan behind, a terrible realization washes over me.

The Scythe's dominance was never just about stalking.

It's about possession.

A claim so all-consuming, so terrifyingly complete, that it threatens to devour not just my freedom but also my very identity.

13
LAYLA

The zip ties dig into my wrists as I squirm against the tight knots, searching for any weakness in their embrace.

The Scythe watches my struggle, his tone a mix of impatience and amusement. "You won't break free."

After a tense, silent drive, we arrived at an old warehouse on the outskirts of town near the rarely used, dilapidated docks. It loomed before me, appearing like a giant, evil castle out of the night. The Scythe pulled me out of the car and ushered me inside, his hand like a shackle on my arm.

In the center of the ground floor, a solitary chair stood like a throne in a neglected kingdom. He tied me to it, his movements swift and precise. I was powerless by alcohol, the vision of my friend abandoned on the street, and all the ways this man could hurt me now that he's hidden me where no one will hear me scream.

"What is the *point* of this?" I snarl, whipping my head around to face him. My hair tangles in front of my face. "If you're so intent on 'protecting' me, why am I tied to a chair?"

"Because you still don't see the gravity of your situation.

Tonight proves that. You think I'm your enemy, but I'm the only one standing between you and death."

I scoff. "My 'knight in shining armor,' right? More like a captor in a Batman suit. You can't keep me here forever."

The Scythe halts in front of me. Before I can blink, his hand snaps out, his fingers and thumbs digging into my cheeks when he forces my gaze to his. "Watch me."

I cry out, and I'm ashamed to admit it's not entirely from fear. "Oh yeah? And what will you do now that you have me?"

His free hand trails down my arm. "Everything you've been too afraid to ask for."

Without warning, he releases me, leaving a throbbing pain in his wake, and retreats into the shadows of the room. I watch through tendrils of my hair as he disappears from sight, wondering what he's up to now.

I try wriggling against the restraints again, but they hold fast. There's little else to do, so I keep trying, testing, kicking and picking at the chair so maybe I can grab a piece of wood for a weapon.

Time passes slowly. The moon's gleam through the small window tells me it's still night, but I don't know when the Scythe will return, or what for. Mumbling curses at him, I fight against the chair, my wrists becoming slick with blood and my palms throbbing with small splinters, none of them weaponized.

The alcohol has faded and left a nasty headache behind. I'm really thirsty, and I need to use the restroom.

Sighing, I let my head fall back, my rapid pulse more obvious in the stretched skin of my neck.

I'm starting to panic.

The Scythe hasn't hurt me before—in fact, he brought me to orgasm instead. But this feels very different.

I'm teetering on the edge of a meltdown when an unexpected sound breaks through the quiet. My body goes rigid and my heart leaps into my throat, expecting the Scythe to emerge from one of the many gloomy corners. Instead, a sleek black cat pads into view, its green eyes reflecting faintly in the light.

Paws land silently on the cold concrete floor as it approaches, whiskers twitching with curiosity and a motorboat operating in its stomach.

"Nice kitty," I croon. "Your stealth matches your owner."

The cat tilts its head at me before resuming its purr-fest. The oddly soothing noise does nothing to ease my predicament. If anything, it seems to emphasize just how hopelessly trapped I am.

With a graceful leap, it lands on my lap. But as it kneads my legs, then curls up and gets cozy, its glowing green eyes meet mine again.

"Are you spying on me for him?" I ask my fellow inmate.

"Reaper," a voice orders out of nowhere, causing me to flinch.

The cat is unfazed, merely tilting its head toward the source of the sound. I watch in confusion as the Scythe steps into the rays of moonlight, looking more human than I've ever seen him.

His mask is gone, his chest bare, allowing the soft light to play over his ruggedly handsome body that would've been considered beautiful if not for the striking display of tattoos and scars covering him, each one telling a story as complex as the man himself.

The Scythe advances slowly, his posture relaxed as he reaches out to rub the cat's sleek black fur, then picks Reaper up, cradling the cat against his chest. I'm taken aback by his gentleness, struggling to reconcile this image with the cold and ruthless man who's tied me to this chair.

His shirt is off. His. Shirt. Is. Off, I needlessly repeat to myself.

And I can't help but ogle.

I've never seen anyone look so deadly and so achingly gorgeous all at once.

He's not bulked up like a bodybuilder, but honed, every inch of him chiseled with potent strength.

A tattoo sleeve on his left arm seems to depict a tragedy. It's a blend of intricate patterns and symbolisms interwoven with images of death and rebirth. Eerie and beautiful. His jet-black hair is tousled, making him seem less like a terrifying figure of the underworld and more ... well, more like a man.

But it's his face that captures most of my attention.

The most striking of all is the scar snaking from his jaw to under his eyebrow, the silvery threads giving him an intense, intimidating allure. It's a painfully familiar mark—a mirror image to the one I saw on my savior the night I was almost run down.

My body tenses as this visual confirmation threatens to drown me like a tidal wave.

"It really is you," I whisper.

His pale-blue eyes stare at me with a force that freezes my lungs, until I remind myself to take a breath.

"I'm getting tired," I say. "And now I'm bleeding, if you're here for a status update on your captive."

No response.

"Can I please have some water?"

I hate saying *please* to him, but maybe that's what he wants. A begging, pleading submissive before he lets me go. "Or use the bathroom?"

"Come," he croons.

Not to me. But to his pet cat.

Then he disappears again.

"Hey!" I call out to him. "Come back!"

A familiar clicking sound draws me away from his

retreating form, and as I turn to look, a match is lit in the far corner of the room. The aroma of a cigarette fills the air, making my nostrils tingle with its pungent scent.

Then slow, unhurried footsteps approach and a figure emerges from the black, sauntering toward me with an arrogance and cruelty that makes my skin crawl.

No burn marks. No scars. No tattoos.

This isn't the Scythe.

His aura is different—more menacing, more volatile. He flicks the spent match onto the cold concrete floor and takes a long drag from his cigarette before he finally meets my gaze.

"Would you look at those eyes." He smirks. "Nature's own little freak show. I always wanted to fuck something rare. Guess it's my lucky day, dollface."

I blink, taken aback. He's taller than the Scythe, larger in build, and his face—though handsome in a pock-marked sort of way—is twisted with barbarity.

Panic surges, but a part of me still believes this is a ruse—until his unfamiliar, rough hand hooks my chin.

"Pretty young thing, aren't you?"

"Who are you?" I manage to choke out.

The man chuckles, an awful, grating sound. "You can call me Bonesaw. And you, dollface, are my new dissection project."

He releases my chin, only to trail his fingers down my neck and over my collarbone. I shudder, trying to shrink away from his touch, but the zip ties' teeth hold me in place.

"The Scythe will kill you for this," I say, mustering up what courage I have left. "He brought me here. I'm his ... captive."

Bonesaw barks out a laugh. "You think he cares about you? Oh, that's precious. The Scythe, if that's indeed who it is, only cares about himself and his precious mission. No one truly knows him. If he had a name he was born with, that's long gone. He goes by reputation only. He's succeeded in every one of his contract kills. Very expensive guy from the sounds of it. Me, I come cheaper, likely because I'm ... messier."

He takes another drag from his cigarette, then blows the smoke directly into my face. I cough and sputter, my eyes watering from the acrid sting.

"Besides," Bonesaw continues, flicking ash onto the floor, "I have an arrangement with the guy who gave me the tip you were at this warehouse, trussed up and ready for me. He won't interfere with my fun so long as I don't interfere with his plans."

He traces a gnarled finger down my cheek, scooping up an errant tear, then raises it to his lips and flicks his tongue out.

"Mm. Tasty, but I bet your pussy has more seasoning."

Ice floods my veins. The Scythe knows about this man? Allowed him to be here, to torment me? The betrayal cuts deep, even though I know I shouldn't have expected anything less.

Bonesaw seems to sense my despair because his smirk widens. He stubs out his cigarette on the back of the chair, inches from my bound wrists, making me flinch. Then he leans in close, his breath hot and rancid against my ear.

"Now, let's see what makes you scream, shall we?"

His hands roam lower, tugging at the hem of my shirt. Bile churns into my throat and I thrash against my bonds, splinters digging deeper into my palms.

"No! Stop!" I'm beyond pride now, openly pleading. "Please, don't do this!"

But he just laughs, his fingers tightening on my hip hard enough to bruise. I squeeze my eyes shut, bracing for the worst—

"Looks like you're all mine now, sweetheart."

I clamp my lips shut, the tears running freely now. Did I

imagine the Scythe without a mask? Was there ever a cat? Am I having a nightmare?

Oh God, please let this be a really bad dream...

My body stays in fight mode, pulling uselessly at the restraints, bucking up and down without actually making any headway. Sweat and blood have made me slippery, but not enough to escape what this man wants to do to me.

A feral snarl rips through the air, followed by a yowl of pain. My eyes fly open to see Reaper latched onto Bonesaw's arm, claws and fangs sank deep into his flesh.

He curses, trying to shake the cat off, but Reaper holds fast. Taking advantage of the distraction, I rear back and slam my head into Bonesaw's nose with a sickening crunch.

He staggers back, blood gushing down his face, and Reaper leaps free. The cat lands gracefully on its feet and races off into the shadows.

"You fucking bitch!" Bonesaw roars, one hand cupping his shattered nose. Murder flashes in his eyes as he lunges for me again.

I brace for impact, but it never comes. Instead, a dark shape blurs past me and slams into Bonesaw with the force of a wrecking ball.

The Scythe.

The two men hit the ground in a tangle of limbs, fists and feet flying in a brutal, no-holds-barred brawl. I can barely track the vicious blows as they roll across the concrete, grunting and snarling like wild animals.

Bonesaw manages to get in a few solid hits, his knuckles splitting open the Scythe's eyebrow and lip. But the Scythe gives as good as he gets, driving his knee into the other man's ribs with an audible crack.

They scramble to their feet, circling each other like wolves, both bloodied and panting. The Scythe's eyes are chips of blue ice, promising death.

"I warned you," he growls, voice guttural, "not to touch her."

Bonesaw spits a mouthful of blood onto the floor.

"Yeah, and what are you gonna do about it?" Bonesaw's split lip curls into a mocking grin. "She's just a piece of ass. Since when do you care about the meat?"

The Scythe's nostrils flare. His muscles coil, every inch of his exposed skin stretched taut over sinew and bone. "You forget your place. I am not one of Morelli's lackeys to be trifled with."

"Fuck Morelli. He didn't say how hot she was. And fuck you, too." Bonesaw lunges, a glint of steel flashing in his hand.

The Scythe twists, the knife scoring a thin line across his ribs. Crimson wells, trickling down his side, but he doesn't even flinch. His hand snaps out, seizing Bonesaw's wrist in a vise grip. Bones grind together as he applies pressure, the knife clattering to the floor.

Bonesaw howls, his free hand scrabbling at the Scythe's iron hold. But it's futile. With a vicious wrench, the Scythe dislocates Bonesaw's shoulder, the wet pop reverberating through the room.

Bonesaw's agonized scream cuts off into a gurgle as the Scythe's other hand clamps around his throat. He slams the larger man against the wall, concrete cracking under the force.

"There's no question that I'll kill you," the Scythe hisses, his face a mask of cold fury. "The only difference is, now I'm wondering whether to feed your entrails to Reaper and leave your carcass for her kittens."

Bonesaw's eyes bulge, his good hand clawing weakly at the Scythe's implacable grip. His feet kick uselessly, dangling a foot off the ground.

"But I don't feed them rotten pork," the Scythe continues, his voice dropping to a lethal purr.

He leans in closer until they're nearly nose to nose. Bonesaw's face is turning purple, spit bubbling at the corners of his mouth.

Slowly, deliberately, the Scythe reaches behind his back and draws a wicked-looking knife from a sheath at his waist. The blade gleams.

Bonesaw sees it.

"Wait," he croaks, throwing up a hand in a feeble attempt to ward off the Scythe. "Wait, we can—"

The Scythe releases Bonesaw's neck to grab a fistful of his hair, wrenching his head back to expose the vulnerable line of his throat.

The knife flashes down. Bonesaw gurgles as the keen edge parts his flesh, splitting him from ear to ear in a gruesome spray. Blood spurts, painting the Scythe's face and chest.

I scream, thrashing against my bonds until my skin splits open. Tears soak my cheeks and blur my vision, but I can't look away.

The Scythe steps back, letting Bonesaw's lifeless body slump to the floor in a spreading pool of crimson. He turns to face me, the knife still clutched in his hand, dripping.

His expression is unreadable, his eyes two clear glaciers in a face streaked with gore.

The Scythe takes a step toward me. And another, his footfalls like gunshots. I shrink back in the chair, my heart rabbiting against my ribs, every instinct screaming at me to flee.

But there's nowhere to go. I'm trapped, helpless, completely at his mercy.

He reaches me and crouches down until we're at eye level. Slowly, almost gently, he reaches out and wipes the tears streaking down one cheek. I gasp in a shuddering breath, tasting salt and copper on my tongue.

"P-please," I whimper, my voice cracking. "Please don't hurt me."

Something flickers in his gaze. His jaw tightens and he looks away, as if he can't bear to meet my eyes anymore.

"I'm not going to hurt you," he says roughly.

The Scythe straightens and steps back, giving me space. He wipes the knife clean on his pant leg before sheathing it at his waist.

"That," the Scythe says to me softly, nodding toward the lifeless form on the floor, "was your future."

I shudder involuntarily, terror gripping my heart. "You … you killed him."

"You really think I'd let anything happen to you, Layla?" He stares down at me, his dark expression severe. "Every word I've told you is the truth. The threat is real. It's deadly. And it's my job to protect you from it."

"You … you really brought him here to do this to me."

It hits me then. This was all orchestrated. The Scythe lured this assassin here, dangling me as bait, to prove his point. It's a brutal, visceral demonstration of the threats surrounding me —and of his willingness to eliminate them.

"Yes, Wraithling. Really. I'm trying to save you from this world, a world where men like him are around every corner."

"Why? I don't even know your name, and you're professing your loyalty to me like we're important to each other, some- how. I've fought you at every turn."

My voice fractures on my next question, from trauma, from hopelessness, from fear. "Why aren't you just leaving me to die?"

Something shifts in his gaze. "I knew a girl like you once. She was much younger, but she was forced into a world she didn't deserve to be a part of, and it was my fault. I'm not making that mistake with an innocent again."

"But I'm not her."

"No," he clips out. "You're not."

His confession only deepens the mystery surrounding him. The Scythe's bitter stare sinks through my skin, seeking understanding, perhaps even absolution. But I have none to give.

"What happened to her?"

The question slips out, unbidden.

A muscle tics in his jaw. For a long moment, I think he won't answer.

"She died."

Two words, spoken with such finality, such grief.

"I'm sorry," I whisper.

And I am. Despite everything, despite the gore still raining down on me, I feel the weight of his loss.

"Her death was..." He pauses, searching for the right word. "Unnecessary. Avoidable. Much like yours would be if I left you to the wolves."

He turns back to me, his expression hardening. "I won't let that happen again. No matter how much you fight me."

I believe him. God help me, but I do. There's a conviction in his voice, an impenetrable determination that brooks no argument. He will protect me, even from myself.

But at what cost?

As if reading my thoughts, the Scythe crouches down once more, bringing us eye to eye.

"You're not my prisoner, Layla."

"What am I, then?"

His lips quirk. "That's what we're going to find out."

This is a man who only refers to himself as the Scythe. If not unhinged, then he's definitely unstable. He just happily supervised an assassin threatening to rape and murder me, then killed him in front of me. Now he's telling me I will only be able to survive if I stay by his side.

And I'm still tied to a chair.

"Untie me."

"Do you believe me?"

"I don't know what to believe."

The Scythe takes his time studying my face. It's a survey that makes me shatter, like he's trying to reach too far inside me to get his answers.

He says, "Normally after witnessing what you just did, a person would easily do as I say."

I shake my head tiredly, adrenaline evaporating as fast as the alcohol did. "You've made it clear that no matter what I say or do, you're going to prove your point, anyway."

"You needed to see what these men want to do to you if they catch you."

"I don't need lessons in murder."

I say it harshly, my voice ragged and emotional. It hasn't hit me yet—that there's a dead man a few feet away from me. And that staying late at work one unlucky night caused a killer to take the wheel of my life.

"Then consider it a wake-up call," he bites out. "Because soon, more than one man will be sent. A group of them will. How do you think you'll fare then?"

I don't realize he's grabbed me by the hair until my head's yanked back, my scalp stinging from how hard he commands my attention.

My stomach lurches under his gaze, but I keep my expression schooled, staring into the power burning in his eyes.

"You're mine. Must I prove that to you as well?" he asks, his stare morphing into something untamed.

"I'm not yours," I spit, jerking my head back. A clump of hair tears free in his fist. "You're insane."

The Scythe's expression crystallizes into exactly what everyone, even fellow assassins, are terrified of. "You still don't understand the danger you're in."

"I understand plenty." My voice shakes. "You murdered a man in front of me. You tied me to a chair. You're threatening me."

He shakes his head. "I'm trying to save your life."

"By terrorizing me?"

"Yes. Because sometimes terror is the only teacher that works."

As he straightens, I notice the bulge in his pants and how it strains the fabric every time he moves. Under my nervous study, he pulls at the zipper, his dick springing out as if released from prison.

With my head back in his vise-like grip, he pushes his hips, rubbing the tip against my clenched mouth.

"Taste it," he commands. "Put the flavor of my growing obsession with you on your tongue."

The heat of his shaft sinks into my lower lip, warming where I once trembled. I should be appalled right now. I should scream and bite his dick off and act so off-my-face crazy he'd have no choice but to release me.

Instead, his pre-cum leaks into the seam of my lips, his salt bursting with flavor. I've wanted to see him—all of him—since we were on top of the lighthouse. And when I touched myself in bed, knowing he was watching.

I open my mouth obediently, but with hesitation, lapping up more of him. I lick it off slowly, savoring the tangy flavor and eyeing him through my lashes to see my effect.

He groans in approval, pushing my mouth open wider to push more of himself into my mouth. My lips part under his demand, my eyes locked on his.

"You like this, don't you?" he asks, his voice a quiet dare.

I nod, unable to speak, my tongue curling under the base of his shaft.

"You want me."

His words are more of a statement of anguish than a question.

I moan in response, unable to deny the truth in his words. He continues his sensual assault, pushing deeper until he's almost at the back of my throat.

I gag, but he doesn't pull out to give me air.

"You look so fucking perfect around my dick," he murmurs, his voice uneven. "You've never been touched like this before, have you? Tied down, helpless, choking on cock."

I shake my head, terrified yet thrilled by the thought.

His eyes darken in approval as he positions himself, spreading his legs enough that I sense what he's going to do, and I brace for him to slam his entire length inside my mouth.

He starts moving, hard and fast, heedless of my choking sounds, the gargle of my voice mixing with saliva as I try to take him in. Strange, panicked sounds escape my throat as he hits the back, again and again, my nails digging into my palms.

My fingers flex against the ties binding my wrists, desperate for freedom, but also needing to connect with him. Each thrust sends waves of shame and pleasure through my body, making him moan my name louder.

He releases my hair and moves to my cheeks, indenting them with his fingers and thumbs so hard, sparks of pain flash into my vision.

This is raw and fierce, fueled by desperation and lust and something more addictive than I can comprehend.

Suddenly, he pulls out, causing me to cry out in both shock and relief.

He makes an agonized sound in his throat, reaching down to pump himself and aiming directly for my face.

"You still want me?" he asks, his voice curt and gravelly. "Despite what I am?"

Blinking back tears, and fairly certain that my eyes need to be pushed back into their sockets, I nod.

Because I can't lie.

"You want a Scythe to fuck you?"

I raise my head, willing to stare him down while he comes all over me, refusing to flinch.

Every breath I take is filled with the scent of the sea air mixed with his musk and sweat, making me drunk off it.

My lips open again, and without waiting for permission, I dart my head forward and take him in my mouth. He groans deep in his throat, too in the throes of ecstasy to scold me for disobeying him as my head bobs up and down, taking him in as far as I can while bound.

Taking control.

My tongue swirls around the head, tasting the saltiness. My eyes close. I feel him grow bigger inside my mouth, stretching my jaw to its limit.

Both of his hands grip my hair roughly this time, pulling me closer to him, his hips bucking forward, demanding more.

I retch and choke as he pushes deeper still, my throat aching from the force of it. But I don't stop, knowing it's what he needs from me. My eyes water as I struggle to breathe, but I take him all the way to the hilt, feeling the balls of his heavy sack press against my chin. I taste the metallic tang of my own blood in my mouth, and when that taste mixes with salt and cream, I force myself to swallow all of it as he shouts indecipherable words above my head and comes again.

My heart races, my chest heaving as he releases my hair, stepping back to admire his handiwork as he tucks himself back in. He gives me the once-over, and I feel like a prize he's caught.

Slowly, he walks around me, circling his prey, his gaze trailing over every disheveled inch of me.

But he's panting.

His cheeks are flushed.

And his eyes are bright with satisfaction and ... apprehension.

His proximity sends tremors down my exhausted body; his presence is a living nightmare, yet I ache for him despite the trauma I've just endured.

He kneels before me, taking my chin in his hand. "Say my name."

"Scythe," I say automatically, my voice a shell of its former self.

His lips form a bittersweet curve, and there is true fear behind his eyes when he murmurs, "Kaden."

"Kaden," I repeat it like an obedient child, but I like the feel of it on my lips. The sound of it with my voice.

He leans forward, capturing my lips in a devouring kiss, his hand roaming down, over my stomach, then around the back of the chair where he snaps my ties open with the same knife that killed a man. Many men.

I make a grieving, pathetic sound when he pulls away.

"That name belonged to a different life, a different world. One I thought I'd left behind."

The Scythe—Kaden—regards me thoughtfully for a moment before helping me stand. "But your voice makes my name sound like a promise. I never thought I'd want to hear my real name again."

I regard him warily. This is the part of him I don't understand—the soft part, the tattered soul hiding within a lethal body with heartbreaking force.

It unnerves me more than any of his threats.

Because now, I need to know why.

14
LAYLA

I'm wrapped in an iron-clad, suffocating burrito smelling of leather and oak.

Kaden doesn't let me leave his side as we trek through the backwoods and he escorts me home, convinced more Bonesaws are hiding in the bushes readying to ambush us.

Actually, *escort* is too nice a word. My left arm is numb from how tightly I'm molded to his chest. Every time I shift, his hand clenches around my arm, pressing me harder against him. I'm afraid if I tell him my left side is asleep, he'll just roll me up tighter and I'll no longer be able to breathe. Death by leather sushi roll.

Not a bad way to go, but I have too much to do before meeting my maker.

"I've been thinking," I venture to say.

He hasn't let me speak since we left his warehouse, but we're far enough into the woods that I'm willing to risk it.

Kaden grunts an acknowledgment.

Kaden. That's his name. Even having my mind whisper it warms my tummy.

"The illegal AI that Morelli wants, I think I can erase it," I say.

Kaden grinds us to a halt. "What?"

Me, ever one to sense when I've stepped over the line, continues on unabashed, "If I can get into Pulse's basement and access their mainframe, I can wipe all the data. We wouldn't have to worry about Morelli getting his hands on it anymore."

Kaden seems to consider this, the muscles in his cheek working as we resume our trek. I crane my neck to study his face, refusing to break eye contact despite the ache building in my spine. His arms latch around me, fingertips digging into my flesh.

Kaden's deliberate silence magnifies the forest's sounds. The clacking of branches, the rustle of nocturnal animals hunting and foraging. The scent of pine trees and wet earth overwhelms Kaden's delicious smell, even with my nose squished against his shirt.

"No," he says at last.

"But why not?" I counter, frustration bubbling up. "I know what I'm doing. I've gotten in their system before."

The scar on Kaden's face seems to darken. "I don't care whether Morelli gets the AI or not."

I plant my feet, my sudden stop causing Kaden to collide with me. When the toes of his boots crash into my ankles, I swallow the howl that wants to escape.

Kaden lowers his chin to glare at me, his breath hot on my cheeks. "Do that again, and I'll truss you up like a spider's meal. You'll dangle from these branches, swaying with every breeze, while I decide whether to come back for you ... or not."

The blood drains from my face, leaving me lightheaded. Kaden's true motives snap into focus with terrifying clarity, each implication more awful than the last.

A villain doesn't want to save the world. He wants to watch it burn. And that's exactly what Kaden is.

He isn't here to truly protect me or save the world from Morelli's machinations. He's here for his own selfish reasons, his vengeance consuming him until nothing is left but its destructive path.

I'd been foolish to think Kaden's actions were anything more than revenge, no matter how many times he's saved me.

A cynical laugh escapes my throat. Kaden furrows his brows.

"Stop that," he snaps before clamping a hand on my shoulder and propelling me forward.

"Why?" I challenge, shrugging off his hold. My voice sounds hollow, even to me. "Is joy and laughter your enemy, too?"

Kaden freezes, his body going stiff. For a heartbeat, his habitual apathy slips, revealing a maelstrom of pain and fury behind his gaze. His hand shoots out, fingers wrapping around my throat—not squeezing.

Time seems to slow. I'm acutely aware of every point of contact: his calloused palm against my jugular, his thumb resting on my pulse point. My breath comes in short, shallow gasps, my chest rising and falling rapidly.

Our eyes lock. This close, I can see flecks of gold in his irises, lightning joining the storm.

I should be terrified. I *am* terrified. But there's also that exhilarating rebellion he brings out in me to stand my ground, to face him head-on rather than surrender.

"You're so fucking clueless," he snarls, voice muted. But there's a tremor there, barely perceptible. "Out here, starry-eyed dreamers like you end up as vulture food. Bury that shit deep."

Kaden's fingers flex against my neck, his grip tightening

incrementally, and for a terrifying second, I wonder if this is how it ends—not at Morelli's hands, but at the mercy of the man who's both my savior and my captor. The man who's awakened something inside me, a reckless disobedience that refuses to cower, even as my pulse hammers beneath his touch.

But then, as abruptly as he grabbed me, Kaden releases his hold, leaving me gasping and unsteady on my feet. He turns away, his broad shoulders a wall between us, and when he speaks again, his voice has returned to that controlled, emotionless cadence.

"Move. Now."

I hesitate, rubbing my throat, the phantom pressure of his fingers lingering on my skin. The smart thing would be to obey, to fall in line and keep my mouth shut. But I've never been one for the easy path.

"Kaden," I push. "This isn't the way. You can't let your hatred consume you. There's still good in this world, still things worth fighting for beyond revenge."

He coils, then rounds on me.

"You have no idea how deep my hatred runs," he says in a lethal whisper, the words grating against his throat like broken glass. "No clue what I've endured, what I've lost. There is no good left in this world for me."

The anguish in his voice, fresh and bleeding, drowns my heart.

But I also fortify myself, squaring my shoulders and lifting my chin.

"Then tell me," I challenge. "Make me understand. Because from where I'm standing, you're just a walking weapon aimed at everyone, including yourself."

Every muscle of Kaden's is primed like a spring under immense pressure. A rhythmic tic flutters along his jawline.

For a moment, he seems poised on the edge of violence. Then, unexpectedly, a bitter laugh escapes him.

"You think you've got me all figured out, don't you? Let me tell you something, Wraithling. Death isn't the enemy here. It's just another tool. And I'll use every damn utensil at my disposal to get what I want."

He pauses, his mask slipping—revealing the man he buried alive.

"As for my humanity?" His voice drops to an undertone, coarse and jaded. "I carved that out a long time ago, along with everything else that made me weak."

Kaden pulls back abruptly, as if realizing he's said too much. His veneer of cold indifference slams back into place. "Walk. We're not having this conversation in the middle of the woods, out in the open."

Pine needles crunch under my feet as I force my legs to move, to follow his retreating form through the undergrowth.

As we trudge onward, I study the rigid lines of his back, the tension in his shoulders. The scar on his face, I realize, is more than just a physical mark—it's a manifestation of the wounds that have shaped him, the violence that has driven him to this point.

The impulse to reach out, to offer comfort or understanding, rises within me, but I tamp it down. Kaden's walls are too high, his defenses too impenetrable. Any attempt at connection would likely be met with scorn or, worse, viciousness.

Kaden maintains a punishing pace, his long strides eating up the distance while I scramble to keep up. Branches claw at my arms, and exposed roots threaten to snare my ankles, but Kaden moves through the brush like a seasoned hunter, silent and relentless, and I have no choice but to follow.

The trees thin out as we near the edge of the woods, moonlight filtering through the canopy. Kaden slows, his head cocked as if listening for predators. I strain my ears, but all I hear is the thud of my own heart and the rasp of my breathing.

We break through the tree line, emerging onto a narrow dirt road. An old pickup truck is parked on the shoulder, its faded blue paint almost silver. Kaden strides over to it, yanking open the passenger door with a screech of rusted hinges.

"Get in," he grunts, jerking his head toward the cab.

I hesitate, eyeing the truck skeptically. It looks like it's seen better days, the tires bald and the windshield cracked.

Kaden's patience snaps. He grabs my arm, hauling me toward the vehicle. I yelp, stumbling, but his grip is unbreakable. He all but shoves me into the seat, slamming the door behind me.

At this point, I'm convinced what happened between us back at the warehouse, where I gave him ecstasy and he gave me his name, was all in my imagination.

The cab smells of stale cigarettes and motor oil, the upholstery threadbare and stained. Kaden climbs in the driver's side, the truck dipping under his weight. He jams the key into the ignition, and the engine sputters to life with a belch of exhaust.

We lurch onto the road, the truck's suspension groaning as we bounce over the ruts. I clutch the door handle, my knuckles white, as Kaden pushes the accelerator to the floor. The speedometer needle climbs past sixty, seventy, eighty, the woods blurring past the windows.

I chance a peek at Kaden's profile, his features harsh in the dashboard's glow, his scar appearing more like a weapon than an injury.

"Where are we going?" I dare to ask.

Kaden's hands tighten on the steering wheel. So many

seconds pass that I think he's ignoring me, when he finally responds. "I told you. Home."

To my utter horror, my stomach drops at the thought of him dumping me at the lighthouse, then walking away. "And then what? You'll just leave me there, go off on your suicide mission?"

"We're not done," he says so smoothly that it's clear he's regained control. "Your little date with Ethan tonight proved one thing: you can't be trusted to stay put and stay safe."

Dread and a perverse fascination war within me, leaving me dizzy and off-balance. "What are you saying?"

Kaden turns to meet my gaze, unflinching. "I'm saying that from now on, I'll be staying there. With you."

The implications of his words make the back of my head slam against the seat. "You're moving in?"

A cold smile flirts with the corners of his mouth. "Consider it a security measure. For both our sakes."

As I sit there, frozen in disbelief, Kaden slows the car in front of my home. "Better make some space, Wraithling. Your new roommate has arrived."

15
KADEN

Layla stands on her porch with her arms folded when I slow my truck in front of her cottage the following morning, the ocean waves frothing against the weathered cliffs below. She's wrapped herself in a soft blanket since I dropped her off a few hours ago and returned to the warehouse for my things, the salty air tangling her hair under the eerie glow of the fog-twisted dawn.

That same brackish tang fills my lungs as I step out, the crunch of gravel beneath my boots the only sound between my grim face and hers.

The darkness in me thrives on this—the intimidation, the control—but there's a shimmering undercurrent of something else. Something disturbingly like guilt that I crush into nonexistence as I hoist a box from the back of the truck and stride up to her door.

"Don't you dare step inside," she hisses as a greeting.

I don't bother with a reply. Instead, I shove past her into the cottage.

The space is cozy, imbued with an inviting warmth that I fight against absorbing. Her scent lingers everywhere, the same way it did when I first broke in to set up surveillance equipment—a disquieting mixture of florals and ocean breeze.

It sinks into my skin.

Unloading the box onto the nearby table, I let my gaze sweep across the room, taking in the peculiar blend of nautical history and her attempts at modern comfort. The ground floor is an open space, combining a small kitchen and living area. Exposed wooden beams crisscross the ceiling, weathered by years of sea air. Layla's added splashes of teal and coral in the curtains and throw pillows in a pitiful attempt to brighten the space.

A narrow, spiral staircase dominates one corner, leading to the upper floors. As I ascend, I note the walls lined with faded nautical charts and her father's amateur watercolor attempts at seascapes. The second floor holds a small bathroom and guest room, with Layla's bedroom occupying the former watch room.

The top floor, a sole octagon shaped room with windows for walls, serves as Layla's home office. Its glass enclosure provides a 360-degree view of the surrounding cliffs and ocean, but the inside is cluttered with more of her father's driftwood sculptures and collections of sea glass.

Layla's at my heels, her face colored and eyes flashing. I pivot, almost crashing into her.

"You have no right to—"

I ignore her unfinished sentence and descend back into the bottom floor. I move briskly through the living room, deliberately knocking over a tower of stacked books and scattering them across the worn hardwood.

It's a cheap power play, but I can't deny the perverse satisfaction it brings.

"You son of a bitch!" Layla shouts from behind me.

I turn to face her, watching as she bends down to retrieve her fallen books. She raises her head to glare at me and something wild sparks between us—a dangerous heat that has me clenching my fists.

"Keep biting at my heels, and I'll go for your father's pretty artwork next."

"I'd rather you went for his stuff," she retorts, her lips shimmering with her spit. "I don't give a damn about his paintings. These books are my favorite of all time, and if you touch them again, I'll—"

I cock my head. "You'll what?"

Her mouth twitches with all the profanities she'd no doubt love to hurl at me.

A burst of laughter rushes from my lips before I can squelch it.

"Are you always this fierce, or is it just for me?" I ask, my tone more mocking than curious.

Instead of voicing any of the ways in which she likely wants me to die, she collects her fallen books, cradling them like wounded animals as she storms over to the corner where a rickety bookshelf leans against the wall.

"Get out," she croaks, pointing toward the door behind me.

My amusement fades as quickly as it came. "You care more about your romance books than your father's legacy?"

Layla pauses and looks at me over her shoulder, a careful expression on her face. "Why should I?"

"They are all that's left of him," I say before I can stop myself.

"My father left behind more than enough baggage," she snaps, her voice brittle.

I arch a brow, advancing closer. Layla has no idea how close she's coming to treading on my weakness, the one aspect of honor I've retained, or how fast she'll trigger me if she so much as scoffs at it. "Family is everything, Layla. You should give a damn."

Her hands curl at her sides, the color draining from her face as I advance.

"My father left when I was a baby," she says in a tight voice. "He chose the sea and this fucking lighthouse over his daughter. Don't lecture me about giving a shit."

I blink, momentarily taken aback by the rawness in her tone. Even so, I press on, my anger flaring, ripping open old wounds. "Yet you live here, in his shadow. Why?"

"I didn't have a choice," she retorts, her voice choked with emotion. "Fictional worlds in books are better than fathers, anyway."

"Watch your mouth," I bite out, stopping only once we're inches apart.

"Oh, did I hit a nerve?" She looks up at me, her blue and brown eye narrowed, but a tremble to her lips betrays her bravado.

I stare down at her with an intensity that has her stepping back involuntarily against the bookshelf.

"You don't know a fucking thing about me or my father," she snaps, her voice quavering despite the fire in her eyes.

I lean in closer, relishing the hitch in her breath. "You're right. I don't give a shit about your daddy issues. But I do care about you getting in my way."

Her gaze darts to my lips before meeting my eyes again. "I'm not afraid of you."

"Is that so?"

Without warning, I slam my palms against the bookshelf on either side of her head. She winces as several volumes topple to the floor. "Doesn't seem that way to me."

Layla swallows hard, her cheeks returning to that beautiful, rosy red. But she tips her chin up. "Do your worst, then. It's nothing I haven't survived before."

A twinge of something unfamiliar stirs beneath my rib cage. I examine her face, taking in the dark circles under her eyes and the way her chapped lips tremble. She looks exhausted. Haunted. And much too young to wear such disillusionment.

Blinking away the alien sensation, I shove off the bookshelf and turn my back on her. "Stay out of my way, and there won't be a problem. For either of us."

I stride for the door to grab my remaining boxes, but her voice stops me cold. "How did she die? The girl you couldn't save?"

My breath stalls. My shoulders go rigid. And a deep black void takes the place of my thoughts.

"That has to be what drives you," she stupidly continues on behind me. "Because you carry your guilt like a shroud. It's in the way you move, the way you speak ... and the way you can't stand to see me reading about happy endings."

My hands fuse to my sides, knuckles turning piercing through skin with restrained fury. I don't know what's more infuriating: her audacious assumption or the fact that she's so close to the truth.

"Or maybe you're just jealous that a bunch of fictional characters are capable of finding the love that you can't."

I turn, slowly, my gaze scorching with a warning. A threat.

"Oh, you are so full of hypocritical shit." She releases an acrimonious laugh.

I snarl, an explosion of pent-up anger detonating in my chest as I storm toward her, forcing her to backpedal until she's pinned against the wall. Heat radiates from her body as mine presses against her, my voice a resonant snarl in my throat. "You know nothing about me."

Her breaths come thin and fast, her eyes wide but steady in the face of my rage. "I only know what you've shown me."

My hand flies to her throat, gripping tightly as my fury blazes unabated. "And what's that? That I'm just some heartless killer?"

Her lips part, but no words escape, fingers clawing at my hand as she gasps for breath. But dammit, it's the distress shimmering in those contrasting eyes that snuffs out my anger like a gust of wind extinguishing a flame.

I let go abruptly, stepping back as if burned. She slides down the wall, massaging her throat.

But those incredible eyes of hers remain bright when she rises, pushing off the wall and standing despite being cornered. "You're just a broken man trying to find solace in his retribution. But here's the truth: it won't bring her back."

Every nerve-ending in my body howls in denial, but instead, I find myself closing the distance between us until we're pressed together, my hands finding their way to her shoulders.

"Exactly," I snarl with enough force that she blinks in surprise. "So don't forget your place. You are nothing but a tool to me. Nothing but bait. Remember, I'm the one with the gun here."

Layla grips my wrist, her nails biting into my skin. But it's her piercing stare that adds to my scars. "Then use it on me already."

Red tinges the edges of my vision. But with a monumental effort, I force my fingers to relax.

"You don't know what you're asking for," I rasp.

I shove away from her and stalk out the door, slamming it shut behind me.

Only when I'm back in my truck, gripping the wheel, do I allow myself to exhale.

Layla's scent clings to my clothes, my skin, and pumps through the very organ I thought long dead.

And I wonder which one of us is more haunted.

16

LAYLA

Kaden nearly chokes me out, then walks back inside my home with his cat cradled tenderly in his arms.

His reemergence causes an electric charge in the air, a smoky blend of danger and impending doom that seeps into every corner of my home.

Carefully, he makes his way upstairs, boots heavy on the creaking wooden steps.

"Where are you going?" I call after him, curiosity creeping into my voice.

He doesn't answer, but continues his ascent.

I've managed to regain enough composure that only my fingers shake as I follow him. Our confrontation was brutal, visceral and so eye-opening, I'm heartbroken over what I saw.

Not terrified, *heartbroken.*

What the hell kind of person does that make me? Am I a masochist now?

I find him commandeering the smaller guest room adjacent to mine. It's barely more than storage space at this point, filled with boxes and my own chaotic clutter.

With Reaper purring soundly in the middle of my bed, Kaden scours every corner of the upstairs, assessing and calculating with a meticulous focus that sends my heart skittering.

The house, he declares in that low rumble of his, needs some improvements.

Then, under Kaden's ruthless efficiency and latent military precision, my spare room begins to transform.

I watch as he hauls in crates filled with equipment I've only seen in spy thrillers—sleek-looking monitors, complex keyboard sets, complicated machinery with blinking lights and whirring sounds.

I don't ask where he got them from. Some questions are better left unanswered.

I gulp when he unrolls a satchel filled with weapons.

He arranges the monitors in a semi-circle on a rectangular fold-out table he lugged up the stairs, adjusting and readjusting the screens to align perfectly with his tall figure behind the table. Kaden's set himself up to face the open doorway, with a direct line of sight into my bedroom.

His logic is sound, unfortunately. The vantage point allows him unobstructed views of my room and the surrounding hallway, but there's something possessive about his actions, a primal marking of territory that has my pulse quickening.

Once everything is plugged in and powered up, it casts a supernatural blue glow, transforming my quaint storage space into a nerve center. I'm both impressed and intimidated by what he's accomplished in mere hours.

"Will this ... invasion affect my internet connection?" I ask as I linger outside the doorway.

It's a poor attempt to inject levity into our tension-charged atmosphere, but I'm at a loss on what else to do. It's clear he's staying. I'm not about to give in to the impulse to try to stop him again. It's clear I need more of a strategy when it comes to this man.

"No," he replies. "It'll improve it to the point you'll believe you're in the heart of a metropolis, not out on a peninsula with constant storms."

His eyes slide over and catch mine briefly before they move to the view of my bed.

"I'll move Reaper and her brood once I've set up their bed in here."

Excuse me?

My attention whips to the furry black ball nestled in my comforter. "Her brood? She has kittens?"

Vaguely, I remember Kaden threatening to feed Bonesaw's corpse to kittens, but I thought he was just being creative.

Risking turning my back to Kaden, I stride toward the bed and notice at least four kittens suckling on their mother.

"I told you," Kaden grunts behind me. "Family is everything. I wasn't about to leave them."

I stare at the kittens, their tiny bodies squirming against Reaper's belly. Their eyes are still closed, pink noses twitching as they nurse. The sight softens something inside me, a welcome contrast to the strain that's been building since Kaden's arrival.

"How old are they?" I ask, my voice barely above gushing.

"About three weeks," Kaden replies, and I nearly jump out of my skin.

He stands just behind me, his hulking frame casting a shadow over my head. "They'll be prowling around soon."

I turn to look at him, struck by the kindness in his voice. It's at odds with the man who nearly strangled me earlier, who's now setting up a military-grade command center in my spare room.

"You knew she had them before you brought her to Grey-cliff," I say. It's not a question.

Kaden keeps his attention fixed on the babies. "Reaper isn't mine. I found her at the warehouse, half starved and trying to feed her litter. They've grown on me."

His expression remains blank. More than anything, I wish I could know what was going on behind those tempered blue eyes.

"You shouldn't put them in that room with you," I say, breaking the moment. "Your equipment generates too much heat. It's not safe for the kittens in there."

Without waiting for my response, Kaden leans over and scoops up the blanket Reaper and her brood are nestled in with one fluid motion. The cat doesn't protest, seeming to trust him implicitly. He places them gently in the corner.

I follow, watching as he arranges pillows around them, creating a makeshift nest. His hands, capable of such violence, now move with surprising delicacy.

"They'll stay here for now." He straightens. "I'll need to procure supplies for them. Food, litter, toys."

The domesticity of his words, said with a confidence that he's done this before and taken care of something vulnerable, creates a cognitive dissonance that makes my head spin.

"Kaden," I start, not sure what I'm going to say.

Yet I have so many questions.

I clear my throat. "I'm sorry for what happened earlier. What I said about—"

"You should get some rest." He cuts in. "I'll stand watch."

"Stand watch?" I repeat, incredulous. "You expect me to sleep while you're ... what? Patrolling the house?"

"Yes," he replies, his tone leaving no room for argument. He moves past me, back toward his newly established command center. "Lock your bedroom door. Don't open it unless you hear me give the all-clear signal."

"What's the all-clear signal?" I ask, trailing him.

He pauses at the threshold of the spare room, looking back at me. "Three short knocks, followed by two long ones. Anything else, you stay put and keep quiet."

With that, he steps into the spare room and closes the door, leaving me alone in the hallway with more confusion than answers.

I retreat to my bedroom, locking the door as instructed. Reaper spies me in her claimed corner of my room. I smile a greeting to my new roommate, then undress, my mind racing with the events of the day.

Who is Kaden, really? What kind of life has he led? And why, despite everything, do I feel safer with him here?

The soft purring of Reaper and the tiny mewls of her kittens fill the uncomfortable atmosphere as I slip under my covers. Outside my door, I hear the faint hum of Kaden's equipment and his occasional movements.

I close my eyes, knowing I'll be chasing sleep long into the night. In the darkness, I strain my ears, listening for any sound that might signal trouble. But all I hear is the steady rhythm of Kaden's footsteps, pacing back and forth, keeping watch over me.

———

The wind howls outside my window.

I turn to my side, tucking deeper under my covers and shivering against a sudden gust that slips through the cracks.

A warning growl sounds near my face, and in a flash of panic, my eyes snap open and I see that Reaper's made herself at home on the empty side of my bed, bringing her babies along with her and burrowing under my covers, too.

Reaper's eyes are open and staring at me with a ferocity that's disconcerting, as if she's trying to warn me about something.

I'm shaken out of our staring contest by a sudden crack of thunder. Almost instantly, the sliver of light under my door leading into the hallway flickers and dies.

I lift onto my elbow, lurching over the cat where my bedside lamp is. My fingers fumble in the pitch-black for a switch, but even after several fruitless seconds of twisting, no comforting light dispels the overwhelming darkness.

"Kaden?" I call out, trying to keep my voice steady.

No response.

Another deafening clap of thunder makes me jump. I decide to brave the inky blackness and crawl out of bed toward the door. But before I can touch the knob, it swings open.

I yelp, stumbling back. A sharp hiss from Reaper warns me not to move another muscle, but the fear of her claws in my flesh is nothing compared to the massive form with glowing, neon green eyes blocking any escape route in front of me.

"Stay calm," Kaden commands behind his mask. "The storm's taken out the power grid."

"No shit," I retort with more courage than I actually feel. "What now? And what happened to your all-clear signal before you come in?"

I don't need to see his face to envision his wry expression when he intones, "It's not all clear."

Then he moves. Quick and efficient, he crosses the room to my window and pulls down the blinds, blocking out the flashes of lightning.

"Security systems are down. We'll have to double up for the night."

"Double up?" I stammer, still half-reeling from his sudden intrusion.

Despite the threat of a power outage, another form of anticipation begins to prickle under my skin.

Kaden nods curtly. "In here. It's safer."

"In my bedroom?" I finally manage to get out.

"Yes."

I don't miss the weighted expectation that follows his reply or the stiffness in his tone.

Kaden, in my bedroom? The very concept raises a myriad of unarticulated feelings—dread, excitement, curiosity—all jumbled and fighting for attention within me.

But somewhere, buried deep beneath this tumultuous medley, there is an undeniable sense of relief.

I don't want to endure this black-out alone.

"Are you, um, going to keep your Scythe mask on?" I ask, horrified at the high pitch to my voice.

"Yes."

"I see." I swallow down the panic threatening to rise in my throat. "And where would you like to sleep? The chair? The floor?"

He keeps his neon-rimmed eyes trained on me, unmoving. "The bed."

In bed with me? I think, my thoughts turning slightly manic.

In response to the unspoken question that's probably written all over my face, Kaden's mask dips down, his apathetic gaze trailing over my skimpy tank top and under-wear, to my bare feet, my toes curling against the hardwood.

"Are you cold?" he suddenly asks, his illuminated eyes the only brightness in the pitch-dark room. There's a note of something indistinct interlaced within his voice, like the sound of a gun's safety being turned off.

I don't respond because, honestly, I'm not sure if I am. My

skin tingles in a way that's reminiscent of the cold, but it's more invasive. More primal. My knees knock together and my breath hitches.

"Answer me."

His command is punctuated by an unforgiving jab of lightning that dances behind the closed blinds. The room plunges into sheer darkness again, and I can feel him—Kaden, The Scythe—close enough to touch.

"I ... yes," I admit, my voice merely a whisper against the drumming rain hitting the roof. "I am."

His next move is as quick as it is unexpected. In one swift motion, he picks me up effortlessly, cradling me against his chest. My surprised gasp is lost against the thunderous backdrop of the storm outside.

The mattress dips under our combined weight, his mask hovering just above my face. The warmth of his body seeps into me, chasing away the chill that had settled on my skin. I squirm at the cool sensation of the sheets against my thighs, blushing in the darkness.

His voice is rough, almost inaudible as he speaks. "Stay under the covers. Keep warm."

Kaden moves around the room, carefully lifting, then depositing Reaper and her kittens back in her corner with additional blankets. In the lightning-streaked darkness, I notice him shed his leather jacket, then settle beside me, above the covers.

His proximity is unnerving. Electrifying. The heat radiating from him is a paradox. Comforting, yet disturbingly extreme.

"I won't touch you," he says. "I have to stay close, now that there's nothing to help me monitor you or your property."

I nod in understanding, my heart pounding an erratic rhythm against my ribs. He's here for his own ends, not for my comfort. I need to remember that.

But his confirmation does nothing to temper the crackling lightning inside me.

Kaden's promise feels empty as the hours crawl by. I toss and turn, throwing off the covers at the increased heat my inner lightning strikes keep reigniting.

My mind refuses to slumber, too consumed by Kaden's proximity, his lethal presence penetrating any dreams I might have. I'm remembering the taste of him, the silk of him, the noises he made when I forced him to come undone.

Surprisingly, it's Kaden who shatters the quietude first, his ragged breath cutting through the room. "Wraithling..."

His voice is a warning growl. Rough, desperate.

"You need to stop—moving around, so much."

I hear a harsh intake of breath, like he's trying to control himself.

I can't sleep, I start to explain, then realize what a compromising position I'm in.

I'm on my back, my legs splayed on top of the covers, my shirt riding up under my breasts with all my twisting.

Right. He has night vision.

"I ... I didn't mean..." I stammer, trying to straighten my top but instead brushing against him.

Kaden's hand snaps out, gripping my wrist. His fingers are cool and firm against my over-heated skin.

"Layla," he says, an undertone of warning detectable even through his neutral mask.

With a slow deliberation born of restraint so iron-strong it leaves me breathless, his scarred knuckles brush against the exposed skin of my abdomen.

I have to remind myself, this isn't the Kaden who saves kittens and pushes me out of the path of oncoming vehicles. This is the Scythe—the trained, cold-blooded killer.

I clench my fists as his hand creeps upward, exploring the

terrain of my body with unerring precision. My breath becomes audible, my breasts rising and falling under his masked gaze.

His thumb circles the edge of my navel as a rumble escapes him. "So soft."

Lightning flares, and in the split-second illumination, I see him leaning a fraction closer, as if drawn by some magnetic force. The glow from his mask reflects off the sheen of sweat on my bare skin.

"Kaden," I whisper.

I've said his name so much since I've learned it. Maybe too much. But I love how it sounds. I love calling him by his true name.

His hand stills.

"What?" he asks, his voice just above a scrape. Dangerously quiet.

"I can't sleep," I admit.

"And why is that?" His thumb resumes its lazy circling of my navel, the heat from his touch searing through my skin.

"Because you're here," I confess, my words breaking through the storm like shattered glass. "And because ... I want you."

Kaden stops breathing.

"*Fuhhck.*" Kaden pulls his hand back and moves to sit on the side of the bed and putting his back to me.

"Wraithling," he warns, an edge of desperation lacing through his restraint.

"I'm not blind. I can see the way you look at me." My voice breaks, aching and exposed. I swallow and press on, compelled by some masochistic instinct. "You want me, too."

His silence is deafening.

"And..." I hesitate, then plunge forward into the abyss.

"And I think about it, too. All the time. About you touching me."

He murmurs my name like a prayer, or a curse, his head bowed. "You don't know what you're asking for."

I somehow find the courage to say, "Then show me."

"Ten years," he says without turning his head. "A decade since I've touched a woman. Since I've allowed that part of me to have even a breath of life."

His voice scrapes over his vocal cords while my heart races and my cheeks flame at the deeper implications.

Whether he's aware or not, Kaden has just bared himself to me in a way that has nothing to do with physicality.

"Why are you telling me this?" I ask.

"You need to know." There's a finality in his tone. "If I start, if I let myself go, I won't be gentle. I won't be considerate. I'll take what I want, how I want. And it will hurt. This is not something you can handle."

I should be horrified, repulsed, and I am a bit of both. But most of all, I'm filled with an insane, overwhelming curiosity.

I want to taste the darkness he's warning me about.

"Let me decide what I can handle."

His chuckle is harsh and devoid of humor. Still, he doesn't turn to me.

Kaden's hand whips out and grips my ankle, pulling until I'm flat on the bed with one leg in his control and the other trying to find purchase.

He keeps his back to me when his hand, warm and firm, runs up the bare skin of my inner thigh.

It's an intimate touch that sends a jolt to my core. His fingers skim over the lace edge of my panties before his hand comes to rest on the fabric against my heated center.

"Last chance."

His voice is thick and heady as his fingers apply an insistent pressure.

"I want this," I say, though it comes out more like a plea than a statement.

Kaden turns to face me then, his night vision eyes two bright, toxic orbs. His fingers stop their exploration, and he looks at me for a long moment, then reaches for the waistband of my panties.

There's no tenderness in his touch, no caution. Just the abrupt, arrogant grip of a man claiming what's his.

The fabric tears away easily under his firm hold, leaving me bare. I'm certain his eyes are roaming my body unabashedly behind his mask, drinking in the sight of me panting and laid out before him.

It should scare me, having to guess at his intentions, but instead, I'm getting wetter at the thought of the unknown.

He returns to my inner thighs, pushing them apart with a force that has me choking on an inhale.

Kaden's spread me so wide it hurts, the dull throb of it stirring an unfamiliar craving for more.

There's a momentary hesitation, then the soft click of a button and his mask retracts, revealing the hardened planes of his face. His eyes meet mine, pinning me in place with their passion. The faint glow from where his mask rests on the top of his head reflects their ravenous shine.

Hungry for more. Hungry for me.

His free hand delves into the slick folds between my legs, smearing the wetness around before sinking two fingers inside me without any warning.

I gasp at the sudden intrusion, my body unable to stifle an instinctive jolt of pleasure. The sudden pain has me biting down on my lower lip.

A desperate cry escapes me when his teeth graze my clit, then clamp down.

And my cry turns into a scream.

The pain blooms warm and quick, a savage bite of unexpected sensation that forces my back flat against the bed. I grab handfuls of the sheets, my hands cramping from how hard I clench them. I can't look away from him, even as he devours me with a lavishness that borders on violence.

Kaden doesn't pause, doesn't relent, even when the stimulation is so much, it hurts to bear it.

His eyes don't stray from my face, as if he's making sure I watch. Watch as he devours me, his mouth glossed with my arousal. I'm bared for him, stretched out and spread wide like an offering. And he's taking everything.

I don't realize I'm arching into him until I feel the strain in my muscles. My hands, which had been holding onto anything they could find for support, fly instinctively to his head.

His mouth leaves me then, first pulling my hands off him, then wiping his wet mouth with the back of one before they grasp my knees and press them into the mattress.

My arms curl into my chest at the thought of what could happen next, but he catches both my wrists and yanks my hands to my pussy, commanding, "Keep yourself in this position. Spread yourself open."

The harshness of his command stirs a wave of heat through my body. I do as he says, parting my slick folds with shaking fingers. Kaden's eyes blacken at the sight, his gaze lingering on my exposed flesh. He releases a low growl, which sends a shudder up my spine.

Then Kaden's hand is back between my legs, his thumb circling my swollen clit with slow, torturous strokes that cause my fingernails to cut into my own flesh. I grimace, the pain-pleasure spiral morphing into a pit of torture.

I let out a broken whimper when he adds his tongue with no buildup, no teasing tests of patience. Just a carnal, ruthless kiss that has my toes curling and my body thrashing underneath him.

He makes no attempt to soothe or slow down, his actions instead becoming wilder, more brutal. A coppery smell hits the air, and I'm pretty sure it's my blood. Whether from my nails or from him, I don't know. I can't think straight.

Kaden pulls away. Immediately, I whine in protest, but he silences any resistance with a single look, his glare flat yet possessive.

"Spread yourself until you're stretching to the point of agony."

The familiar indifference seeping back into his features makes me pause, but then he thrusts his fingers inside me again, harsh and fast.

My quiet whimper transforms into a desperate gasp when his thumbnail finds my sweet spot. The intensity of it is suddenly too much, and I'm borderline sobbing with the overwhelming flood of sensations when I do as he asks.

My body, under his command, opens further, my fingers trembling as they pull apart my folds. Kaden's tongue is unforgiving, each lash sending sparks and igniting a flame that rapidly grows into an uncontrollable inferno.

I'm not sure when the tears began to fall, but I taste salt on my lips as I throw my head back and surrender to such unrelenting exposure. The edges of my vision blur and I can feel the pressure building, the knot in my stomach ready to snap any moment.

My body jerks as a wave crashes through me, but Kaden pulls back at the last moment, denying my release. He rises from the edge of the bed, observing my blubbering form.

"This is a mere sliver of what I want to do to you. I'm going to take you apart, piece by agonizing piece, until there's nothing left but what I've given you."

I can't think, can't speak. The room spins and I can still feel his heat against my skin.

Just when I'm about to beg him for my release, a sudden creak sounds from downstairs. Kaden's head whips toward the closed door.

His face shows no emotion when he does it, but I can read the subtext.

Intruders.

"Fuck," he says.

17
KADEN

"Fuck."

The word rushes from my lips, sharp as a blade slicing through hot air.

Layla's bare skin shimmers beneath me every time lightning flashes, her fingers digging into herself, opening her pussy with pleading eyes.

I press my hand over her mouth, my fingers spanning half her face, and I relish the soft gasp she emits against my palm.

Layla's wide eyes stare into mine, shining with quiet hesitancy.

I use my other hand to skim my fingers over the length of bare skin stretched taut across her hip bone, tracing a soundless promise—*I'll protect you*—before I pad silently to the door.

The faint noise downstairs has amplified into an unmistakable shuffling. Not loud enough to be a breach, but too obvious to ignore. It's the sound of uncertainty tiptoeing through the seams of the old cottage, and my gut tells me it's human, not a lost fox from the woods.

I'm always ready for death—my own or someone else's.

The Reaper is an old friend, after all. But Layla, she's still a stranger to his grasp.

Crouched into obscurity by the door, I extract a pair of sleek Glocks from the jacket I discarded. Their cold, metallic weight is a familiar comfort. Though it doesn't come close to Layla's warm skin, she's a luxury afforded to men not hunted by the monsters of their past.

Silently, I beckon Layla closer. She's so out of sorts, she tiptoes over without bothering to cover her bottom half. Once she's kneeling beside me, I press one weapon into her palm.

"Stay here," I order, "and shoot anyone who isn't me."

Her brows furrow and her throat bobs, but she nods, clutching the weapon like hope itself. I'd wager she's never handled a gun before, yet there's a delicious irony in arming an angel.

"How do I...?"

Her voice shakes but carries a soft acceptance of the inevitable.

"Keep your finger off the trigger until you intend to shoot. Aim low, center mass."

The paleness to her face intensifies, but she nods again, gripping the Glock tighter.

I rise to slip out of the bedroom, but Layla hooks my elbow.

"Are you going to be okay?" she whispers.

I smile before my mask comes down. "The idiot doesn't know it yet, but he's not breaking in—he's locking himself in here with me."

I brush my fingers against her cheek once, a silent guarantee that I'll return. "Secure the door after I leave."

Then I'm creeping down the stairs, nimble and silent as a cat. This intruder thinks darkness is his ally. I was born in it, molded by it. The fool is walking into my playground.

As I descend, each step below creaks slightly beneath my

weight, but I time it with the storm outside, using the crashes of thunder and buffeting wind to my advantage. Leaves are whipped off trees, and rain peppers the glass windows.

Night vision illuminates my path forward, but I can't shake the taste of Layla's concern along with her arousal off my tongue. It's a sweet mixture that sticks in my throat, but beneath it lies something else: trust.

It's an unfamiliar flavor, and it distracts me for a moment too long.

The intruder lunges from the side, crashing into me with a grunt reminiscent of a wild boar ramming into its enemy. We stumble against a wall, his sweaty palm pressing against my throat as he tries to kick my legs out from under.

But I stand, immovable as the roots of the old oak out front. His body struggles against mine, and the taste of blood—that alloyed tang—singes my tongue as his fist connects with my mouth.

But he's just another raindrop in the storm outside. He is not my equal.

Faster than he can track, I twist, snapping his hold on my throat. I hammer my elbow into his gut, savoring the pained wheeze he emits as I drive it home again and again—until he doubles over. A swift knee to his face sends him sprawling across the hardwood, his body thudding painfully against a corner table.

Before he can recover, I'm on him. One moment he's struggling to rise, and the next his world is reduced to agony and blindness as my boot connects with the side of his skull.

His body crumples beneath me, twitching feebly in its death throes.

There's an odd comfort in the stillness following such violence. The cessation of movement, the fading heat from a body now slowly cooling.

I rummage quickly through his pockets, discovering nothing but a cheap wallet and a burner phone with a single number dialed multiple times. No ID. They never carry identification.

One down. How many more to go?

I toss the wallet onto the dead man's chest, then go still. The hair on the back of my neck rises. It's too quiet. I turn, scanning the room for any signs of movement.

The unmistakable footsteps of another prowling hunter draws my attention to the left. There's a second living pulse in this house.

Can he hear my heart pounding with adrenaline? Or does he mistake it for fear?

I drag the first intruder's body into the open, arranging him on the living room floor, before searching one of Layla's side tables, finding what I need, then procuring a knife from my boot and driving it through his hand, pinning a note between.

She's protected.

A brief glance tells me his time of death: 1:03 a.m. I take a cheap plastic watch out of my pocket, wind the hands to that time, then drop it on the note, rivulets of blood winding through the ink.

I'm sending a clear message: this is the Scythe's territory.

Breathing heavily, I turn my back on the lifeless intruder sprawled out behind me. The silence stretches thin again, only punctuated by the soft patter of rain against age-old glass and wood. Yet beneath its rhythmic lull is the slight rustle of fabric and a muffled breath.

I allow myself a small, brutal smile behind my mask.

Positioning myself at the end of the long hallway, I wait for him to come to me. The intruder's flashlight beam sweeps across the walls, inching closer until he pauses with a quick inhale of breath.

Looks like he found his friend.

The beam of light arcs toward me with an unsteady sweep.

"Who's there? Who the *fuck* did this?"

I press against the wall, keeping quiet.

As the flashlight nears, ricocheting between the walls without caution, I reach out, lightning-fast, and break the flashlight's lens. The sudden plunge into darkness is followed by a startled curse.

Before the intruder can say more, my hand clamps over the man's mouth, muffling any sound. The other drives a knife between his ribs.

I lean in close, my mask's lips brushing the dying man's ear.

"She's mine," I whisper, twisting the knife. "You never stood a chance."

I ease the body to the floor, already alert for the next target. The entire encounter has lasted less than ten seconds.

My pulse quickens, a mix of bloodlust and another, deeper starvation.

Layla's scent is still on my fingers, a soft, delicious overlay to the tinny stench of blood. But it's a fatalistic distraction. I'll never see killing in the same way now that her name is forever etched upon it.

A muffled explosion reverberates through the house, shattering my contemplation.

I'm moving before the sound fades, taking the stairs, a knife in one hand, gun in the other.

A telltale sizzle of circuitry fills the air as I step onto the second floor. I round the corner, taking in the scene in an instant, and note the broken lock on Layla's door, still smoking after the charge used to destroy it.

Layla's set up her phone to act as a spotlight and blind the assassin's night vision goggles. That assassin's now on the floor, goggles flung off and his body convulsing. Layla's backed against the side wall, dressed in an oversized sweater hitting her mid-thigh. I zero in on the wires trailing from the damaged lock to a battery pack in her hand.

Clever.

Layla must have tampered with the battery-powered lock to give a jolt of electricity to anyone who tried to sabotage it. And this guy was the lucky recipient of her surprise.

The tension in her body relaxes when she spots me.

"Scythe," she breathes out, her voice ragged as she drops the battery pack onto the floor with a loud thunk.

Her hands are shaking, but her gaze is deadly calm, a distinction that sparks pride as I assess her for any injury.

I nod at her, an acknowledgment of a job well done. She'd surprised me when she rammed her forehead into Bonesaw's nose, keeping her sense of self-protection despite her terror. Now, she's downright impressed me.

"Are you all right?"

My voice comes out rougher than intended, my concern seeping through.

Layla opens her mouth to respond, but in that split second, the intruder recovers, and with a wet growl, he lunges at Layla.

On instinct, I start forward, my gun already lifting. But Layla is moving as well.

With a merciless grace she shouldn't possess, she sidesteps his reckless charge, using his momentum to shove him face-first into her bedroom wall. He grunts in surprise and pain as she wrenches the arm he'd used to reach for her up behind his back.

My steps falter in disbelief.

And then ...

Then she swings.

In the span of a heartbeat, she slams her laptop into his face with a well-aimed *crunch* of bone against aluminum. The blow sends the assassin sprawling, his body going limp.

For a moment, there's only the sound of Layla panting, her chest palpitating with exertion. Then she's lowering the laptop to her side and looking at me with wide eyes.

"I'm ... I'm okay," she says, her voice wobbling.

I can't hold back my grin beneath the mask.

"Nice swing."

Gently taking the laptop from her, I guide her to sit on the edge of the bed. She allows this without protest, her gaze never leaving me.

I turn my attention back to our uninvited guest.

This guy isn't going anywhere soon, but if he and his friends knew about the power outage and wanted to take advantage, there are bound to be others. We need information —fast.

I cross the room and drop my knee into the assassin's back to secure his wrists in handcuffs.

As I pat him down for weapons, Layla asks, "Aren't you going to kill him?"

I glance up at her question. When I do, I realize I've made a grave error, for I'm incapable of averting my eyes from this woman who is so much more than she appears.

"Do you want to watch while I do?"

Her throat moves with a gulp. Then she seems to blink out of it. "No. Of course not. But isn't that what you do, as the Scythe?"

"Most of the time," I confirm, patting down the unconscious man one last time. "But right now, he's more helpful to us alive than dead."

Her hand flies to her mouth. There's a faint tremor to her voice when she asks, "Are you going to torture him?"

I pause. The question sounds almost accusatory. When I turn my head, studying her, I notice that her expression is frightened, but also curious. A morbid fascination with the monster she's allowed into her bed.

"Yes."

The barely audible gasp she emits shreds through me like a freshly sharpened blade. If gasps could be translated, hers would say, *What would your daughter think of you now?*

But that's impossible. Layla doesn't know enough about Cassie. No one does, except for me and her killer.

I'm doing this for you, baby girl.

Before Layla can interject further, I turn my attention back to the unconscious man. Abruptly, I flip him onto his back, eliciting a groan as his eyes flutter back to the present.

Using a sterilized blade from my gear, I cut open his jacket and shirt to reveal a tattoo etched on his chest—Morelli's sigil.

I grip the collar of his scuffed leather jacket with barely restrained fury, lowering my masked face to his. A single bead of sweat drips down my temple and into one eye.

The assassin's darting gaze steadies, then widens when he realizes who hovers above him.

"I have questions," I say. "And you're going to give me answers."

18

LAYLA

Kaden's voice is a deathly hiss cutting through the room.

The figure beneath him squirms in a futile attempt to free himself before he sags against the floorboards and spits, "Go to hell."

Kaden stiffens.

"I've been there," he responds. "I received the economy experience. You should be thankful. Yours is a first-class ticket."

Despite the clear threat, the assassin's lips twist into a defiant smirk. Kaden doesn't seem surprised by the stubborn resistance.

Kaden reaches out, pressing the surgical blade against the skin above Morelli's sigil tattoo.

A tremor courses through me. What I'm witnessing is far beyond any shady dealings I've stumbled upon at work. I clutch the hem of my sweater, struggling to keep my own fear in check as my moral reservations clash with a morbid fascination.

"Listen carefully." Kaden's words ring out like an executioner's sentence. "You failed. The girl is under the Scythe's protection now."

The assassin's eyes dart to me, then back to Kaden's mask.

Kaden digs the edge of the blade deeper into the man's skin, enough to draw blood. The man beneath him breathes through clenched teeth but says nothing.

A bead of crimson blooms beneath the blade and drips down the man's torso, staining my bedroom floor. Kaden angles his masked face to watch it spread as if he were observing a curious phenomenon rather than inflicting torture.

He angles the blade, pulling up a piece of skin inked with the tattoo. "Tell Morelli if he wants Layla Verona, he'll have to come get her himself."

Now, the man screams through his teeth.

When Kaden relents, a laugh bubbles from the assassin's throat, wet and clogged.

"Morelli? Come himself?" He coughs, spitting blood. "You're out of the loop, Scythe. The old man's dying. Terminal. He's not going anywhere."

Kaden goes rigid. Even through the mask, I sense the shock rippling through him.

"What did you say?"

The modulator barely conceals the disbelief in Kaden's voice.

The captive laughs, a harsh sound. "You think I'm going to explain?"

"You seem to have misunderstood your situation."

Kaden presses the blade deeper, slowly, as though he were slicing off a pad of butter. The captive's laughter dies, replaced by an anguished squeal.

A sick dread crawls up my spine. I press my lips together, keeping down the vomit threatening to rise.

"Still nothing?" Kaden's voice suddenly becomes distant, as if his spirit is the one being tortured instead of his captive. "Then let's keep playing."

With a fluid maneuver that belies his imposing size, Kaden shoots to his feet and paces around his victim, whose face blanches with panic.

Kaden kneels back down, his knee crushing into the man's sternum. "You are here because I allowed it. And you will leave only when I've had my fill."

He traces along the man's jawline. As Kaden leans in, his blade cuts along the man's cheek, lifting skin. "Tell me, or I'll replace my mask with your face."

Between gritting his teeth and arching off the floor, the assassin wrenches his lips open and sucks in a sharp breath, choking on fear and a rank mouthful of defeat. "Cancer's eating him alive. Got a few months, tops."

When Kaden's scalpel pauses, the assassin's grin is red-stained. "But don't worry. Someone's waiting in the wings. Someone who'll make you wish it was still Morelli."

Kaden flings the blade aside, its metal pinging against my window and cracking the glass. His hand shoots out, gripping the man's throat.

"Who?" he snarls, composure cracking. "Who's taking over?"

"Don't know," the assassin wheezes. "Nobody does. But the word is, they're something else. Cold. Brilliant. Morelli's perfect successor."

Kaden's breathing shreds through the mouth of his mask, the sound harsh underneath his disguise. His mind seems to be racing, grappling with the news—the revenge he so meticulously planned for is slipping away in the form of a dying enemy.

His fingers tighten around the assassin's throat, a terrible keening sound coming from behind his mask.

Seeing Kaden falter catches me off guard. Kaden's always been the epitome of control. For the first time, I notice the cracks in his armor, fissures revealing a man driven by grief, vengeance ... and futility.

My voice is a thin whisper, lost under his thunderous rage. "Stop it, Kaden."

He doesn't let go. The assassin's face is turning an ugly shade of purple, his eyes bulging. His struggles are growing weaker, flailing hands reaching for Kaden's arm with less and less conviction.

"Kaden, stop!"

My voice strengthens. I push off the bed and step into the man's pool of blood, desperate to pull Kaden back from the precipice he's teetering on. "You need him alive!"

Something in my plea seems to reach him. As if emerging from a trance, his fingers slacken, and he releases his hold on the assassin's throat.

The man collapses against the floorboards, rolling to his side as he sucks in jagged gulps of air. Blood oozes from the gash on his cheek, mingling with the rivulets of sweat that course down his ashen skin.

Kaden rises to his feet, his movements stiff and mechanical. He retrieves his scalpel from the floor, the blade glinting in the light that filters through the retreating storm clouds and into my window. When he turns to face me, the emotionless mask that conceals his features seems more ominous than ever, a barrier that shields him from the truth.

He may not win this war.

When Kaden faces the assassin again, his voice is ice. "Tell Morelli Death's coming, and it wears my face. For him, his successor, all of it."

The assassin gives a rapid nod.

Kaden snarls, "I'll desecrate every trace of him until even his memory will bleed out and die."

Kaden stands motionless as the assassin stumbles to his feet, then limps out.

Then, when we're alone, a sound rips from him—part wounded animal, part breaking man. His fist collides with the wall. The impact shudders through the room, through me. Again. And again. Plaster rains down, pink with his blood, a macabre snowfall.

I'm rooted to the spot, lungs forgetting how to work. Each blow seems to punch through my own chest, a skewering of splintering drywall and disintegrating control.

When his assault on the wall finally ceases, his mask swivels to me. The blank face is more haunting now than ever before. In its emptiness, I see a truth laid bare: the Scythe—the name that makes hardened criminals tremble—is a man undone.

Pain slices through my heart, white and sharp.

Kaden's shoulders rise and fall with each labored breath, his fists still pressed against the crumbling wall. The sanctuary of my bedroom has become distorted, as if the violence has left an electric residue in the air.

An irrational urge to comfort him surges through me.

It's madness. Kaden's a killer, a threat. Yet my feet carry me forward, ignoring every instinct screaming for self-preservation.

"How many more will die?" I whisper, staring at the blood on his hands.

"As many as it takes to keep you safe."

I should be horrified, but instead, I feel ... protected. Cherished.

"And what happens when there's no one left to kill?" I whisper.

"I will always kill for you."

Kaden doesn't move, but the set of his shoulders tells me he's acutely aware of my approach. I pause just behind him, close enough to catch the scent of blood and sweat clinging to his tactical gear.

My hand hovers near his shoulder, uncertainty staying my touch. When I finally make contact, the Kevlar feels cool beneath my palm. He tenses but doesn't pull away.

"Face me," I say. "I need to see you."

He pivots slowly, the expressionless metal on his face a safeguard against the devastation I sense lurking beneath. But I've seen enough cracks in his facade, glimpsed the festering anguish he hides, and that knowledge hardens my determination to stay firm.

My fingers find the edge of the mask, tracing its contours.

Kaden's hand clamps around my wrist, halting my movement. His grip tightens in warning. But before fear can fully take hold, his fingers loosen, thumb brushing over my pulse point.

I lift the mask, revealing him gradually. The sharp angle of his jaw. The jagged scar carving a path on one side of his face. And finally, his eyes—blue as frosted cyanide and brimming with emotions too complex to name.

The mask clatters to the floor, forgotten. His exhales are warm against my palm.

"Talk to me," I say, cupping his face, my thumb following the ridge of his scar. "Let me in."

A muscle in Kaden's jaw twitches. He leans into my touch, the movement so subtle I almost miss it. His eyes flutter closed, a shuddering breath escaping his lips.

He leans forward, his forehead resting on mine. The

contact makes my heart leap, sparks racing through my veins, and I shut my eyes, too, just to know what it's like to feel the man and not the monster.

My forehead goes cold, and I open my eyes to see that Kaden's lifted his head, the anguish in his eyes hardening into such rage, it's like staring down the barrel of a gun.

"I need to get to Morelli before he dies and kill him myself. I'll kill them all," he grinds out. "Every last one."

I take a deep breath.

"I know." My thumb traces the ridge of muscles in his scarred cheek. "But you've never told me why."

I brace myself for the surge of anger at the question, the intrusion into his life. But Kaden doesn't recoil. His gaze remains steady, his hold on my wrist reassuringly firm, before something breaks in him, like glass against steel.

"There was a time I believed in honor," he begins. "I was a soldier once, who believed in duty and country. Ten years ago, I was ... someone else. A second lieutenant in military intelligence. Analytical operations, threat assessment, data mining —the kind of work that shapes wars."

A shiver cuts through me at the detachment in his voice.

"I was good at it. Seeing patterns, predicting moves, unraveling complex networks of information." He pauses, a muscle working in his jaw. "After my tour ended, I transitioned to civilian life. Landed a position as a cybersecurity consultant for a tech firm dealing in government contracts. High-stakes work, but it felt tame after the military."

Kaden's focus drifts over my shoulder to the window, focusing on something I can't see. "I had a routine. Up at 0500 every morning for a run along the coast. The sea air, the sunrise, it centered me. Reminded me why I did what I did."

A smile touches his lips, there and gone in an instant. "Then home to my daughter before heading to the office."

Daughter.

The word arrows into my mind, and suddenly I'm six years old again, standing in my first-grade classroom. Miss Hanson is asking everyone to draw their families for Parents' Day. I remember the waxy smell of crayons, the scratch of paper, the excited chatter of my classmates.

I'd drawn a stick figure of myself, alone.

Looking at Kaden, I see a different little girl in his eyes. One who had a father who came home to her, who probably colored family portraits with too many crayons and hung them on the fridge.

I want to ask about her. What was her name? Did she have Kaden's eyes, his rare smile? Did she wait by the window for him to come home, the way I used to imagine a father would come for me?

But the words stick in my throat, because I know. I know with a certainty that chills me to my marrow that this story doesn't have a happy ending.

Kaden's voice grows harder. "I thought I'd left the war behind when I was honorably discharged. I was wrong. The enemy was closer than I ever imagined, and I didn't even know I was still fighting."

He takes a deep breath. "There was an operation back when I was in the military. We disrupted a major overseas criminal network. Drug trafficking, arms dealing. It was all data to me then. Numbers on a screen, connections to be severed. We cost them millions. Crippled their operations. I never considered the face behind the data. Until that face found me."

"Frank Morelli," I whisper.

Kaden gives a short nod, his eyes a bottomless black. "One morning, I went for my run. Fog thick as soup. Came back to..." His voice falters for a split second. "To make my kid a pancake breakfast for graduating middle school. But the house was empty. Cassie was gone."

I forget how to exhale, my body frozen mid-breath.

The pieces start to fall into place.

"We mounted a search. Every resource, every favor called in. Nothing."

Kaden tears from my hold, pacing like a caged animal.

"I resigned that day. Liquidated everything. Called in every contact from my military days. But I refused to leave it in someone else's hands. Strangers, friends ... not one of them was me. No one understood the need to find Cassie more than *me*. But I needed skills. So I went off-grid. Found teachers. Former special forces. Retired assassins. Learned every method of killing, tracking, disappearing."

Kaden stops, his back to me. "My first job was to track down one of Morelli's human traffickers in Bangkok. He told me Morelli sold her to him. That she was pumped full of heroin and handed around to rich, foreign executives and nothing was left of her." Kaden's voice breaks. "His death was sloppy. Messy. But effective. And I was nowhere near done."

There is literal blood on his hands as he speaks.

"I refined my methods. Became a ghost, like Morelli. The Scythe." A humorless laugh escapes him. "Ironic. I became the very thing I once hunted."

Kaden turns, and I force myself not to flinch from the cold fury in his eyes.

"Morelli was impossible to locate, but I convinced myself that every job brought me closer. Every kill honed my talent. I dismantled his network piece by piece. Year after year, hoping he'd resurface. I'd immersed myself in the disguise of an assassin for hire. So much, I didn't just wear the Scythe's mask, I *became* him and would take jobs unrelated to my goal just to stay believable. Until I started to enjoy it. Then one of my contacts slipped me a photograph. A picture of you. You were the unexpected variable. The key I've been searching for all these years."

I wrap my arms around my waist, hugging myself.

"Your face..." Kaden shakes his head, as if dislodging the unwelcome tenderness in his voice. "You were an innocent. I verified that by learning everything about you, including how you accessed company servers after hours. It was crafty of you, using your skills to protect yourself from that lech of a supervisor."

I ignore the flattery, my stomach churning. How long had Morelli been watching me?

"But you stumbled onto something bigger, didn't you?" Kaden continues, his words precise. "Security footage. Your boss and an unknown figure, discussing some 'cleanup operation' involving AI tech."

The memory of that night makes me grimace. The stupidity, the confusion, the weight of the USB drive in my pocket.

"That unknown figure?" Kaden's voice drops to a near husk of itself. "It was Morelli. After a decade of chasing phantoms, there he was. On your company's servers."

Blood drains from my face as I jerk my chin up and stare at him. "But you said Morelli never shows his face. Why would he —*how*? In Greycliff?"

"I wondered the same myself. It didn't occur to me that the man in the footage could be the Ghost Leader. Until we got our answer today."

My mind goes quiet at his meaning. Too quiet. "Morelli's dying, so he's personally making sure his enterprise lives on. He's preparing for a power transition and wants to ensure his successor is ready for the role. That's why he's showing his face. Because it doesn't matter anymore."

The cottage's lights burst on. I squint, adjusting to the

sudden glare, but notice how the shadows seem to shrink away from Kaden, leaving nothing but the solid form of a man who's walked through hell and emerged bearing its scars.

Kaden rakes his fingers through his hair and releases a sound halfway between a sigh and a lament. "The AI tech is a trigger to guarantee his monopoly. He's using your company as a shield until his successor finishes what he started. You're a witness who could dismantle all of that. No wonder he wants you so badly."

My stomach flutters as Kaden crosses the room, each step measured. He's a man of precision, every movement deadly. It's both terrifying and mesmerizing when he holds my stare. "I'm not going to let that happen. Not again."

"But I'm still bait," I say.

Kaden's scar seems to shift to a stark white. Every inch of his frame radiates with menace. "I'm not a hero, Layla."

"I can see that. And I'm certainly not your princess."

I'm not sure whether it's the adrenaline or the insanity of my situation giving me this newfound courage, but I welcome it.

"Your hatred for Morelli is palpable," I add. "But what about after? When you've had your revenge? What then?"

Kaden's focus doesn't waver from my face. "He took my daughter away from me when she was barely twelve. She was innocent, Layla. Just like you."

The vivid picture of a twelve-year-old girl on the cusp of becoming, her future mutilated before being snuffed out, punctures any defenses I had left, acid-sharp. Kaden isn't just a steel-edged assassin, he's a man hollowed out and carved to the bone with loss. I'm drowning along with him in the depths of his anguish, at a love so violently severed, because the image of a younger Kaden cradling a baby swathed in soft blankets brings me to tears.

"Tell me about her. Tell me about the day she was born."

Tell me how you love, I add silently. *Instead of just hate.*

Kaden softens for the barest of seconds. "The day Cassie was born, it was chaos. I was deployed overseas and had to catch three different flights to make it back in time."

He pauses, two fingers brushing his lips as if to suppress a smile. "I burst into the hospital room, still in my fatigues, covered in dust from God-knows-where. And there she was. Tiny. Perfect."

Kaden's voice grows quieter. "Cassie's mother, Angie, we weren't together. It was complicated. She was a journalist, always chasing the next big story. When she found out she was pregnant, she told me she wasn't cut out for motherhood, but she'd carry the baby to term if I wanted to raise her."

Kaden's jaw shifts slightly. "Angie signed over full custody the day after Cassie was born. Last I heard, she was covering conflicts in some war-torn country. But Cassie, from the moment I held her, I knew. She was my whole world."

Then he sighs, the past pulling him under. "I'd give anything to hold her again."

His confession hangs in the air, a fragile thread connecting two broken souls.

And then I close the distance, sealing his pain with a kiss. His lips are soft, hesitant at first, as if he's afraid I'll shatter beneath his touch. But as I wind my arms around his neck, pulling him closer, he responds with a fervor that turns my exhales into his inhales.

Kaden's hands find my waist, fingers digging into my flesh as he deepens the kiss. It's a clash of teeth and tongue, a desperate need to feel something, anything, beyond what he's buried in.

When we finally break apart, both of us panting, I notice a forgotten piece of his past anchored in his gaze.

Hope, perhaps. Or the beginnings of reliance.

I tilt my chin, keeping the Kaden-that-was close to my heart. "I'll be your bait. I'll help lure Morelli to you."

Kaden stills. "You're sure?"

I nod, no longer weighed down by terror.

Because looking at the man before me—the killer, the protector, the stolen father—I realize that I would wade through rivers of blood, stain my soul beyond recognition. In Kaden, I see a love so fierce that a little girl and her crayon scribbles rewrote his entire existence, and for the first time, I'm ready to color myself into someone else's world, even if it's painted in shades of black.

19
LAYLA

Kaden's hands are washed of blood, gore, and dirt. By the time he returns from the woods, his tall figure emerges from the dense fog like a demon born of shadow and sea. The soft morning light streaming in through the misted window illuminates the scar that splits his face, a testament to his darker talents of being able to bury his enemies, then stride into my kitchen and put together a hot breakfast.

My cuticles are still stained with dried blood after bleaching and wiping down the floors, but instead of attempting to scrub the blood off my hands (again), I watch him move behind the counter with surprising grace, the juxtaposition of his lethal skills and his current domesticity almost laughable.

The aroma of sizzling bacon and freshly brewed coffee fills the air, mingling with the earthy scent of moss-covered cobblestones outside and contrasting with the latent stench of death that clings to our clothes.

After setting down plates laden with food, Kaden joins me by sitting on one of the worn wooden chairs at the small table.

"Thank you," I murmur, picking up my fork and pushing the scrambled eggs around.

Our conversation consists of the clinks of metal on ceramic until Kaden lifts his head and searches my face. "Morelli knows I'm the one protecting you now. His interest isn't just in the AI anymore. He'll come after us doubly as hard."

I pause, my fork halfway to my mouth. Then I place it back down.

"You've been provoking him," I counter, trying to hide the sting of my words behind a casual shrug.

Kaden rubs his fingers over the stubble on his jawline and nods in agreement.

"Yes." His acceptance of guilt surprises me. "And I'm sorry."

A truly fleshed-out apology from Kaden is as unusual as a sunny day in Greycliff. My gaze lingers on Kaden's face, on the lines of concentration that crease his forehead and the constant storm brewing in his vibrant blue eyes.

"Why do you look so calm?" he asks, lowering his fork onto the plate with a clatter and leaning back with a frown.

Because I have you, I want to respond. But I only shrug again and offer him a small smile.

"I'm not helpless, Kaden. Besides," I add, feeling a flush creep up my neck. "I'm starting to trust you."

Kaden stares at me, his eyes reflecting a rare mix of shock and confusion. Then he gives me a curt nod.

"Good," he mutters under his breath.

"The AI," I say, trying to veer the conversation back into less treacherous territory. "We need to figure out how to neutralize it."

His focus sharpens on me. "As I've told you before, I don't care about the damn AI, Layla. All I want is Morelli."

"But you can't just kill him and walk away. This isn't just about revenge. A lot of people will suffer if we don't destroy it."

"He killed my daughter and made her suffer. That's all that matters."

"I can do more than just wait around for you to end Morelli."

"I won't put you at risk—"

"But I'm already at risk!"

I stand, my chair scraping abruptly against the floor.

"Because of you," I repeat, my voice louder than intended. "In case you forgot, you walked into my life and turned it upside down!"

The following silence is painful, broken only by the hissing of the overflowing coffee pot. Kaden's jaw tenses as he gets up and moves to the drip machine, yanking the pot off the hot plate.

His back is to me, but even from here, I can see how rigid his posture is.

"I didn't plan for this, either," he says after a while, his voice barely audible in the deafening silence.

Turning back to face me, he takes a deep breath. "You've become..."

Kaden rakes a hand through his black, disheveled hair, releasing a frustrated growl. He walks over to the sink, dumping out the burned coffee, then filling the pot with water and washing it out. The sound of running water fills the uncomfortable silence.

The meager sunlight hits his profile, lingering on the scar that bisects his face, a constant reminder of his past, just like my inherited lighthouse is to me.

He says, "For what it's worth, I stopped seeing you as bait last night, when they..."

Kaden sets the clean pot on the drying rack, then turns

around to lean against the sink and crosses his arms over his chest, his muscles tightening beneath his shirt.

"The way you handled that man in your bedroom like a goddamned warrior even though you had every reason to be terrified. You're not just a pawn, Layla. You never have been."

His confession hits me as hard as the waves hitting Greycliff's jagged rocks. I'm frozen in my spot, my heart thundering in my ears.

I want to respond, to tell him that I'm only a warrior because I have him at my side, because of him. But before I can form the words, he pushes away from the sink and strides across the room toward me.

"But you are still my responsibility," he grinds out.

"I don't need a knight!" The words burst from me, raw and angry. My throat burns with their release, but it feels good.

The look of surprise on Kaden's face is almost worth it. Almost.

"Maybe I don't want to be saved," I go on when he doesn't respond. "Maybe I want to fight by your side instead of being the damsel locked in the tower."

"Is that what you think this is?" Kaden asks, his tone brimming with restraint.

"That's exactly what this is," I retort, matching his icy tone with my own. "You've been treating me like some clueless civilian who can't handle the truth, who can't fight her own battles. But I'm not a little girl, Kaden. I'm not your daughter."

I flinch as my words strike him, as he absorbs their impact, his piercing eyes blinking rapidly as if in pain.

"I didn't mean—" I backpedal, realizing too late that I've crossed a line.

"I'm well aware you're not my daughter," he says after a moment, his voice far too calm.

Kaden's jaw tightens, the muscle twitching beneath the

jagged line of his scar. His gaze breaks away from mine as he takes a step back, pinching the bridge of his nose with fingers that tremble ever so slightly.

"I didn't bring you into this mess," he says quietly, almost in defeat. "I found you in it."

His unspoken accusation of carelessness is like cold steel sliding between my ribs, severing the tenuous thread of hope I'd been clinging to.

"Why?" I demand. "Why can't you let me in? Why can't—"

"Why can't we be partners?" He finishes my question with a painted smirk that doesn't brush his eyes. "Because this isn't some sort of romantic adventure. I'm a killer, same as the men who broke in last night to kill you. I was originally hired to *murder* you. It's only because you're more valuable to my plans alive that you're even arguing with me right now."

"I know what you are," I say defiantly, "But I also know who you are."

Kaden's face is a mask of stone as he rakes his gaze over me.

"For God's sake, Kaden," I breathe out, frustration and hurt surging. "I'd do anything to help you. Can't you see that?"

"I see it, Layla," he says quietly, his brows smoothing just a fraction. "I see it more clearly than I want to."

"Then why—"

"Because I don't want you in the same room as him!" he roars suddenly, slamming his hand on the table, making the mugs and dishes rattle. "Because I can't bear the thought of something happening to you! Because..." He takes a deep breath. His expression is pained, tortured. And as much as I hate to see him hurting, I can't deny the shiver of relief that courses through me at his outburst. "Because I can't lose you, too."

I resist the urge to close my eyes and crumple to the

ground. The room spins in tandem to the relentless churning of the ocean outside.

"But…" My voice is barely a whisper, struggling to find form in the thick fog of emotion choking me. "But what if I lose you?"

His eyes snap to mine, wide and unguarded for the first time since we met. They're no longer just the color of a storm-tossed sea but full of its turmoil, too.

Then he's moving away, distancing himself from me as if afraid of what we've just admitted.

"Kaden," I prompt softly, trying to reach him.

But he's erected his walls, making himself impenetrable.

"There is no 'we', Layla," he murmurs. "You don't even know my fucking last name."

"I know your pain," I say, talking past the stab of hurt at his statement. "I know your thirst for justice, your rule against harming innocent people, and your urge to protect. Isn't that better than a surname that tells me nothing about you?"

He chuckles bitterly. "And what if my last name is all that I am?"

"I don't believe that."

"It's not enough!" Kaden snaps, his voice rebounding off the aged walls of my once peaceful cottage. There's no malice in his outburst, only a sore desperation that sends a tremor of empathy through me.

He spins away from me, shoulders set as he looks out toward the fog-shrouded lighthouse looming in the distance.

"Do you think this ends with Morelli?" he asks, his voice a hollow imitation of itself. "Do you think there will be some sort of happily ever after once I've gotten my hands on him?"

"Then how do you want it to end, Kaden?" I manage to choke out.

He glances at me over his shoulder. "It only ends one way for men like me."

"You're wrong," I whisper. "It could be different. It *can* be different..."

"No," he rumbles, shaking his head. "I'm beyond redemption."

Suddenly, the room feels too cold, too bleak.

In a last-ditch attempt to bridge the growing chasm between us, I reach out for him. "Kaden..."

But he's already moving to my front door, his pace as firm as a soldier heading to the battlefield.

With no plans to return.

20
KADEN

Layla has me in a chokehold.

I catch her silhouette through the kitchen's window as I stand outside, staring at her rather than the expansive view of the peninsula. I take a quick drag from my cigarette, letting it fill my lungs before exhaling slowly. It's been ten years since I quit, but this morning is an exception, and I need a fucking smoke.

The sea-sprayed fog seems to be seeping into my eyes as I study her through the glass. The soft glow of dawn illuminates her, turning her into a ghostly wisp of golden hair and pale skin.

It's a vision that sears itself into my obsession ... and fuels more agony.

The nicotine calms the thrumming in my veins, numbing my senses just enough to focus on the task at hand—setting up additional surveillance around the property to further control the environment, with Layla as the main attraction.

I'm not the only one tempted by her. Once Morelli realizes his three thugs failed to acquire her, he'll want to ensure the next attempt will be a success. He did the same with my daughter, and the more difficult a mark Layla becomes, the more likely he'll want to eliminate her himself.

I grimace at the memory, crushing the half-burned cigarette under my heel before moving toward the shed housing more tools. The early morning sunlight glints off the familiar shape of my sniper rifle, stashed away for a time like this.

My fingers itch to reach for it. But that's not what I'm here for right now. I'm not hunting today, I'm fortifying. My gaze skims over the various gadgets strewn across the workbench: tiny cameras, tripwires, and packets of C-4, each instrument another layer in my plan to protect Layla from Morelli's clutches, even while I make her a target.

I set to work on rigging up an extra network of cameras over the dense forest surrounding Layla's house. Each time I drill a hole into the bark, I envision just one more eye watching over her. Beads of sweat trickle down my back as I spend hours scaling trees and rerouting wires, the physical labor a welcome distraction.

At some point, the cold morning gives way to a sunny afternoon. The salty tang of the ocean breeze clashes with the earthy scent of soil and pine. The cries of seagulls carry into the coast, mingling with the whir of my drill.

A fevered urgency to my work propels me forward, my body moving with trained precision despite the ache that begins to creep into my limbs. I ignore it, pushing myself to finish before nightfall.

As I finish installing the last camera, I glance back at the cottage, envisioning Layla inside, her soft blond hair falling around her face, those contrary eyes of hers—one as bright as the future I once had, the other as dark as the one I've chosen. I can almost hear her quiet sigh as she traces my scar with her slender fingers, her lips parted in pure fascination.

I shake my head, dispelling the image that burns too vividly against the backdrop of the darkening forest. The deep moan of a foghorn rolls in from the sea, bringing with it a wave of isolation that mirrors my emptiness within.

"I don't want you, Layla," I murmur to nobody but myself, recalling the harsh words I'd thrown at her during our heated argument.

Each syllable was a lie. Lies formed from a need for self-preservation that came easier than admitting the truth—that every time I look at her, I see what I'm not. A beacon of hope, an undeniable spark of life that hovers above the ashes of my desolate world.

The connection between us is growing, and I can't allow it to go any further. The distraction is too much. Too sweet.

You are just a means to an end, Layla.

Those words resonate in my head like a distorted carousel ride.

Leaping off the final tree, I make my way back toward the house. My feet crunch on the gravel pathway leading up to her front door. Beyond it, I hear snippets of Layla's voice carrying through.

"No, I don't think that's a good idea," Layla says, her voice strained. "I understand it's important, but I can't—"

She falls silent, listening. I can practically hear the gears turning in her head.

"Yes, I know it's crucial for the company, Mr. Dawson," she continues, a note of resignation creeping into her voice. "But surely someone else can handle it? I've documented everything thoroughly."

She's on a work call, trying to assert herself, trying to

pierce through her own cloud of isolation. By now, I'm aware that giving up isn't in her nature.

"I appreciate the opportunity, but given my current situation…" She takes a deep breath. "No, I'm not asking for special treatment. I just need you to understand that I can't be there in person."

Her fingers drum against her thigh as she listens, her frustration palpable. I pause at the threshold, listening to her steady voice and the measured way she speaks, even when she's frustrated. It's a stubbornness that keeps her pushing forward despite the hazards.

Through the mudroom, I catch sight of Layla pacing back and forth in front of her couch. She throws a hand up in exasperation, almost knocking over a lampshade that casts long shadows on the floorboards.

"Did you just ask me on a date?" she asks into the phone.

I want to rip that man apart.

Layla says, her voice ice cold, "My personal life is not up for discussion. Now, about the remote access—"

She's cut off again, and I can see the tension in her jaw as she clenches her teeth.

"Fine," she says finally, defeat evident in her tone. "Goodbye, Mr. Dawson."

Layla ends the call and tosses her phone onto the couch.

An acrid taste swirls in my mouth as rage bubbles, at the thought of her so-called supervisor.

I've read up on him—Emmett Dawson—and I don't like what I've found. He's not just a sleazy boss who can't keep his hands off Layla; he's also deep in the pockets of Morelli.

Swallowing down the rancor, I step over the threshold. Layla spins around at the deliberate creak of the floorboard under my shoe. Her gaze narrows, her plush mouth settling into a thin line. With her hands on her hips, she takes me in from head-to-toe, noting the sweat glistening on my brow.

"You're back," she says.

"Yes."

"Is everything ... secure?" she asks, not entirely meeting my stare.

"As secure as it can be," I reply.

I drop my drill on a nearby table and unlace my boots, pretending ignorance. "Who was that?"

Layla sighs. "That was Emmett Dawson. He's insisting I attend this corporate event tonight. Some kind of tech show-case the company's hosting."

She moves to the kitchen, busying herself with pouring water into a kettle. "It's just a glorified PR stunt, really. Showing off our latest security protocols to potential clients. Normally, I'd be all over it. It's a chance to present my work, network, that sort of thing. But given that I'm not allowed to leave my house ... are you going to say anything?"

I blink, realizing I've fallen into the soothing cadence of her voice and was unintentionally mesmerized by her graceful movements as she goes about her nightly routine of hot tea and a book.

She asks over her shoulder, "No disapproving grunts? No snippy orders reminding me to stay put?"

"Isn't that understood?" I say, my voice gruff even to my own ears.

"Right," she whispers after a while over the low rumble of the boiling water.

Layla turns when she notices me crossing the room, tracking my movements with a steady intensity that makes my trigger finger twitch, a reflex I can't quite control. It itches to eliminate anyone who dares to threaten her.

I stop at the entrance of the kitchen, leaning against the doorframe, watching her.

"Did he say anything else?" I ask.

She diverts her attention to the steaming kettle.

"No," she says too quickly, her voice a notch higher than usual.

"Are you sure, Wraithling?"

My question is as musical as ice cracking under heated pressure.

"He asked me to be his date to the conference," she admits, her voice steady despite the flush creeping up her neck.

Something snaps inside me. In two strides, I'm across the kitchen, crowding her against the counter. My hands slam down on either side of her, caging her in.

"If he ever asks you that again, I'll peel the skin from his fingers. I'll carve out his tongue and feed it to him. I'll make him beg for death long before I grant it."

Layla stops breathing, the whites of her eyes visible. But there's no trepidation in them, only a fervor that matches the inferno raging inside me.

"You are not his to pursue," I continue, lowering my head. Her scent—coconut and sea salt—fills my senses. "You are under my protection. My ... care."

My focus drops to her open mouth, and it takes every ounce of willpower not to claim it, not to hoist her onto the counter and show her exactly who she belongs to.

Instead, I force myself to step back, my hands clenching into fists at my sides.

"Do you understand?" I ask, my voice rough.

Layla nods, her chest rising and falling rapidly.

"I understand," she whispers, a mix of emotions I can't quite decipher flitting across her face.

I give her the cold shoulder, needing to put distance between us before I lose what little control I have left.

"Good," I mutter.

"Where are you going?" she asks behind me.

"I still have work to do."

The lie slips out smoothly.

As I stalk out of the kitchen, I can feel Layla's eyes burning into my back.

And I know, with a certainty that terrifies me, that this woman will be my undoing.

21

LAYLA

My body screams for Kaden to return even as my mind races with plans to defy him.

His stifling presence lingers in the kitchen, the scent of his cologne, the taste of his exhales on my lips, a cocktail of heat and adrenaline that leaves me dizzy and bracing against the counter.

I shake my head, banishing the fantasy. I don't have a lot of time.

The rhythm of my pounding heart plays out beneath my skin, but I force myself to calm. I need to be quick, efficient.

My bare feet hardly make a sound up the rickety stairs. I reach my bedroom and start rifling through my closet, pulling out an old black lace dress that's been gathering dust in there. It's a bit too fancy for me, but tonight it may just pass for acceptable at a formal conference.

The thought that Kaden could walk in at any moment and stop me tightens my chest. But this is something I have to do. For me. For anyone who thinks they don't matter and can't save the world, when actually, they damn well can.

I slip into the dress and look at myself in the full-length mirror. The lace clings to my curves, the plunging neckline boldly revealing more than I'm used to, but there's a power in my reflection that straightens my shoulders.

Gathering up my long hair, I twist it into a loose updo that falls over one shoulder. A quick makeup application to enhance my eyes, cheeks, and lips are next until I can delay the inevitable no longer.

I pick up my phone. Kaden's tracking software is undoubtedly running, but I don't have a choice. I open my messaging app and type:

Ethan, can you pick me up at the old boat launch? ASAP. Don't reply.

As I await his read receipt, it feels like I'm counting down the seconds on a ticking time bomb. I nervously bite my thumbnail, fixated on my phone's screen as if I could telepathically send a message instead. But Ethan's always glued to his video games and never off-line, even when he needs to attend a conference in an hour.

At last, the checkmark appears. He's seen it.

"Thank God," I mutter, then turn the phone off and toss it on the bed.

There's no doubt that Kaden will find the phone and go through it. He'll know I've left, but at least he won't know where I'm going. Not yet.

I peer out the window. The lighthouse cuts a lonely silhouette against the roiling clouds, its feeble light penetrating the mist of tempered rain, but it's the smaller shadow prowling over the rocks that catches my attention.

In less than a minute, Kaden will disappear behind the lighthouse for no more than thirty seconds. I've been watching him all day, inadvertently learning his surveillance routine. It's my only opening.

Three... Two... One...

With my heart spilling out of my chest after every beat, I grab my clutch purse then fling open my bedroom door and race down the stairs toward the front door.

On the modern security panel next to the door, the red warning lights glare at me like accusatory eyes, but I quickly mute them with practiced hands. There's no way to shut down Kaden's multiple cameras and no time to mess with the footage, but when he checks them, he'll know I haven't been taken against my will. A small consolation, because he'll be furious either way.

For a fleeting moment, I feel a pang of guilt for betraying his trust. But this isn't about Kaden. He's made it clear he doesn't care about the ramifications of Morelli's illegal technology.

I do.

Through the front door, across the cobblestone path slick with sea spray and rainwater, my heels click softly as I crane my neck to keep the lighthouse in my view and ensure I stay in Kaden's blind spot before pushing through the wooden gate separating my property from the woods. Starting a car would draw his attention, so I skirt past my old girl and his sleek truck and disappear into the dense foliage.

The smell of seaweed and wet earth fills my nostrils as I navigate through the underbrush in the light drizzle, my dress getting splattered with droplets falling off the leaves until I find the small path leading to the boat launch, its once lively energy now nothing more than a desolate shoreline dotted with rotting skiffs and long-forgotten buoys. The weathered sign creaks and groans from the cold wind as I pass under it, a relic from fifty years ago when fishermen hauled their vessels to sea at dawn and returned at dusk. Now, the place is hidden under a blanket of fog and decaying planks.

A set of headlights cuts through, disturbing the peaceful melancholy. Ethan's van pulls up, his engine humming like a dying animal. The sliding door squeaks open, and there he is—looking like he's about to piss himself.

"Hey, Layla," Ethan grates out, hunched behind the steering wheel like he's expecting to be ambushed.

"Thanks for coming," I say, stumbling into the passenger seat.

The van is a crammed spaceship of digital paraphernalia: consoles, keyboards, and monitors flicker with lines of encoded gibberish. A glowing unicorn bobblehead vibrates merrily on the dashboard, while empty soda cans and chip packets roll underfoot.

"Don't mention it," he murmurs, pushing up his glasses and casting a sidelong glance at me. "Though it would help if you would explain what the hell is going on. Last time I saw you, I got an impromptu acupuncture session to the neck, and you were carted off like some twisted *Beauty and the Beast* story."

I cringe. "Thank you for not calling the cops."

"Oh, don't worry about it. Your 'friend' paid me a visit and explained things. Said you were fine, and that my continued ability to type might depend on my discretion."

"I'm so sorry, Ethan."

The van lurches forward, making me grip the edges of my seat as we bounce over the uneven terrain. Ethan's driving skills leave much to be desired. It feels less like he's navigating the coastal track and more like he's trying to take down Bowser from *Mario Kart*.

"You and me, we're fine," Ethan says, though his voice wavers. "Your hulking bodyguard, on the other hand..."

"He's not my—well. He's complicated."

"There it is," he mumbles, his eyes never leaving the road.

"Your defense of him already. You do realize there's a difference between 'complicated' and 'probably going to murder me in my sleep,' right?"

"Ethan, Kaden isn't going to murder you."

"Of course not. Not if I don't ever sleep again."

The weight of his curious gaze falls on my shoulders as I gather my thoughts. How much should I tell him? Ethan's my friend, and the last thing I want is to drag him deeper into this mess than he already is.

"Hey, no need to look so grim. I'm not mad at you," he says, flashing me a wry grin. "Just ... start from the beginning, yeah?"

"It started with Dawson," I mutter, keeping my attention firmly trained on the foggy road ahead.

"Our creep of a boss?" Ethan wrinkles his nose, the windshield wipers thrumming against the rain-slicked glass. "Why am I not surprised? Go on."

I nod. "He's involved in something. Something really bad."

Ethan snorts and looks at me sidelong. "What, like embezzling company funds? Creating a Ponzi scheme? Bitcoin fraud? What is it with start-up tech guys?"

"No," I say, trying to suppress a laugh despite myself. It feels strange and foreign to laugh at a time like this, but there's something comforting about Ethan's natural humor. "Like illegal AI tech that could crash our economy and be sold to the Mafia level bad."

Silence.

"Wait ... are you *serious*?"

"Dead serious." I shiver as I look out the van's window.

"But ... why would Dawson be involved in that?" His voice is small now, filled with confusion and a touch of fear. "He's a terrible boss, but a criminal mastermind?"

"He's not the mastermind," I clarify. "Just a peon."

"So who's the king, then?"

"His name is Frank Morelli. The Ghost Leader." I let the name settle between us like a poisonous cloud. "He's the head of a Mafia syndicate, and he wants to take the world to hell along with him when he succumbs to cancer."

A beat of silence passes.

When I don't fill it, Ethan says, "Oh my God. You're serious. You're seriously serious."

He clamps one hand to his mouth, looking distinctly green around the edges.

"This isn't like you, Layla," he says softly. "I mean, you're a kick-ass coder, not some super spy. This isn't our world. Where the fuck do you come in to all this?"

I find myself confessing, "I overheard something I shouldn't. Morelli's men have been after me ever since. Kaden's been protecting me from them because he has his own vendetta to settle with Morelli, but he refuses to help stop the AI from falling into the wrong hands. *That's* where I come in. I can't just sit back and let it be handed to the Mafia."

Ethan sighs and rubs his forehead with the heel of his free hand. "I'm regretting the edible I ate before coming to get you. Or maybe I didn't have enough."

"You don't have to be involved. I just need a ride to the conference. And maybe your security pass so I'm not flagged by using mine to access the basement, then plant a virus in this AI that every employee at Pulse, including you, has helped create."

"Excuse me, *what*? I've been creating *what*?"

I can't help the laughter that bubbles up. It's not funny, not really, it's dangerous and potentially life-ending, but the look on Ethan's face is too much. "Keep your eyes on the road before you get us both killed."

He throws up his hands defensively, although one quickly

returns to the wheel. "You tell me you're breaking into a high-security tech event held by our boss who's apparently involved in some Mafia scheme and expect me to just drive perfectly? I'm stressed, Layla!"

"No one will know," I reassure him.

Ethan scrubs a hand down his face and mumbles something that sounds suspiciously like '*why me?*'.

"You realize this is not like hacking into your neighbors' Wi-Fi because they forgot to lock it, right? This is some James Bond level shit and there's no way you can do this alone. I'm coming with you."

My stomach drops. "No. No, you're not. You're going to go to the event and mingle and kiss ass like every other employee and stay safe."

Ethan catches my hand, his fingers wrapping around mine tightly. "James Bond needs a Q, Layla."

A surge of warmth floods my chest at my friend's steadfast support. "You would really want to be Q?"

He shrugs nonchalantly, a hint of a smirk playing on his lips. "Well, he's a genius who saves Bond's ass multiple times, so..."

That earns him a chuckle. I squeeze his hand before letting go. "I could use someone as a lookout for anyone who goes into the basement, but at the first sign of trouble, you have to promise me you'll find someplace safe."

"Only if you promise the same," he counters, and I can see in his eyes that he means every word.

We pull into Main Street, and the suspicion that pulled me to this conference tonight settles around me again. Greycliff is an abandoned fishing town recently discovered by millennials and Gen Zs, both for the crazy deals on real estate and the idealism attached to reviving and modernizing a quaint, spooky town. It's why Pulse Dynamics moved in. The start-up company bought up an entire building with six floors and renovated it to their specifications for a quarter of the cost a start-up in New York City would require. After establishing their success, no doubt Pulse would move to a better location, but that begs the question: Why hold a conference here?

Greycliff is not yet a town you invite prospective clients to, unless they enjoy ghost tours and the stench of dead fish.

Pulse has never hosted clients before or had parties beyond its first December holiday last year that Ethan told me about, consisting of a single keg and tinsel along the walls.

The only explanation is that someone in the clientele they're courting enjoys the thrill of investing in a risky, fledgling town and the clandestine meetings it promises. It offers the kind of privacy that backing illegal technology and being shown how it operates would require.

As Ethan and I park the van, the sprawling Pulse Dynamics building comes into view. The high-tech glass structure seems almost out of place against the old-world charm of Greycliff. Its sleek metallic lines reflect the blue LED lights inside.

When we come to a stop, I rummage through my purse, then use the sun visor to put in a brown contact over my blue eye. Then I turn to Ethan, blinking a few times. "How do I look?"

"Wait, you do that? I've never seen you camouflage your awesome eye colors before."

"I gave up a long time ago. It was too expensive to buy lenses without insurance, and when I tried the cheap Halloween ones, well, I almost blinded myself."

Covering the true colors of my eyes started as an attempt to be less desirable and less stared at by Mom's "friends." I was too young to know that it wasn't my uniqueness that drew them to me. It was my age.

I was forced to learn how to stay away from home fast.

Even this contact is too old. I can feel its edges every time I blink, giving me a tic. It's better than being recognized on sight, though.

"Gotta say, you look pretty boring now. Zero superhero aura about you," Ethan adds.

I laugh, but my smile dies as fast as Ethan's does. His face is a sickly shade of white, and he's chewing on his lower lip nervously.

"You can stay here." I lay a comforting hand on his arm. "I just need your security pass."

He hesitates.

"You'll get it back, I promise."

Ethan's expression is filled with worry, but there's trust too. A trust I don't deserve but am grateful for.

"My pass should be a backup plan," Ethan says as he twists between our seats and grabs his laptop. He uses the lever to push back his seat granting him room to open his computer and mutters over the electronic whir of the chair, "Time to be Q."

"What are you doing?"

"Figuring out how to keep you safe during this insane operation you've talked yourself into."

Ethan's fingers fly over the keyboard with soft clicking noises. Lines of code fill his screen and I lean closer, interpreting the numbers.

"You're creating a backdoor in Pulse's security system. That's brilliant," I say, my heart picking up on the excitement. *I can actually do this.*

"It'll give you maybe twenty minutes before they detect it and shut it down."

My excitement pops and fizzles away.

20 minutes.

That's barely enough time for me to get to the server room,

install my malware, and find an escape route before it all goes sideways.

"And here." Ethan reaches under his seat, sifting through empty chip bags and soda cans before tossing something at me that I catch in mid-air. "My smartwatch. Put it on so I can track you."

Watching Ethan work, the glow of the screen illuminating the taut concentration on his face, causes a lump in my throat to form.

I've never needed anyone. Never thought it necessary. But here, with Ethan's guidance and Kaden's protective lessons, they're both spurring me on. I may have slipped away from Kaden, but ironically, it's his influence that's given me the edge I need to pull this off.

It also makes me realize that if anything happened to either of them, I would fight the asshole responsible to the death.

Is this what it feels like to have a family?

Ethan looks up and must notice the sheen to my eyes because he says quietly, "Hey, what are friends for if not to commit felonies together?"

I respond with a small smile. "Thanks, Ethan. I owe you big time."

With a final keystroke, Ethan says, "Your time starts now. And Layla, be careful. Please."

I nod, reaching for the van's door handle. "Promise."

"And if we pull this off, drinks are on me. You know, assuming we're not in witness protection or something."

Despite everything, I find myself grinning before stepping out. "I'll hold you to that."

22

KADEN

As I step into the house, I immediately sense that Layla's not here. A half-drunk cup of tea now cold, the lack of her perfume's aroma, and a book lies open with a bookmark hastily placed between its pages, slightly crinkled from what may have been a stray teardrop.

The stillness in the air is broken only by the soft tick of the kitchen's wall clock, a constant reminder that seconds are slipping by, time is ebbing, and with it, my chances.

I rip my gloves off, discarding them on the wooden table next to her abandoned cup, my fingers running across the smooth ceramic surface as if to feel where her mouth lingered.

"Layla?"

No answer.

"Wraithing, where are you? Don't make me start a countdown before I find and punish you."

Nothing.

Gritting my teeth against the rising unease, I stalk past the table and into the kitchen, devoid of her presence. I check her favorite reading chair in the main room—empty. After listening for the creak of footsteps on the second floor and hearing nothing, I storm up the staircase, gripping the banister as I leap over steps three at a time, the hard thud of my boots showcasing a warning to whomever might have her and what I will do to them when I catch them.

I envision their bones snapping under my strength, blood splattering on the walls I've promised to keep safe. My mind spirals into the abyss, picturing sick scenarios laid out by the demons that haunt me: Layla taken by someone, her fear-stricken face, the sound of her screams muffled by a calloused hand.

God*damn* it. I punch the wall next to me, the pain coursing through my knuckles doing little to distract from the open terror clawing at my insides.

Not again. Fuck, not again...

"LAYLA!" I bellow.

It slithers down the hall, unmet by any response. I grip the first doorknob, Layla's room, rattling it in its socket.

Locked.

I yank back my fist and ram it against the wood, cracking under my force, then kick it open.

Her room is untouched.

The bed is neatly made, the curtains drawn back revealing the panoramic view of Greycliff. My eyes scan wildly over the room and over her belongings like her favorite lip balm on the dresser, her glasses on her bedside table, her coat hanging from a hook on her closet door, but no Layla.

Until I notice a slash of pink nestled in her comforter. The phone I made clear that she have on her at all times.

Gripping it until the screen cracks from the force, I pull up her most recent text message asking Ethan to come pick her up. The screen blinks out just as I finish reading, the broken glass under my fingertips a mocking reminder of how I've lost control. Of everything. The phone, the woman, the situation.

Tossing the dead phone over my shoulder, I turn and stalk into the guest room where all my equipment is and sign in to the surveillance feed.

Images flicker across the multiple screens, each representing a different part of the house—from the front porch to the staircase, the living room to the bedrooms. My fingers play the keyboard like an instrument, uploading, then rewinding the feeds and setting them to play as I watch with a vulturine intensity.

There she is.

On screen, Layla moves about in her usual manner—alive and vibrant. Her hair is messily pulled into a bun on top of her head, tendrils escaping to frame her face in a way I find irritatingly endearing. She's wearing her favorite oversized sweater I left her in before doing perimeter checks.

I swallow hard, allowing myself a second to just watch. To see her alive and well, unharmed. It's a comfort that does little to quell my soaring anxiety.

Then I see it—the moment she stares at bit too long at my retreating form out of the house, then bolts into action as soon as I shut the door behind me.

Oh, you little...

Layla races up the stairs and into her room. I flip the screen to the cameras in her bedroom, my vision turning into slits as she peels off her sweater and steps into a pretty, sexy dress.

A thousand questions ricochet through my mind. What was she thinking? Where is she going? Why did she leave without telling me after the recent hell she's been through? I'm stunned into silence as she reaches for her purse, pulls on a coat, and stares at her phone, likely sending that message to Ethan before tossing it onto the bed.

She then steps into the hallway and pauses in front of the guest room, biting her lower lip before she strides down the staircase.

But she doesn't stop there.

My throat tightens as I watch her move with purpose toward the front door, deftly disarming the security system. She casts one last look around her home before she steps outside and shuts the door behind her.

I slam my fist on the table, cracking the wooden surface. A choking sound comes out of me that's halfway between a laugh and a scoff. Layla's audacity baffles me, infuriates me.

My hands ball into fists, and I hurl the mouse across the room. The device shatters when it hits the wall, plastic shards raining down onto the worn carpet.

I rise so abruptly that my chair skids backward and topples over.

"Goddamn it, Layla!"

With serrated breaths, I swipe my arm across the table, sending the screens teetering before they crash to the floor, shattered glass spreading out like a spiderweb.

My chest heaves as I stare at the wreckage of my control center—my connection to her. In Layla's dewy-eyed bravery—or is it utter recklessness?—she's torn that away from me, left me blinded in a world dangerous beyond her comprehension.

I kick over the last of the monitors as I storm out of the room, the final image of Layla flickering into black as it topples.

"Foolish girl," I hiss under my breath, gripping the banister as I thunder down the stairs.

My boots hammer against the old floors until I push open the front door and step into the foggy Greycliff air. My hands are unsteady, but my mind—my mind is pinpoint sharp.

I huff out a breath, running a hand over my stubble-clad

jaw before glancing up at the quiet lighthouse standing sentinel over me.

With nothing but instinct to guide me now, I head for my black Lincoln parked nearby. Once planted in the driver's seat, a bitter taste rises in my throat, souring the surrounding air.

Of course it had to be Ethan coming to her rescue. Always lurking around Layla like an annoying pop-up notification, even though I'd warned him off. Even after I'd left him gasping on the ground from one mean hook to his windpipe. But perhaps the fool thought I wouldn't find out. Or worse, he didn't care.

I slam the dashboard with my palm, rattling the vehicle, a dangerous fury threatening to burst from my chest. I don't bother to suppress it. I need it. It fuels me, pushes me onward as the engine roars to life.

Gravel pings against the undercarriage like gunfire as I peel out of the driveway and take the winding road into town, all while my GPS begins to churn.

Finally connected to a secure server, my dashboard's screen flickers to life, displaying a live feed from a tracking device I slipped into Ethan's van during our last encounter. A precaution. A prediction. And now, it seems, a prophecy fulfilled.

Then I slip on my mask.

23
LAYLA

If there's one thing about Ethan, it's that he could never understand the glorious thrill of doing something bad.

There's a rush, a wave of adrenaline that blooms out of my chest when I merge with a cluster of caterers dressed in a monochrome of black to line up at a service door at the back of Pulse's building.

I first experienced it when I met the Scythe. The feeling escalated when the Scythe kidnapped me, tied me to a chair, and let me believe a man was about to kill me before interceding and slaughtering that same man in front of me. It didn't go away when the Scythe gave me his real name, theoretically softening the threat against my life to a more palatable, heartbreaking revenge scheme of a devoted father, even after his daughter's death. The need for more of a kick, more adrenaline, stayed with me, and now I've left the safety of Kaden's fortress to experience more of it.

Ethan is grounded, intelligent, and uses rational thought to make his way through life. He wanted to work for the CIA but a poorly timed prank involving hacking his university's grading system branded Ethan as a security risk, dashing his dreams. So he pivoted in a reasonable fashion, working in the private tech industry instead.

Me? I've led an independent, lonely life whose excitement consisted of punching my mother's boyfriends in the nuts if they came too close. I enjoyed the rush then, too, but stayed the course, graduated with honors, and nurtured my talent with computers.

Kaden changed all that when he didn't just redirect my moral compass, he annihilated it. Thinking of him stops my breath. Picturing Kaden's punishment when he ultimately catches me tonight, which he will, sparks that glorious thrill. I just hope it's *after* I tank Morelli's AI and render it permanently useless.

When I slip in with a group of catering staff, my black dress allows me to blend seamlessly into their ranks. We approach the service entrance, and I discreetly reach out and press my thumb against the electronic lock's sensor, my touch delicate and fleeting. A faint blue light flickers beneath my fingertip, and the lock's LED shifts from red to green for the briefest of moments before reverting back. To anyone watching, it would appear as though I had swiped my access card along with the others, when really, I piggy-backed off the guy in front of me.

The servers and I walk into a portable kitchen built for Pulse's event, with chefs barking orders and dishes clattering, the air thick with savory aromas that make my empty stomach grumble. I duck and weave through towering hors d'oeuvres balanced precariously on silver trays, ignoring my stomach's demands and heading for the next corridor. I'll steal some food later as a nod to my rogue teenager days, because fuck Dawson and this event.

As I slip out of the bustling kitchen and into the hallway, my heart pounds with a mix of exhilaration and apprehension.

The high of infiltrating Pulse's event undetected lifts my chest like a balloon, urging me forward.

The deserted hallway stretches long, its walls adorned with prints where art, technology, and the brightest colors possible collide. Standard office carpeting muffles my heels while I half run, half power walk through it.

I'm so focused on my destination, mentally rehearsing the steps to access the server room, that I nearly collide with a figure when I round the corner.

The stench of expensive whiskey and cigar smoke assaults my nostrils as I instinctively recoil and wrinkle my nose. He sways on his feet, his suit jacket unbuttoned and his tie hanging loosely around his neck as he steadies himself against the wall and struggles to focus.

"Yum," he slurs, a lecherous grin spreading across his flushed cheeks when he spots me. "What's a pretty little thing like you doing back here?"

My stomach churns as his eyes rake over my body, lingering on the curves accentuated by the fitted black dress. I take a step back, trying to maintain a professional demeanor despite the alarm bells ringing in my head.

"I'm sorry, sir, but this area is off-limits to guests. If you'll please allow me to escort you back to the main event space..."

He lurches forward, trapping me against the wall with his bulk in a heartbeat, his breath hot and sour on my cheek. "Nah, I think I'd rather stay right here with you, sweetheart. How about you show me a good time, huh?"

One meaty hand comes up to stroke my cheek, and I barely suppress a shudder.

"You shouldn't be wanderin' around all alone. Never know what kinda trouble you might run into."

My insides revolt, churning with caustic disgust. I force a

smile, my mind whirring as I try to find a way out of this situation without blowing my cover.

"That's very generous of you, sir, but I really must insist that you return to the party. Mr. Dawson wouldn't want one of his esteemed guests to miss out on the festivities."

The man's grip on my arm loosens slightly at the mention of Dawson's name, and he leans in closer, his whiskey-soaked breath making my eyes water and my contact shift. I rapidly blink it back into place.

"Dawson, huh? You one of his special girls he promised to bring into the VIP room?"

I nod, playing along. "That's right. And he wouldn't be happy if he knew you were back here, keeping me from my duties."

A conspiratorial grin spreads across his ruddy face. "Well, we wouldn't want to upset the big boss man, now would we? 'Specially not tonight, with all the big deals he's got goin' on."

My curiosity piques despite the precarious situation. I feign wide-eyed innocence.

"Big deals? I'm afraid I don't know what you mean, sir. What could be so important?"

He grins, his teeth stained with tobacco.

"Oh, you know," he drawls, his words slurring together. "All the hush-hush stuff happening in that fancy VIP room. Dawson's got some real important people in there if you catch my drift."

He taps the side of his nose with a clumsy finger, a gesture that might have let me in on his secret if he weren't so drunk. "People you don't wanna mess with if you know what I mean. And I should know, I'm what they call a 'made man,' you see. Part of the family."

My knees buckle at his revelation. A made man—a fully

initiated member of the Mafia. What are the chances this man is from Morelli's?

High. Very high.

At the stunned look on my face, he follows up with, "Wanna see my gun?" then cups his crotch and gives it a wiggle.

I force a laugh, hoping it doesn't sound as brittle as it feels. "Well, aren't you just full of surprises!"

All while my brain ignites, synapses firing like a lightning storm that this man is connected to Morelli. I can't risk asking more questions and blowing my cover or arousing his suspicion, but the temptation to dig deeper, to uncover any scrap of intel that could help Kaden, is nearly overwhelming.

I flutter my lashes and aim for a breathy, adoring tone, channeling every bad noir film I've ever seen. "You must be so busy, what with all your important responsibilities. I'd hate to keep you from your obligations."

His chest puffs up at the praise, and he releases his grip on my arm to straighten his crooked tie. "Damn right, I am."

I nod eagerly, subtly shifting my weight to one side in an attempt to edge away.

My watch vibrates with an incoming text from Ethan. I discreetly read it by placing my hand on the man's chest. His heart races beneath my palm, the heat of his body seeping through his sweat-dampened shirt.

You ok? You've been in 1 place for a long time.

I take a deep breath, schooling my features into a mask of demure subservience. "I really must be going now. Mr. Dawson is expecting me, and I wouldn't want to keep him waiting. Us girls are meant to give you men a big, sexy surprise later."

The man's bleary eyes narrow, and for a heart-stopping moment, I fear he'll refuse to let me go. But then his face lights up like a toddler on his birthday. "Like dirty and sexy?"

I wink with my good eye. "Absolutely."

"Off you go, then." He flaps his hands. "I gotta leave, anyway, because, uh, I was sent here to, hmm ... I can't quite remember. Grab another bottle of whiskey from the kitchen?"

Leaving him to his problem-solving, I slink past and stride as fast and as calmly as my legs can carry me before I'm out of his sight. Hopefully forever.

My steps slow when I hear a loud crunch, then gagging sounds coming from his direction, but I don't dare backtrack to inspect it or see how badly he's fallen or passed out. As soon as I spot the emergency exit door, I push through and enter into the stairwell.

Lifting the watch close to my mouth, I dictate a response to Ethan in a whisper. "I'm fine. Sidelined by a drunk prick, but on my way to the basement now."

But Morelli's name won't stop circling my mind. I pause on the landing, my hand gripping the metal railing as I wrestle with two decisions that pull me in opposite directions. On the one hand, I came here tonight with a singular purpose—to destroy the illegal AI that Dawson, Morelli, and his cronies have been developing in secret. It's a noble cause, one that could prevent untold harm and suffering if this technology were to be leveraged by the Mafia.

Except Frank Morelli, the monster who murdered Kaden's daughter, the man he's devoted his life to destroying, is here in this very building. Conducting his business in a private VIP room, no less.

A sitting duck.

Kaden, Morelli's here.

The mere thought of bringing Kaden the news sends a shiver trickling down my neck and a delicious ache blooming deep in my chest. If I could just get eyes on Morelli and confirm he's here ... it would mean everything to Kaden. To us.

The temptation is too much, luring me away from my original mission with whispers of Kaden's praise, his approval, his touch...

I close my eyes and imagine the look on Kaden's face if I were to present him with a lead, something concrete he could use to get one step closer to Morelli. The way his icy-blue eyes would warm, just a fraction, as he regards me with a mix of surprise and grudging respect. The ghost of a smile that might play at the corners of his sensual mouth, a rare display of pleasure in a man so tightly controlled. And later, when we're alone, the way he might show his gratitude with those skillful hands and wicked tongue...

God, what I wouldn't give to please him, to be the one who delivers Morelli to him on a silver platter. To see the look of fierce pride and possessive hunger in Kaden's eyes when he realizes what I've done for him.

No.

I'm becoming as obsessed with Kaden as he is with me. Unhealthy and toxic.

The *world* matters, not just one person. I have to stick to my plan.

I descend the final steps into the basement where a blast of frigid air greets me, chilling the sweat that had begun to gather at the nape of my neck.

The hum of countless servers fills the cavernous space, a constant drone that vibrates in my chest. Rows upon rows of tall, black server racks are lined up in front of me, their blinking lights creating an eerie, artificial field of stars.

I pause, orienting myself. At the far end of the room, I spot my target, a glass-walled control center, its interior lit with a soft, bluish glow.

But before I step toward it...

"*Dammit,*" I hiss, unabashedly annoyed with what I'm about to do, but unable to stop myself.

I lift my wrist to my mouth again. "Hey, is this line secure for, uh, classified intel?"

Ethan responds immediately. **Damn right babe. I mean, respectfully, yes. It is.**

After blowing out an exhale that puffs my cheeks, I make my confession. "I need you to drive to my house and get Kaden. Morelli's here."

WUT. DO U WANT ME TO DIE.

"Well, I'm 90 percent sure Morelli's here. Kaden will want to check it out."

No way. Not leaving you.

"I'm fine. I made it to the basement. I'll be done in fifteen minutes."

You only have 10 left.

"Soon to be nine if you keep making me reply to you."

A few seconds, then: **Fine. I'll go. If I don't hear from u in 10 mins, I'm calling the police.**

I'm forced to accept his deal. Like Ethan said, I don't have a lot of time and can't waste any more seconds, especially considering what I've just added to the mix.

I lower my arm, fully aware of the hell I just unleashed upon myself once Kaden arrives.

My heels click across the concrete floor as I approach the glass-encased control room. As I reach the clear door, I pause, my hand hovering over the handle.

This is it. The moment I've been preparing for, the reason I risked everything to infiltrate Pulse tonight. With a deep breath to steady my nerves, I grasp the handle and pull, surprised when the door opens with ease.

A cocky grin tugs at my lips. They never expect a woman in a pretty dress to be a threat.

The door clicks shut behind me with a soft hiss of hydraulics. A quick glance confirms the room is empty, the sole occupant being the massive computer terminal that dominates the far wall. Its array of screens flicker with lines of code and complex diagrams, a silent concerto of data waiting for the right conductor.

An ethereal blue sheen reflects off the skin of my arms as I approach the main terminal and reach into my purse to pull out a small, foldable keyboard.

The device is sleek and lightweight, its matte black finish absorbing the ambient light rather than reflecting it. I unfold it with a practiced flick of my wrist, the keys clicking into place with a satisfying snap.

Connecting the keyboard to the main computer is a simple matter, the USB cable snaking out from the device and plugging into an open port.

The arrogance of it all, the sheer hubris of thinking themselves untouchable, sends a surge of righteous anger that boils.

Until the numbers on the screen shift and morph before I touch a key.

For the second time tonight, I curse out loud. My contact is dry to the point that it's nothing but a knife to my cornea, so I pull it out and flick it into my purse, never to be used again.

Now that I can see properly, my fingers fly across the keyboard. I'm not just deleting the AI; I'm obliterating it. My custom-made virus will spread like wildfire through the Pulse Dynamics' servers, corrupting the AI's core and poisoning its data beyond repair.

But I'm not stopping there.

With each line of code, I'm weaving a digital trap, ensuring that any attempt to recreate this monstrosity will trigger a devastating system-wide meltdown. I think of how Dawson manipulated me and my colleagues, using our innovations for his twisted agenda, and the contract they put on my head because of it. This isn't just about destroying a dangerous creation—it's personal.

With three minutes to spare, I'm about to seal the fate of Morelli's illicit empire. Let Dawson try to do a test run tonight. Let him try to rebuild from this, I think, a fierce smile playing on my lips. I've just turned this technological nightmare into digital dust.

But in the space between one heartbeat and the next, everything changes.

The lights cut out with a sickening electronic whine, plunging the room into a darkness so absolute, I let out a squeak of surprise. The servers fall silent, their constant hum snuffed out.

And then, before I can even process the sudden shift, a strong hand clamps over my mouth from behind, stifling the scream on my tongue.

24

KADEN

I picture my next home with a white picket fence staked with all the heads I'll collect tonight.

Wishful thinking, since I haven't had a place to call my own in over a decade. Homes are for people with families, with lives. Not for soulless monsters who leave trails of blood and screams in their wake.

I stalk through the darkened halls of Pulse Dynamics, my footsteps silent as a reaper's sigh. The office rooms and cubicles I pass are quiet at this late hour, save for the distant hum of servers and the occasional flicker of fluorescent lights. I can feel the weight of my blades against my forearms, hungry for flesh. Everyone's on the sixth-floor rooftop, enjoying Dawson's event where he promises to unveil cutting-edge technology and put it up for bid to the wealthy, elite clientele stumbling about the building, drunk on champagne and power.

I've learned a lot in the thirty minutes since Layla gave me the slip, tracking Ethan's van to a spot across the street from Pulse. It wasn't there when I arrived, but that's no matter.

Ethan got lucky. I'm confident Layla's not inside the vehicle anymore.

The second I laid eyes on her office building and recalled her brief, frustrated phone call to Dawson, it all fell into place. Wraithling is using the opening that a party gives her to destroy Morelli's new technology, with everyone gathered in one room and the rest of the building empty.

If I weren't so furious with her, I'd be impressed at her gall.

I'm a fool for letting my guard down and allowing Layla to worm her way under my skin. When I returned to her house and found her gone, a cold, familiar wrath gripped my heart. The kind of ferocity I haven't felt since Cassie.

In a blind rage, I lashed out, shards of glass and broken tech slicing into my knuckles, but I barely feel the sting. The pain inside is far worse.

How could I have been so careless? I should know better than to trust Layla, to care for her.

Attachments are a liability. They make you vulnerable, distracted. And now, because of my foolishness, Layla is out there alone, unprotected, and at the mercy of men like Dawson who make friends with the Mafia.

The nightmare of my daughter's lifeless eyes, her tiny body broken and bloody, floods my mind. I never got to say a final goodbye to her. Never got to hold her one last time, warm or cold.

I can't lose Layla, too.

I move through the shadows of the service corridors like a phantom, my tactical suit and mask obscuring any move I make. The layout of the building is etched in my mind from when I initially stalked Layla, memorized from blueprints and hours of surveillance. I know every blind spot, every potential choke point.

As I round a corner, I recognize a lone security guard

patrolling the hallway ahead. He's young, barely out of his teens, with a bored expression on his face as he scrolls through his phone. Poor kid. Wrong place, wrong time.

I wait, still as a panther spotting a rabbit, until he's just a few feet away. Then, with a burst of speed, I lunge, one hand closing over his mouth while the other finds the pressure point at the base of his neck. He struggles for a moment, eyes wide, but my grip is iron. In seconds, he goes limp.

I ease the unconscious guard to the floor, propping him against the wall as if he merely dozed off.

Old habits die hard. I could have easily snapped his neck, but I'm trying to avoid unnecessary kills tonight. The urge to end him still lingers though, like a dark whisper in the back of my mind. It would be so easy, so satisfying to feel that familiar crunch of bone and cartilage...

I shake my head. *Focus.* I'm here for Layla.

I continue my silent prowl through the building, senses heightened for any signs of trouble. The sound of my heartbeat echoes in my ears, a metronome of calm. The server room should be just ahead, down a flight of stairs and through a reinforced door. That's where Layla will likely be, trying to sabotage Dawson's grand unveiling.

And when I get my hands on her...

"Nah, boss, she wasn't the one."

The voice stops me short, and I dart into a cubicle room, the lights off, and press against the wall near a window overlooking the hallway.

I peer through the slats of the blinds, making out a figure striding down the hallway with his phone to his ear. His shirt is untucked and hair mussed, like he's had one too many to drink, but his gait is too steady, his eyes too focused as he talks.

"I'm tellin' ya, it wasn't the girl," the fake drunk insists, his words crisp and clear. "I got a long look at her when I grabbed her. Both her eyes were brown, and the boss said the Verona girl's got one blue eye and one brown, like a circus freak or somethin'."

I should rip his stomach open and tie his intestines around his flaccid dick. Layla is worth a thousand of him.

I'm about to do just that, and more, when I hear the fake drunk chuckle and say, "Nah, I played it up real good. Stumbled around, got a little handsy. She bought the drunk act hook, line, and sinker, but the broad is just one of the whores who got lost on her way to the VIP room, as a gift to Morelli. Those chicks are hot but ain't too bright. Yeah, I'm headed there now. Later."

Crimson bleeds into the edges of my vision and a roar fills my ears. Rage courses through my veins, heating my blood to a volcanic level.

Morelli.

I've been chasing the Ghost Leader for years, coming close, but never close enough. And now, one of his lackeys is right here within my grasp.

I move without thinking.

In one fluid motion, I'm behind the fake drunk, one hand covering his mouth, the other pressing a blade to his throat. He starts to struggle, but I dig the knife in deeper, drawing a thin line of blood.

"Quiet," I hiss in his ear, my voice a guttural rasp through the mask. "Or I'll paint the walls using your intestines as my paintbrush."

The man stiffens, phone clattering to the floor.

With a flick of my wrist, I have him flying face-first into the wall with a satisfying crunch. He yelps in pain and surprise, but I'm already wrenching his arm behind his back, twisting until I feel the pop of dislocation.

"Where's Morelli?" I snarl through the mask's voice modulator.

The man whimpers, tears and snot mixing with the blood dripping from his broken nose. "I don't know, I swear! I'm just a grunt. Morelli don't tell me nothin'!"

I slam his face into the wall again, relishing the wet fracturing of cartilage. "Wrong answer."

Keeping his dislocated arm wrenched behind him, I drag the man into the empty office and throw him to the floor. He scrambles back against a cubicle wall. The green slits of my mask's eyes track him in the dark.

"Last chance," I growl, flicking out another knife. The blade gleams hungrily. "Where is Morelli hiding?"

"I'm just the muscle! I follow orders, and I was told to come to this floor to check out a girl coming through the service entrance who matched the description of the one he's looking for. That's all. I don't know where he's at right now."

I hunch down in front of him, and with methodical precision, I dislocate each of his fingers one by one, the snap-crackle-pop a morbid rhythm. His cries escalate into shrill, agonized shrieks that reverberate off the walls. It's a miracle no one comes running.

Probably because he's not worth it.

"The VIP room!" he gasps out between sobs, snot and blood dribbling down his chin. "Top floor, northwest corner. But you'll never get in. It's guarded to shit for the auction."

"Auction?"

"Yeah, the black market tech being auctioned off. A bunch of the crime families are here. Morelli's got some sort of bid war going on for—fuck, I don't know the exact stuff. I'm no techie."

Grabbing a fistful of his hair, I yank his head back, exposing his neck. I lean in close, so he can feel my breath through the mask. "And the girl? Where was she headed?"

"The girl!" the man gasps out as if overjoyed that he can provide the answer without difficulty. "She went through the exit door to the stairs. That's all I know. I fucking swear. Please, guy..."

I press the blade to his throat, the steel kissing his skin. "If you touched her..."

The man's eyes widen in terror, pupils constricting to pinpricks.

"No, no, I didn't!" he babbles. "I just grabbed her arm, that's all. I swear on my mother's grave!"

"Swear on your own grave," I say with enough malice to split our shared air in half. "You'll be in it soon enough."

I slash the knife across his throat, crafting a scarlet smile from ear to ear.

Blood gushes, splattering the cubicle walls in abstract arcs. His body convulses, his useless, crooked fingers scrabbling at his neck.

I watch dispassionately as the light fades from his eyes.

I feel nothing. No remorse. No satisfaction. Just a cold, empty void where my spirit used to be.

I leave the corpse sprawled on the office floor, blood puddling around him, then stride down the hallway to the stairwell door and yank it open, the metal clanging against concrete. The stairs are somewhat lit, the fluorescent bulbs flickering and buzzing like dying fireflies.

I pause, head cocked, listening for any sign of Layla.

Peering over the railing, I gauge which direction I should go. Up to the VIP room to confront Morelli directly? Or down to the server room to protect Layla?

The basement or the rooftop. Of course it has to be opposite ends of the building.

I weigh the possibilities. Layla is brilliant but guileless, driven by a misplaced sense of justice. She doesn't understand the true depths of human depravity, the lengths men like Morelli will go to protect their interests.

If she tries to take on Morelli alone ... if she's cornered by any member of a crime family, idiot brute or otherwise, she may not be so lucky next time.

I clutch the banister to the point that it whines in distress, torn between two conflicting desires. The primal, vengeful part of me yearns to charge up these stairs and continue to add crimson pieces to my museum of art, the most prized being the blood of the man who murdered my baby girl.

But downstairs contains another precious gift. Layla.

My phone buzzes against my thigh, drawing my attention. I frown when I pull it out and read the screen.

It's a text from Layla, which is impossible because she purposely left her phone at home, but I read it anyway.

Hi so this is Ethan. I found Layla's phone on the floor and plugged it in to charge. Layla told me to come back and tell you Morelli's at Pulse somewhere. She's there too and I'm worried about her. I don't have your number but saw that the only contact in this phone other than me is Jerk and I assume that's you, Kaden? I'm sorry please don't kill me.

I suck on a tooth while scrolling through the message. The kid's terror is palpable even through a screen. Layla certainly knows how to pick her accomplices. This one's about as threatening as a marshmallow. My thumbs tap on the screen, composing a terse reply.

I'm already here. And Ethan? Breathe. If I wanted you dead, you wouldn't have had time to send that text. Stay at the house to remain safe. And feed Reaper.

I pocket the phone and take a step, but it buzzes again almost immediately. Sighing, I fish it back out.

Ethan: Feed Reaper? Is that some kind of assassin code? Like, am I supposed to lure someone named Reaper with snacks so you can … you know what, I don't want to know. I'll just stay here and definitely NOT google "how to feed the Grim Reaper" or "do supernatural entities prefer wet or dry food." Nope. Not me. I'm just a simple coder who's suddenly very interested in learning SQL injection. For completely innocent reasons.

I pinch the bridge of my nose, exhaling slowly. This kid might give me an aneurysm before Morelli ever gets the chance. With a swift, annoyed motion, I type out one last message.

It's my cat, you idiot. Dry food. Top shelf.

Shaking my head, I silence the phone and shove it deep into my pocket. Enough distractions.

I'm at war with myself, the Scythe and Kaden battling for dominance within the fortress I've made of my mind. The Scythe demands blood, craves the visceral satisfaction of watching Morelli choke on his own stomach acid as I gut him.

But Kaden, the broken man beneath the mask, the father who failed to protect his little girl, needs something else entirely. He needs to shield the woman who's come to mean more to him than vengeance itself. The one who's slowly, painfully, stitching his shattered heart back together with her quicksilver smiles and unbreakable spirit.

I take the stairs two at a time, my boots scarcely making a sound on the concrete steps.

To the server room.

25
LAYLA

Kaden will never stop haunting my dreams.

I'm one of those sleepers who are aware when they're dreaming and can usually control the outcome. Like, if I'm approaching an ending I don't like, or plopped into nightmares that have become progressively more violent now that the Scythe has infiltrated my life, I can get out of them by redirecting the narrative or simply waking myself up.

But when it comes to Kaden, my lucid dreaming power fails me.

Tonight, he came up behind me in Pulse's server room, blacking out the lights and clamping a hand around my mouth, pulling me into his infernal depths. The server room's emergency lights bathe everything in a red glow. The hum of machinery fills my ears.

I realize I'm suspended in the air, my body stretched out in a way that makes my muscles scream in protest. Fiber optic cables, usually so delicate in my hands, now bite into my skin like steel wires, arms and legs spread wide.

I'm maybe three feet off the ground, held up by thicker

bundles looped under my arms and across my back. They must be anchored to the server racks on either side of me—I can feel the strain when I try to move. Thinner cables wrap around my wrists and ankles, spreading my limbs wide and leaving me horribly exposed.

And naked.

My underwear, dress, and smartwatch have been removed.

Below, I can see a haphazard pile of computer parts. Sharp edges of heat sinks and metal casings glint menacingly. If I loosen myself enough to fall, it's going to hurt. A lot.

The Scythe circles me like a hunter toying with his next kill, drawing my head up.

"Look at you," he purrs through his mask, his deep, modulated voice acting like a vibrator against my core. "The brilliant Layla Verona, caught in a web of the very technology she adores. Poetic, isn't it?"

I should be terrified, but a traitorous heat blossoms low in my belly. Kaden is the twisted hero of my deepest, most shameful desires. But in this dreamscape, I can indulge my darkest fantasies without consequence.

Kaden slinks closer, running a gloved finger down my trembling body. I shudder at his touch, a whimper escaping my lips as he traces the curves of my breasts, waist and hips. His fingers dance over my inner thighs, teasing but not quite touching where I ache for him most.

"So responsive." He chuckles darkly. "Even when you're at my mercy, helpless and exposed, your body sings for me, doesn't it?"

I want to deny it, but the evidence of my arousal glistens between my spread legs. Kaden cups my sex possessively, pressing the heel of his palm against my clit. Sparks ignite my nerve-endings and I arch into his touch with a desperate moan.

"That's it, my little captive," he encourages, rubbing firm circles that make my toes curl.

His fingers delve into my slick folds, two digits pumping in and out, curling to hit that magic spot inside. I try to angle my hips, to force him deeper.

My head falls back as Kaden finger-fucks me relentlessly, his thick digits stretching me wide and delving so deep. Slick, filthy sounds fill the air, blending with my needy whimpers and his sinister amusement. He adds a third finger, pumping them in and out of my clenching pussy, his thumb mercilessly circling my clit.

"Look at you, dripping all over my hand like the greedy little slut you are," Kaden growls. "I bet you're fantasizing about my cock right now, aren't you? Imagining me filling up this tight cunt, fucking you so hard you forget your own name."

My brows come together.

That isn't right. Kaden's never called me those things before.

Redirect the narrative.

With my forehead smoothing, I demand my dream to rewind.

"You're nothing but a filthy whore," he spits out viciously. "Getting off on being tied up and used like the cheap slut you are. I always knew you wanted this, wanted to be put in your place by a real man."

His fingers twist cruelly inside me, and I cry out in pain mingled with unwanted pleasure. "Bet you've been gagging for my cock since the moment you laid eyes on me. Well guess what, you're going to choke on it before the night's through. I'm going to fuck your slutty holes until you're a ruined, sobbing mess."

Kaden's venomous words slice through the haze of lust, so jarringly out of character that I freeze.

This isn't a dream.

The stinging bite of the cables, the acrid smell of hot metal, the hellish red glow—it all crashes into me with a sudden, sickening clarity. This is real. I'm not in control.

A cold sweat breaks out across my skin as my heart rate skyrockets. I twist against my bonds, desperately trying to free myself, but it only makes the cables cut deeper, turning my struggles into a mockery of my earlier writhing.

With a sense of creeping dread, I crane my neck to look at my captor.

He steps into the red light, revealing a face I hate all too well.

Emmitt Dawson.

"Surprise," he drawls, beady eyes gleaming. "Bet you didn't see this coming, did you?"

"Dawson?" I rasp out, my throat dry and an awful taste scraping against my tongue. "What ... what are you doing?"

He laughs, continuing to circle me. "Did you really believe you could interfere with my plans and get away with it? That I wouldn't find out about your pathetic attempt at corporate espionage?"

Dawson smirks, clearly relishing my confusion and fear. "Oh Layla, you have no idea how long I've waited for this moment. To see you helpless and at my mercy, after all the trouble you've caused."

He pulls a small glass vial from his suit jacket, the liquid inside glinting as he shakes it. "A powerful sedative, courtesy of my associates. One little prick and you were out like a light, allowing me to arrange this delightful tableau."

My stomach turns as hazy memories surface. I was one button away from dismantling Morelli's AI tech forever, until the lights went out, a hand came over my mouth, and there was a sting in my neck...

How could I have been so careless, so blind?

"Why are you doing this?" I whisper.

He leans in close, his acrid breath washing over my face. "You never even felt it, did you? Too caught up in your ridiculous fantasies about the Scythe having your back. Yes, we know he's with you. Well, I have news for you, sweetheart. He's not coming to your rescue. No one is."

It takes all my mental energy to ignore the awful fluttering of panic in my chest and keep the conversation going so he can't do worse things to me.

"Why would you work for the Mafia? You're the son of a millionaire. You made this company a success. You don't need Morelli."

"You're such a dumb cunt. *Fuck*, it feels so good to say what I really want to you without all that HR bullshit. You have no idea how the real world works, Lay. Money and power are the only things that matter. And the Mafia? It has both."

"Morelli's dying. Did you know that? You've chained yourself to a man whose empire won't survive without him."

Dawson grips my chin, forcing me to meet his cold, dead eyes. "Who said I was working with Morelli?"

Tears prick at the corners of my eyes. Dawson's nails cut into my cheeks, forcing my lips to purse and saliva to overflow.

"That's right. Get your mouth nice and lubed for me, bitch. Morelli isn't at the top anymore. You fucking whore, you really thought you could stop me? That your stupid little cyber tricks could take down an operation a decade in the making?"

He releases my face with a cruel shove, making me swing in my bonds. The movement sends shock waves of pain radiating through my strained shoulders.

"Morelli's time is almost up, but his legacy? That lives on.

And I'm going to help carry it forward into a glorious new era. With that AI tech, we'll have the world's governments, militaries, corporations, all dancing to our tune."

"You're insane," I choke out.

Dawson rakes his gaze over my naked, bound form. "Not to worry, baby. You'll be lucky if I let you live long enough to witness it. But I do get to take my time with you while the auction goes on upstairs."

Dawson reaches for his belt buckle with a leering grin. "When I'm done, maybe I'll let Morelli have a go at whatever's left. Give the geezer a proper farewell."

I wrench my mouth open to scream. The pain is too real, Dawson's sour scent too pungent. This is my reality now. Betrayed, alone, and about to be brutalized in the cruelest way imaginable.

Just as Dawson frees his dick, the server room doors explode inward with a deafening bang. Shards of metal and plastic rain down, sparks flying from destroyed circuitry.

Through the smoke and debris, a figure emerges, clad in sleek black tactical gear, a matte onyx mask obscuring his features. Twin green slits blaze with unholy fury as the Scythe stalks forward.

Dawson stumbles back, his small, thick dick bobbing. "Fuck me. The Scythe himself. Guess I should be flattered."

Kaden advances on Dawson. "Your first mistake was thinking I wouldn't come for her."

Dawson scrambles to tuck himself away.

"You're too late," he sneers. "The AI is already—"

Kaden ignores him. "Your last was laying a finger on what's mine."

Dawson barely has time to raise his fists before Kaden's on him, a flurry of precise, brutal strikes raining down.

Dawson staggers back, blood spraying from his nose and

mouth. He spits out a tooth, lips curling into a feral snarl. "You think you can stop this? It's already done! That AI is going to make me a god!"

He fumbles for the gun holstered beneath his suit jacket, but Kaden is faster. In a blur of black, he disarms Dawson and slams him against the server racks with bone-crushing force. Components shatter and spark.

Kaden catches Dawson's arm, wrenching it behind his back until the joint pops with a sickening crack. Dawson howls, crumpling to his knees. Kaden twists his arm farther, forcing his face to the ground.

"Look at her," the Scythe commands. "Look at what you did to her."

Through tears of pain and humiliation, I lock eyes with Dawson's bulging, bloodshot ones. His face is a ruin, his nose crushed and lips split, yet still he leers at my exposed body like a rabid dog eyeing a fresh steak.

"Should've heard the way she moaned for me," Dawson slurs through a mouthful of blood. "The slut loved every second of it."

Kaden's fist connects with Dawson's jaw in a brutal uppercut, snapping his head back. Teeth and blood splatter across the floor.

"You don't get to speak to her," Kaden snarls, punctuating each word with a vicious blow. Dawson's head lolls, barely conscious, yet still he grins through his broken mouth.

"Too late," he gurgles. "Already had my fingers in her sweet cunt."

Kaden's entire body goes rigid, a chilling stillness settling over him like the calm before devastating lightning strikes.

His grip on Dawson's mangled arm tightens, leather gloves creaking.

"Say that again." Kaden's tone is a low, deadly purr.

Dawson, even through the haze of agony, has the audacity to chuckle wetly. "You heard me. Fingered her till she was dripping all over my knuckles. Would you like to smell them?"

Kaden moves, blurring until he's not Kaden anymore. He's the black harbinger of death.

His hands clamp around Dawson's head, one gripping his hair, the other digging into Dawson's mouth and hooking his bottom teeth. With a roar of pure, unbridled rage, Kaden pulls Dawson's jaw out of its socket.

Dawson's scream cuts off abruptly as Kaden rips his jaw completely free with a grisly tearing of flesh, sinew, and bone. Blood spurts from the gaping wound, spraying across the Scythe's mask and chest.

He tosses the mangled jaw aside. It hits the floor with a wet slap, the remaining teeth scattering like gory dice.

Dawson gurgles and chokes, drowning in his own blood as it pours down his mutilated neck. His eyes roll wildly, bulging from their sockets as he claws at his ruined face with his one good hand.

But the Scythe isn't done.

He seizes Dawson by the hair, wrenching his head back at an impossible angle until vertebrae pop and crunch. With his other hand, he plunges armored fingers into the gushing ruin of Dawson's lower face, hooking them under the tongue and ripping it out by the root with a brutal yank.

Dawson convulses, a high, thin wail escaping through his windpipe as the Scythe slams Dawson's head against the unforgiving metal of the server rack again and again, until the sickening crack of his skull splits the air. Bits of bone and brain matter splatter across the humming machinery, gore mingling with sparking wires and crushed circuitry.

Dawson's body spasms, limbs jerking in a macabre death-dance as Kaden releases his ruined head. It lolls at an unnatural angle, eyes bulging and glassy, jowls hanging by threads of torn flesh. The Scythe steps back, chest heaving, fists clenching and unclenching at his sides. His tactical suit is drenched in blood, droplets sliding down the black mask like ruby tears.

For a long, tense moment, he stands over Dawson's mutilated corpse, a dark avenging angel painted in viscera. Then slowly, so slowly, he turns to face me.

Pinned beneath that ferocious gaze, I feel stripped bare in a way that has nothing to do with my physical nakedness. It's as if he can see straight into my battered, quivering soul.

His heavy combat boots crunch through the grotesque debris. I quail instinctively, my abused body trying to curl in on itself despite the biting restraints.

For a heart-stopping moment, I fear the Scythe's bloodlust hasn't been sated, that he'll turn that brutal strength on me next.

A whimper escapes my raw throat as he looms over me, one gloved hand reaching out...

And then, with a gentleness that unmoors me, Kaden cradles my tear-streaked face. The coppery scent of blood mingles with the warm, familiar scent of leather as his thumb brushes over my bruised cheekbone.

"Layla."

My name is a broken whisper.

Kaden's touch is impossibly tender as he trails his fingers down my face, tracing the paths of my tears. The brush of leather against my sensitized skin sends involuntary shivers through me, and my mouth trembles with his name on my lips.

His other hand reaches for the cables binding my wrists, snapping them effortlessly. Each loop of cable falls away, and with it, a small measure of the crushing terror that had gripped my heart.

Kaden works in silence, his hands steady and sure despite the fine tremors that wrack his powerful frame.

As the last of the restraints fall away, I pitch forward, muscles too weak and traumatized to support my weight. But Kaden is there to catch me, enfolding my abused body in his strong arms. He holds me close, cradling me against the solidity of his chest as if I'm the most precious thing in the world.

Hot tears spill down my cheeks. "I failed. I'm sorry. I shouldn't have left you—"

"Shh, it's okay," Kaden soothes, his deep voice fluttering the hair at the top of my head. "Your bravery is one of the many things that draws me to you."

I feel small and fragile in his powerful embrace, but also impossibly safe. Protected.

I burrow into his chest, desperate to hear the steady thrum of his heartbeat.

He strokes my hair with a trembling hand. "I've got you, Wraithling. I won't let anyone hurt you, ever again."

The words are both vow and prayer, whispered like a benediction against my temple. I clutch at him, fingers digging into Kevlar, terrified he'll dissipate like smoke if I let go.

"I'm sorry," I rasp, throat raw from screaming. "I shouldn't have come here alone. I thought I could handle Dawson, that I could stop the AI launch, but I—" A damaged sob wrenches from my chest. "I was so stupid..."

Kaden lowers us both to the floor, settling me in his lap as he leans back against the server rack.

He starts to remove his mask, until I reach up with shaking fingers.

The mask comes away under my hand, revealing the face

I've come to know so well. Those piercing blue eyes, now bloodshot and glistening with unshed tears. That proud, aquiline nose, flaring with each ragged exhale. Those sensual lips, usually quirked in a sardonic smirk, now pressed into a thin, bloodless line. And that jagged hook of a scar, a silver river on a flawless face.

His thumb brushes over my lower lip as his gaze roams over me, his eyes twin pools of torment as he takes in every cut, every bruise, every smudge of grime and blood. His throat works as he swallows hard. "I'm so sorry. I failed you when you needed me most. I don't expect you to forgive me, but please, let me help you now. Let me take care of you, in whatever way you need."

Kaden's voice breaks on the words, a hairline fracture in his usual iron control. "I swore to protect you, to keep you safe from the monsters in my world." His hand fists in my hair, clenching almost painfully. "When I saw what he did to you, what he was about to do..." A shudder ripples through his powerful frame. "I have only felt such fear, such blinding rage, once before. The thought of losing you, of being too late..." He squeezes his eyes shut, brow furrowing as if in physical pain. "It unmade me."

I reach up to touch his face, my fingertips grazing his scar. "But you weren't too late."

His eyes snap open, blazing with a ferocity that steals my air. "I will always come for you, Layla. No matter what. No matter the cost." His grip gentles, hand cupping the back of my head. "It's taken me too long to realize that you are everything to me. I'd scale the heights of heaven, rip the wings off angels and use their feathers as a bed for you to dream on. I'd dive into the depths of hell, steal the devil's horns, and crown you queen of my underworld. That is my promise to you."

I'm so filled with emotion, my throat is too clogged to

respond. How could I form what I'm feeling into words, anyway? It's too much, *so* much, that I give him my soul through a kiss, instead.

My lips mold against Kaden's, soft and pliant, seeking to convey all the things my voice cannot. He responds with a groan, his mouth slanting over mine, tongue delving deep to stake his claim.

The taste of him floods my senses, whiskey and smoke, danger and devotion. I cling to his broad shoulders, fingers digging into muscle as he devours.

It's a kiss of absolution, of forgiveness for perceived failures and unspoken fears. It's a kiss of gratitude, of awe at the lengths he would go to protect me, to avenge even the slightest harm done to me. It's a kiss of possession, claiming him as mine just as surely as I am his.

The harsh clang of metal on concrete jolts through both of us, and we pry apart.

Kaden's arms tighten around me as his head snaps up, eyes narrowing to slits.

Slow, mocking applause echoes through the ruined server room. A man in an immaculate suit emerges from the remaining smoke, stepping over Dawson's amputated jawbone.

He surveys the scene with a cold, assessing gaze, taking in Dawson's mutilated corpse and my bruised, naked form cradled against Kaden's blood-soaked chest.

"*Brava*," he drawls, still clapping. "Quite the performance. I must say, I'm impressed."

Kaden tenses, coiling beneath me like a snake tightening its scales.

"Morelli," he snarls.

Morelli smiles, a razor-blade slash of white. "Hello, Kaden.

Or is it Scythe now? I can never keep it straight. It's been too long."

His gaze flicks to me, trailing over my nakedness with a proprietary air.

"I must say, when Dawson proposed this little scheme, I had my doubts." Morelli strolls forward, heedless of the blood and entrails staining his handmade Italian leather shoes.

"But he was right," Morelli says, his voice gravelly from years of cigars. "Dangling the auction as bait for both of you. It was inspired." He chuckles, a sound like gravel in a meat grinder. "His present condition notwithstanding. You see, Kaden, in my line of work, you learn to read people. Their weaknesses, their ... pressure points." His cold eyes flick between Kaden and me, calculating. "I've seen empires rise and fall. Built a few myself." His gaze lifts over my head and snags on Kaden, a cruel smile forming on his lips. "Buried more than a few daughters, too."

26
LAYLA

Nothing else exists except for Kaden's frenzy. I'm certain he can't feel my weight on his lap any longer.

The air I'm sharing with him sizzles with neon hate, years of torment and agony threatening to explode out of his body.

Morelli's flat gray stare holds Kaden's, a smile playing at the corners of his mouth as he savors the anguish etched into every line of Kaden's face.

"That's right," Morelli says, talking slow as if to savor every syllable. "I buried her myself."

Very carefully, Kaden nudges me aside. I don't take my eyes off him when I shift off his lap.

As soon as I'm clear, an unnatural roar tears from Kaden's throat and he lunges, a blade in each hand like talons ready to rip Morelli's throat out.

But Morelli's men are faster, appearing out of obscurity and slamming Kaden back against the wall, their guns pressed to his head.

I scream, the sound bursting from my chest, but no one so

much as glances my way. I'm nothing, insignificant in their final showdown.

Kaden's neck bulges with tendons, his eyes wild and filled with a madness worse than what he possessed when mutilating Dawson.

"I will kill you," he seethes, his words a blood oath.

Despite Morelli's too-lean frame and gaunt cheeks, his suit drapes over him like armor. He exudes victory, reveling in the agony he's inflicting upon his nemesis.

"To think I believe you a mere fly to swat all those years ago," Morelli muses while Kaden spits hatred. "Little did I know how successful I would be in forging the ultimate thorn in my side. You've been after me for some time, Mr. Black. Does it feel good to face me now? With your woman stripped and bleeding, your daughter long gone, and my men's guns at your temple?" Morelli scans the floor, noting the bits and pieces of Dawson with a slight nose wrinkle. "I see you lost your temper."

A strangled cry leaves me when one of Morelli's men yanks me to a stand by my hair.

"Bring her to me," Morelli commands.

My scalp burns as I'm dragged forward. Morelli's man drags me to the center of the room, my bare feet slipping in the slick of Dawson's blood. He positions me in front of Morelli like a human shield, one arm locked around my neck.

My pulse thuds in my ears and each breath saws at my lungs. Fresh tears sting my eyes, but I blink them back in refusal.

Kaden follows it all, straining against the two men holding him against a server tower. A maelstrom of emotions swirl in his cutlass blue depths. Anguish, fury, and beneath it all, terror.

Terror for me.

"Let her go," Kaden says between his clenched teeth.

Morelli's answering laugh is devoid of humor. "You hurt one of mine. It's only fair I do the same to one of yours."

I can barely breathe, my lungs constricting as if Morelli's man is squeezing my very organs. But I can't look away from Kaden. If I do, I'll shatter.

Kaden's lashes flicker even as a vein pulses from his forehead as he struggles. A silent communication passes between us in that split second. Apology and a promise. A reminder from him to remember his vow to me. His oath that he will get me out of this, no matter the cost.

But how?

He's outnumbered, outgunned. Trapped.

Just like his daughter was. Buried by Morelli's own hands. My stomach clenches, a violent upheaval threatening to erupt.

Morelli's expensive shoes splash through the carnage as he inches closer behind me. He reaches out a hand, trailing a finger down my cheek, his touch like ice against my flushed skin.

I jerk my head away, but the arm around my neck holds firm.

"Spirited. I can see why you like her, Kaden."

I feel more than see Morelli giving me the once-over, lingering on my private areas.

"Though her current state leaves something to be desired."

Despite the paralyzing fear, I hiss through gritted teeth, "Go to hell."

"Oh, my dear. We're already there." His chuckle cascades across my shoulders like hundreds of spiderlings exploding out of their nest. "And I'm the devil himself."

I swallow against the pressure around my throat and pour every ounce of contempt into my voice when I respond, "Then Kaden promised me your horns as my trophy."

A sickening sound draws my attention in time to watch Kaden wrench free of the men holding him, moving faster than I thought humanly possible. The guns at his head go off but somehow miss, bullets sparking off the server towers in a shower of metal and plastic.

Kaden's twin blades flash as he slices through the first man's neck, a crimson arc spraying the wall. He pivots, burying his other knife to the hilt in the second man's eye socket with a precise squelch.

The arm around my neck turns into a vise, cutting off my air and jerking me back. Spots dance in my vision.

Morelli barks an order, and suddenly, more of his men flood in, piling onto Kaden.

But Kaden is an unleashed beast whose family is threatened, slashing and tearing with savage ferocity, his face a rictus of primal rage. Men fall in pieces, their screams cut short as Kaden slings their blood around, and I fully accept that I'm in shock when I compare the scene to an assassin breaking into an art room and getting into the paint.

I'm seeing so much violence. It's not stopping. It keeps coming, relentless and determined to break me until there's nothing left but a hollow shell for Kaden to weep over.

"Enough!" Morelli bellows.

Cold steel presses against my temple and I still, whimpering.

Kaden freezes. His blades drip gore as he catches his breath, his gaze locking onto the gun barrel digging into my temple, Morelli's fingers clenched white around the grip.

"Drop the weapons, Mr. Black," Morelli commands, his voice oil-slick with triumph. "Or I'll add her brains into your corpse soup."

A muscle in Kaden's jaw ticks, a war raging behind his visceral stare. The urge to rip Morelli to pieces versus his desperate need to protect me. To not lose another loved one to this monster.

"Kaden," I rasp, his name barely squeezing out. I can't breathe. I'm trembling so violently my teeth chatter. "Don't…"

But Kaden's already loosening his grip, letting the knives clatter to the blood-slicked floor. He raises his hands in surrender, his shoulders slumping in defeat.

Morelli's lips curl in a vicious smile. "Good dog."

Yet there is no submission in Kaden's stare as he regards Morelli. "Where is she? Where did you bury my daughter?"

Morelli's triumphant laugh grates against my eardrums, each guffaw laced with sadistic glee. "Where, you ask? Why, in the very place you least expect. The one location you'd never think to look because it's too close to home. Though I did enjoy all those baubles you left on the bodies you collected over the years. And the creativity in your kills. Death by licorice. That was a good one. And I can't disregard those cheap, cutesy time-pieces you'd leave behind, similar to the ones Cassandra loved to wear, am I right? That alone is my final gift to you, Mr. Black. I noticed your vengeful clues, I realized who the Scythe truly was, and I relished the day I could confront and then end you myself. Your obsession with me was truly flattering."

Kaden's lips twist into a humorless smile. "Enjoy it while you can, Morelli. We both know you're a dead man walking. The cancer eating away at your insides, turning you into a shriveled husk. I can smell it on you, the stench of decay. You reek of desperation, clinging to your last shreds of power. But in the end, you're nothing more than a rotting shell, a tragic parody of the man you once were."

Morelli's papery skin stretches taut over his skull as he snarls. "My health is no concern of yours."

Kaden coughs, a wet and ragged sound that sends alarm bells in my head warning me that he's injured, but he keeps his attention on Morelli. "But it is. Because I want to know exactly how long I have to make you suffer before you take your last breath."

Fury contorts Morelli's features into something inhuman. His finger twitches on the trigger and I squeeze my eyes shut, bracing for the bullet to tear through my skull.

But the bang never comes.

In a blur of motion, Kaden snatches a gun from the limp hand of one of Morelli's fallen men and shoots with deadly precision. The bullet ruffles the hair at my temples and buries itself in the forehead of the henchman holding me hostage.

The pressure around my neck vanishes as the man crumples, his body spasming. I stumble forward, gasping for air, my vision swimming. Kaden is there in an instant, his arm encircling my waist, holding me upright.

He kisses my temple, then murmurs, "Just stay with me, Wraithling. You're almost out of this."

I nod weakly, clinging to him as he turns to face Morelli, shielding me with his body. Morelli's face is twisted with outrage, his gun still trained on us. But there's a flicker of distress in his cold gray eyes now, a realization that he may have underestimated Kaden.

"I'm not one to torture the terminally ill," Kaden says. "But for you, I'll make an exception."

Kaden squeezes my arm, and too late, I realize it's a symbol of farewell before he's on Morelli in a whirlwind of savage fury that doesn't care whether it lives or dies.

His fists thump against Morelli's gaunt face, the sound of fracturing bone and loosening muscle filling the room. Morelli staggers back, his face a pulpy mess, but Kaden is relentless. He grabs Morelli by the lapels of his suit and slams him against the wall, the impact rattling the shelves.

"Where is she?" Kaden roars. "Where's my daughter's body?"

Morelli's lips pull back in a bloody grin, his teeth stained crimson. "You'll never find it."

Morelli's expensive suit is now a tattered mess, soaked through with his own blood. But still, he laughs, a gurgling, choking sound that makes me shudder.

"You ... can't ... win..." Morelli gasps out between bloody coughs. "I've already ... won..."

Kaden's hands wrap around Morelli's throat, squeezing with all his strength. Morelli's eyes protrude, his face turning a mottled purple as he claws at Kaden's iron grip. But Kaden doesn't relent, his eyes rabid with a decade's worth of a grudge.

"This is for Cassie," Kaden growls, his voice unrecognizable. "For every day you stole from her. For every nightmare you gave me. For every piece of my soul I sold off to get to you."

With a sickening crunch, Morelli's neck snaps under Kaden's hold, his knees buckling and his body sliding to the floor in a heap.

I make an audible gasp, then I'm reaching forward, as if my arms could get me to Kaden faster than my legs, when a deafening crack splits the air.

Kaden's body jerks. He stumbles back, then turns, his hand clutching a spot near his shoulder, blood seeping through his fingers. He goes for his holster with his injured arm, trying to raise his weapon, but his fingers won't respond. The gun clatters to the floor as he staggers, his left hand instinctively pressing against the wound that made it through a gap in his protective gear.

He falls to his knees.

"*Kaden!*" I scream, sprinting toward him.

His face pales and he sways to the side. I get there in time to catch him and gently lay him down, my tears mixing with his blood. "Kaden, no, please…"

My heart is in ruins as I cradle Kaden's head in my lap, my fingers stroking his sweat-damp hair. His breathing is labored, each inhale a wet rattle that sends iced-over vines of dread into my stomach.

"Stay with me," I whisper, my voice cracking.

His eyelids flutter open, revealing those captivating blue eyes I've come to cherish, now glazed. "Wraithling…"

His hand, slick with his own blood, reaches up to cup my cheek. I lean into his touch, uncaring of the wet streaks he leaves on my skin.

"Shh, don't try to talk." I attempt a watery smile. "Save your strength. I'm going to get you out of here, get you patched up."

A ghost of a smile flickers across his lips. "Always the optimist."

"One of us has to be."

Kaden's thumb strokes my cheek. "I'm sorry I … couldn't keep my promise."

"Don't say that." I shake my head vehemently, refusing to accept the finality in his tone. "You're going to be okay. Keep pressure on it. We'll get you help. We'll—"

My conviction dissolves into a sob, the enormity of the situation starting to close in on me.

I glance around frantically, searching for something, anything to stem the flow of blood. But there's nothing except carnage… and the person who fired the gun.

The acrid scent of gunpowder stings my nostrils.

That shot, it didn't come from Morelli.

It came from behind me.

I dive for Kaden's fallen weapon, my fingers closing around the grip. The cool metal slides against my sweaty palms as I raise it, aiming at the columns of servers, some sparking with broken wires, others blinking frantic green lights. The overhead emergency lights cast an unearthly red over this entire hellscape, and I can't pinpoint a thing.

I whip the gun to the left, then to the right, my arms trembling as I hold them stiff.

Casual footsteps echo straight ahead. I grip the gun tighter, my gaze darting through the spaces between the servers. My breaths shorten.

A figure steps out of the shadows, the dim light glinting off the barrel of a pistol. Slender fingers wrap around the grip, wisps of smoke curling from the muzzle. Their silhouette becomes clearer as they step directly under an overhead light, and she takes stock of Morelli's lifeless body.

She.

A woman.

She's tall and lithe, her stride relaxed yet predatory, and dressed in tactical gear not unlike Kaden's, her dark hair pulled back in a severe ponytail. She gives a quick survey of Morelli's corpse with pursed, disappointed lips, then turns to me.

My arms begin to ache from holding the gun steady, but I don't dare lower it.

"Who are you?" I demand, my voice shaking despite my efforts to keep it level.

The woman stops a few feet away, her head tilting as she regards me with an eerie calm. Her face is angular, all sharp cheekbones and a pointed chin, her features strangely familiar, yet I've never seen her before.

"Layla Verona," she says, her voice a smooth alto. "The innocent little coder caught up in the big, bad world."

I flinch at the use of my name, my finger tightening on the trigger. "How do you know who I am?"

Her lips curve into a smile devoid of warmth. "I know everything about you. Just like I know everything about him."

She nods toward Kaden, who shifts in my lap, groaning in pain as he tries to lift his head. His gaze locks onto the woman, and a tattered sound escapes his lips. "Cassie?"

The name slams into me, the gun nearly slipping from my grasp. "What?"

Kaden struggles to prop himself up, his face ashen. I try to hold him still, terrified he'll bleed out faster if he moves, but he's determined.

"Cassandra?" he asks again in a wet whisper.

My head spins as I look between them, the pieces refusing to click into place. This can't be right. Kaden must be hallucinating. It's impossible...

Cassie's grin widens, but there's no joy in it. "Hey, Dad. It's been a long time."

"Cassie ... how?" Kaden grits out between labored breaths. "Morelli said..."

"That he buried me?" Cassie finishes, a harsh laugh escaping her. "Oh, he did. In a coffin, with nothing but the dark and the sounds of my own screams for company."

I stop breathing, horror seizing my lungs at the image she creates in my head. Kaden's face drains of what little color it had left, his lips parting in a silent cry of anguish.

Cassie continues, her voice flat, detached. "He kept me in that box for days, letting me scream myself hoarse, letting me shit and piss myself, the hunger and thirst gnawing at my insides until I thought I would go mad. And just when I was on the brink, when I thought death would be a mercy, he dug me up."

Kaden makes a strangled sound.

Cassie begins to pace, her movements languid, almost hypnotic. The gun dangles loosely from her fingers. "He broke me, piece by piece, day after day. The beatings, the starvation, the isolation. He would leave me in that dark hole for weeks, until I forgot what sunlight looked like, until my own name felt foreign on my tongue. And then, when I was nothing more than an empty doll, he would bring me out. Clean me up, dress me in pretty clothes. Parade me around like a prized pet."

I swallow and blink back tears. I can't even begin to imagine the hell she endured. Kaden's threadbare breaths fill the space between her words, each inhale a painful reminder of his fading strength.

Cassie stops in front of us, then lowers until she's resting on her haunches. "Do you know what it's like, Dad, to have every shred of your identity stripped away? To be dismembered and put back together as something unrecognizable? No, of course you don't. You were too busy playing the vengeful assassin, leaving your little trinkets on the bodies you dropped, never once considering that I might still be alive. That I needed you."

Kaden shakes his head weakly, tears clearing a path through the blood on his face. "I searched everywhere for you. I never stopped looking for you. Never stopped hoping..."

A mirthless laugh escapes her. "He molded me. Reshaped me into his perfect little soldier. His Mafia princess. He taught me to kill, to torture, to revel in the agony of our enemies. But that's not the worst part, Daddy. He buried me half a mile away from you. Next to the lighthouse. There were times you would've walked right on top of me."

My mouth goes dry. The lighthouse. *My* lighthouse. All those weeks Kaden spent searching, hunting for clues, and she was right there, suffering unimaginable horrors so close to home.

Kaden's anguished moan rips me apart. "*No...*"

His voice breaks off into a wet cough, more blood bubbling

past his lips. I press my hand against his wound, my own tears blurring my vision.

Cassie watches him struggle with cold indifference.

"Cassie, we need to get him to a hospital," I say.

She tilts her head at me. "Considering I'm the one who shot him, I'm going to go with a *no*."

"Why?" I demand. "How could you do this to a man who spent a decade searching for you, dead *or* alive? Your father changed his life, he gave up everything, to try to find you. He became a killer. Look around you. *Look*. All this carnage was for you. He tears people apart *for you*. Help him. *Help him!*"

By the time I'm finished, I'm screaming at her.

Cassie's emotionless gaze flickers from Kaden's labored breaths to my desperate, tear-streaked face. She leans in closer, keeping me in her sights with an intensity that makes me want to shrink back. But I force myself to meet her stare head-on, clenching my teeth hard.

"Who are you to him?" she asks.

I take a shuddering breath, choosing my words carefully. "I'm ... I'm his partner. His friend. His..."

"Is he your savior?" Cassie asks sweetly. "When your world fell apart, when you were thrust into this nightmare that you couldn't wake up from, was he there? Did he protect you, shelter you, even when you fought him every step of the way?"

I feel all the blood leaving my face.

Cassie offers a triumphant smile at my physical reaction. "Exactly."

She's right. Kaden saved me, protected me. The realization that it should've been her twists something inside me.

Kaden's breathing grows more labored. Blood seeps through my fingers as I press against his wound. His skin pales, taking on a grayish tint.

"Please," I beg. "He's dying."

Cassie's eyes narrow. She reaches into her pocket and pulls out a small vial filled with clear liquid, as well as a flip-phone. "This is the antidote to the poison coating the bullet. And my men can call an ambulance. Without either, I give him about ten more minutes."

Poison? My heart races. "Give it to him!"

"Not so fast," Cassie says. She holds up the vial, examining it in the poor light. "I want something in return."

"Anything," I say without hesitation.

Kaden's hand weakly grasps my arm. "No, Layla, don't."

I ignore him, focusing on Cassie. "What do you want?"

Her lips pull into a hapless smile. "I want you to feel what I felt. To know what it's like to have your identity stripped away. I want you to come with me."

The thought of going anywhere with Cassie makes my chest constrict, dread overriding any other thought. But I look down at Kaden, at the life draining from his eyes, and I know I have no choice.

"If you agree, Kaden lives. If not..." Cassie shrugs. "Well, at least you'll be together in death."

Kaden coughs. "No. I won't let you."

"Okay," I whisper. "I'll do it."

Cassie gives an approving nod. She tosses me the vial. I catch it and quickly uncork it, lifting Kaden's head to pour the liquid into his mouth.

It's not that I trust what she says. The vial she gave me could kill Kaden faster, for all I know. But I've run out of options.

"Good girl," Cassie says, standing. She pulls out her phone, tapping the screen. "My men will be here in one minute to collect you both. Don't try anything stupid."

I hold on tight to Kaden, already grieving.

His eyes flutter closed, but they open again and find mine.

"Why?" he croaks.

I brush a strand of hair from his forehead, leaving a smear of blood, then lean down, my tears falling onto his pallid face. "You saved me. Now it's my turn."

A lump of emotion burns my throat. I keep my focus on Kaden, memorizing every line and plane of his face, the exact shade of blue in his eyes, the way his hair curls at his nape. I want to sear him into my memory, to carry it with me into the void that awaits.

"I love you," I whisper.

Kaden's glazed eyes clear enough for me to catch the shock, wonder, and despair in their depths. "Layla..."

I press my forehead to his, savoring the connection. "I know."

Cassie watches our exchange behind the cold mask of her features. Her clipped stride toward us makes me raise my head.

"Time's up, Layla. On your feet."

I press a fierce kiss to Kaden's lips. "Hold on."

"I'll find my way back to you," he says hoarsely against my mouth. "Both of you."

My breath hitches as Cassie's men flood into the room, their boots scraping and pounding. They surround us, their weapons trained on Kaden and me.

Kaden's hold on my arm suddenly digs into my flesh with an adrenaline-induced desperation that borders on painful.

"Layla, don't go." His voice scrapes against his throat. "She'll destroy you."

Cassie's men advance, reaching for me, ready to drag me away. I cling to Kaden, my fingers twisting in his shirt, desperate for one last moment.

But Cassie nods to the men and they seize my arms, hauling me to my feet with a force that makes my bones ache.

I cry out, scrabbling to keep my grip on Kaden. "Please! Just let me stay with him until help comes!"

Kaden lunges for me, his hand outstretched, but he crashes to the floor, his blood smearing across the concrete.

"No!" The word slices his throat, a howl of agony and rage. "Layla!"

"I'm sorry," I sob to him, my voice hitching. "I'm so sorry."

I scream his name, thrashing in my captors' hold as they drag me backward, away from him. The distance between us yawns wider with each step, an unbridgeable chasm.

Cassie watches our struggle with a twisted smile, her eyes glittering with a perverse satisfaction.

She turns to Kaden, her head tilting in a mockery of sympathy. "Don't worry, Daddy. Your new girlfriend and I are going to have so much fun getting to know each other."

The last thing I see before they wrench me around the corner is Kaden's face, contorted in anguish, his hand still reaching for me as he mouths my name.

And then he's gone, and I'm being dragged through the shadows and into a nightmare that I won't be able to control.

ALSO BY KETLEY ALLISON

all in kindle unlimited

If you want more secret societies, read:

Rival

Virtue

Fiend

Reign

The Thorne of Winthorpe:

Thorne

Crush

Liar

If you want mafia with your dark, why choose romance:

Cruel Promise (M/F)

Broken Beauty (Why Choose)

Loyal Vows (Why Choose)

also writing as S.K. Allison,

contemporary romance:

If you like your bad boys and bullies as standalones (no series, one book, a happy ending), read:

Rebel

Crave

If you like a grump turned into a protector for his woman, read:

Rock

Lover

If you like your playboys with tormented hearts and scars, read:

Trust

Dare

Play

If you like small-town, angsty vibes:

You Will Want Me

www.ingramcontent.com/pod-product-compliance
Lightning Source LLC
Chambersburg PA
CBHW011807200726

48289CB00016B/3045